FOLLOW A WILD HEART

Wild Cow Ranch 3

Natalie Bright
Denise F. McAllister

Follow A Wild Heart
Natalie Bright
Denise F. McAllister

Paperback Edition

CKN Christian Publishing
An Imprint of Wolfpack Publishing
6032 Wheat Penny Avenue
Las Vegas, NV 89122

Paperback ISBN: 978-1-64734-661-4
Ebook ISBN: 978-1-64734-660-7

FOLLOW A WILD HEART

Dedication

To the hardest working man I know, who never stops dreaming.
Thanks Chris, for all that you do for us. All my love.

— Natalie Bright

The year 2020 was life-changing for the entire world due to the pandemic.
Our thoughts and prayers go out to all who have been affected by the virus.
May God bless and keep you safe.

— Denise F. McAllister

Chapter One

Present Day
Rafter O Ranch, Texas Panhandle

Shifting in his saddle, Nathan Olsen looked out over the early spring range—his father's ranch and three grandpas before him—from the top of a hill. Red Angus spread out nibbling at bits of new growth which cast a tinge of light green onto the scene. The unbroken horizon burned bright orange and gold with streaks of purple-gray clouds.

Winter had not disappeared yet; the penetrating chill seeping under his wild rag was proof. Pulling up the Carhartt collar and tugging down on his ballcap, he loosened his grip on the reins. Nathan flexed his achy, cold fingers and yanked lined deerskin gloves from his pocket. He breathed in the scene, wanting to commit it all to memory. If he were a painter, he could preserve the scene forever.

Some people might be bothered by the silence,

but to Nathan's ears the prairie was loud and restless. Meadowlarks answered each other's call, and the wind kept the dead weeds swaying in constant motion.

As he surveyed the scene his chest filled with pride. It always surprised him, this emotion he felt for a patch of dirt. Generations of Olsens had honored this treeless place, devoting their sweat and tears, and the land had blessed them in return.

A hawk soared across the sky, his wings outstretched to catch the updraft. At the top of the ridge Nathan watched a group of mule deer as they cautiously eased into a chinaberry grove, seeking their hideout for the day after grazing all night. He saw the beauty in the land, but the scene did not feed his soul.

Aggravation hung over his head like the patches of fog that clung to the lows with a gray shroud. Darn cold this early, but his dad had insisted they be in the saddle just after first light. In Nathan's mind, they had plenty of time, all day in fact, to cruise through the heifers. But it seemed his father insisted on creating a list of chores before going to bed to make sure his oldest son stayed occupied. In fact, it was March; birthing season would start any day now. He or his sister Angie had already been making a pass through this group of first-time little mommas several times during the day and night.

Nathan was closing fast on thirty, old enough to know what needed to be done without his father laying out a chores list. There was never a discussion, never a chance for him to give any input. The idea that he might have made other plans for the day never came into question.

About the time he thought to dig out his phone to snap a picture, one of his sisters rode up alongside and halted her horse next to his. "What're you doin'? Dad'll be on your tail soon. Better not let him catch you bein' idle."

Despite the early hour, Angie appeared alert and fresh-faced with cheeks pink from the cold, long blonde hair in a neat braid reaching to her waist. Bright purple shirt, red wild rag, red gloves, red vest, black canvas jacket. As usual his sister was riding his favorite blue roan mare, looking like the perfect models for a Western photo shoot.

He always thought Angie was the better ranch hand. In his mind, he didn't even add, "for a girl." He been doing ranch work his whole life, but she was just better at everything—riding, roping, gathering, branding, and also had a head for business. Of course, he'd never tell her that. She had a natural instinct about cows and loved every minute of it. His brother, Travis, had a knack with horses. His other two sisters were gifted with talents in the ranch kitchen or branding pen. Their dad had taught all of them well about how to manage and sustain the family business.

Nathan, on the other hand, was an observer. They were his family and he loved them, but at times he felt like an outsider, hovering on the edge of every conversation—always there, but not really an integral part of the entire operation. He wondered if any of the bunch had actually admired the view from their horse or watched a sunrise. Not just an occasional glance out a window, but really studied the colors and patterns in the clouds.

"Are you listening?"

Her voice grated on his nerves. It annoyed him that his sister felt a need to interrupt the silence.

"I'm just being still for a minute, that's all. Appreciating nature. God's the best painter, ya know."

"Oh, that's a good one," Angie laughed. "Not the part about God, but I don't think Dad'll like you bein' still. C'mon, let's go. We only have a few heifers that seem to be in trouble. One is ready but I can see a nose instead of feet. If we can get her into the chute, maybe I can turn the little bugger around before he's born."

He rarely shared his inner thoughts or argued because what was the use? There was always work to be done. Nathan turned his horse to follow Angie towards a group of cattle where his father sat patiently. With a smirk and giggle she called out over her shoulder. "Do you have a date with Carli?"

"She might come by later. I'm taking her to lunch."

"Well, better get your work done then."

Nathan clenched his jaw and reined his horse to follow. Life was much easier if he did what Angie said, as well as his father, his mother, even the rest of his younger siblings. Even though he was the oldest it seemed everyone else was in charge but him. "Let's get Nathan to do it," seemed to be their solution to everything. Today was no different than any other day, but he seemed to be more agitated than usual. He shook the troubled thoughts from his mind. No use in wishing for what would never be. A moment of peace to enjoy the coming day was not on the schedule.

Prodding her horse gently with a spur, his sister took off ahead of him. Always full of energy and ready and able to lead, Angie could surely take over the ranch one day. Nathan felt certain of that. He thought about this a lot. As the oldest of five kids, it was expected that he'd be the next generation of cowmen to oversee the Rafter O into the future. If they all assumed he'd take over, maybe it was time he did. Truthfully, he was best at avoiding confrontation, particularly with his father. Blessed are the peacemakers, his grandpa Olsen had always said. Sometimes knowing when to remain silent proved more the man than jumping into the fray.

Trotting his horse to catch up, he filled the gap between his father and sister. They successfully drove four little heifers into the pens at Olsen Ranch headquarters.

Nathan made quick work of running the heifer into the snake and then chute. Angie gloved up and worked her arm into the cow in an effort to push the calf's nose back and find his front feet before he smothered. After a few minutes, the mother gave a grunt and a push, and a newborn calf spilled out.

"It's a she and she's beautiful." Angie wiped the mucus from a shiny, wet nose and pulled the newborn out from behind her momma. They opened the chute and placed the calf in front of the mother's nose. She got a good whiff and began licking the slick, wet hair of her new baby. Silently they all backed away and climbed out of the pen.

By the time they assessed the other heifers, filled the water tub, unsaddled, and put tack back in its place, it was midmorning. Nathan longed for that second cup of coffee which had been interrupted earlier.

He went into the barn where his father and sister, Angie, stood, heads together, laughing about something. They always had shared a special bond. The laughter stopped when they noticed him, which happened often and made him feel like a third wheel.

Mr. Olsen's expression changed to a more serious one when he turned to look at his son. "You have a date in the middle of a workday?"

Nathan and Angie exchanged glances, but she did not speak. She shrugged her shoulders and half-grinned.

"We're almost done here, Dad. Besides it's just lunch. We'll run into Dixon real quick. I won't be gone long."

"You know that running a ranch is a 24/7 job." Skip Olsen gave his oldest son a menacing stare.

Nathan braced himself for the lecture that was sure to come, but instead his father added, "Say hello to Carli for me."

"Yes, sir." Even though Nathan was well past his irresponsible, adolescent days, his father still had the power to make him feel like an eighth grader.

He loved his parents and his family. He really did. They were kind, hardworking people. Salt of the earth. And his dad was never harsh or unkind with any of his five children. But the patriarch of the Olsen family wanted things done his way and could get downright ornery about it. His father had taught each of them well—how to respect the earth, the livestock, and people, but it was like an act of Congress if Nathan had other plans. Maybe he wanted to do things a little different than they'd been done before. On some days he felt like a stranger. He yearned for another life. Any kind of life except the one he had.

As he emerged from the tack barn, Carli's truck bumped across the cattle guard into Rafter O head-quarters and pulled to a stop. She gave a wave in his direction. No matter what, she always looked pretty to him. Whether she was spic 'n' span shiny and joining his family for dinner, or dirty and sweaty when she pitched in on working cattle. The honey-colored hair that spilled over her shoulders, and those hazel eyes that haunted his dreams. He lifted his arm in greeting and gave her a wide smile.

She'd had a tough year, her first one in Texas as the new owner of the Wild Cow Ranch. The whole town was taken aback when she appeared out of nowhere, from Georgia, and the Last Will was read that named her the rightful heir of the Wild Cow Ranch after her grandpa, Ward Kimball, had died.

She'd been through a lot since moving to Tex-as. Even a disastrous fire which destroyed the hay barn, ruled arson later. Then, just recently, caught out in the pasture during a life-threatening Texas norther, a freak snowstorm that would be talked about for years to come. But Carli Jameson seemed to get through it all, stronger than ever, with grace and calm, ready to take on the next thing. Nathan admired her.

And they'd become friends, but he wondered if she might be the answer to his problems. He could imagine a life with her. Combining their ranches, raising Angus cattle, a solid ranch horse stock, and hopefully a few kids. Being married might get him out from under his father's thumb. It would quiet his mother's incessant hints at wanting grandkids.

With Carli at his side, he could settle into ranch life. Only thing standing in his way was Lank Torres, the Wild Cow Ranch hired hand. He could tell Carli was drawn to him. Nathan also sensed that she was guarded and cautious. His relationship with her was not yet on solid ground and a long way from the proposal stage. But the smile she flashed in his direction that morning gave him hope. For today at least, Nathan felt he stood a good chance.

Chapter Two

Carli Jameson gave a wave to Nathan Olsen as she pulled her truck to a stop at the Rafter O headquarters. She was a bit early for their lunch date, but she enjoyed hanging out with the Olsen family. Right after moving to Texas, she had accepted a neighborly invite to a going away party for one of their daughters who had joined the military. It was hard to cast aside her tendency to remain a loner after moving here, but her hired hand Lank Torres insisted she go with him. She felt welcomed and at home the minute she walked into the Olsen's house. Hopes for a closeness with Lank turned out to be a huge disappointment that night, but it was a worry for another time. She was his boss after all, and even though Lank brought her to the party, Nathan had driven her home. Their friendship had only grown from there.

The Olsen's rock house had been occupied for five generations. Towering elms and bushy oaks encircled the old homestead, with one side sloping down into a grove of trees shading a carpet of grass.

It was even pretty this time of year with budding branches and early signs of spring peeking through the crunchy brown lawn. Oldest son Nathan told her they set up tables under those trees during the summer for cookouts. His mother loved to entertain.

Carli waited in the vehicle but rolled down her window.

"Hey. Thanks for meeting me here," Nathan called in greeting as he emerged from the barn and walked towards her.

"I'm looking forward to hanging out today. I want to talk to you about some research I'm doing."

"Research? Something to do with your ranch?" Nathan asked through the open window as he rested his arms on her truck's door.

"I'll explain on the way."

"Let me wash up and I'll be right back. My truck's unlocked."

"Looks like you had a busy morning already. Take your time." She noticed what looked like cow manure covering one sleeve and the sheen of sweat on his face. Carli hopped into Nathan's pickup and waited until he appeared from the house in a clean shirt and leather vest.

"Is Dixon all right for lunch? Since you're early we can grab a coffee first," Nathan added as he filled the cab with a musky scent of men's cologne. "We have heifers calving and I hate to get too far away."

Zipping down the road, she wondered how he had cleaned up so fast. She couldn't ignore his muscled arm on the steering wheel, the other resting on the armrest between them. His light blue pearl-snap shirt was rolled up at the elbows showing off his sturdy, tan forearms. Despite the early spring chill, he didn't wear a jacket. She remembered he had told her about playing football for Dixon High School. The all-star quarterback, and, no doubt, small town hero, fit him. Over six feet, with that chiseled jaw and perfect teeth, the subject of every teenaged girl's love-sick dream. Ranch work only made the boy into a leaner and stronger man.

She had to smile at the thought of her dorky younger self never imagining a moment like this. Carli had always been a loner, definitely never one of the popular crowd, and certainly not the type of girl who would garner the attention of a football quarterback. She had suppressed her loneliness into horses. Thinking back now, she was so fortunate the Fitzgeralds had allowed her to pursue her passion.

They rode in silence for some distance. He suddenly turned and flashed her a bright, wide grin that didn't reach his eyes. She didn't return what she thought was a fake smile. "You seem a little lost in your thoughts, Nate. What's up?"

It bugged her that she could read him so well because she rarely got involved in other people's lives. She grew up with older guardians, and after they passed, Carli accepted her lot in life that she was alone and would never know her birth family. Until a grandpa appeared out of the blue and left her a cow ranch. So here she was in Texas, getting entangled with everyone who lived in and around her ranch, including a little town of interesting characters. It wasn't that long ago she had never even heard of Dixon. It could all be a bit overwhelming at times.

Nathan and Carli had become good friends,

as neighbors and over a common bond of horses, ranching, and so many other things. It was comfortable to spend time with him. She knew he wanted more than friendship. She sensed it in the way he watched her. Her heart still stung when she thought about that Georgia boyfriend. He was "the one", her soulmate. Yeah, right, lesson learned. Once again, she promised herself not to give in. She wouldn't let her guard down so quickly this time.

Nathan stared at the road ahead for several minutes before answering, "Just got some stuff on my mind. What about you? How's everything at the Wild Cow?"

"Things are going great actually. I can't believe I'm feeling more and more like it's my home now. Honestly, I never thought I'd say that after moving from Georgia. I kept thinking I should go back, that I didn't belong here. It was like two people were at war inside of me."

"Man, I know what that's like," Nathan said quietly, in a low whisper as if just to himself.

Carli saw the worry etched on his face and sensed he was troubled about something. She liked him and wanted to help. But she wasn't sure if he would be willing to tell her anything. Men rarely shared what was going on emotionally in their head. She decided to ask anyway.

"What's going on, Nate? Spill. You can tell me anything."

"It's nothin'. What about you? You said you had something you needed my help with."

"Oh, yeah. I wanted to ask you about a family from this area. If you knew of them." Before she could say anything more, Nathan parked right at the front door of the B & R Beanery and Buns. The place looked empty. Business was slow on a weekday morning.

A young woman Carli had never seen before took their order. They settled in a corner. Carli loved the quiet and took a deep breath of the aroma from the roasting coffee berries. The minimal decorations, natural wood tables, and comfy sofas and easy chairs made for a relaxing atmosphere. She pulled out some papers from her tote and spread them all over the table.

Nathan's eyes opened wide. "Wow."

She couldn't suppress her excitement or giggle at his reaction. "As you can see, I've been sorting through stuff at my grandparents' house and I actually found my birth certificate in an old trunk. Apparently, my mother, Michelle, rebelled against her parents, liked to party, and got into drugs."

"Your grandparents, Jean and Ward, never told you who your real father was? Seems your foreman and wife, Buck and Lola, would have known your mom at a young age. Did they know about you?"

"I'm not sure." Carli stared blankly at the table. "I haven't talked to Buck or Lola about it yet."

"This is a lot to take in." Nathan let out a big sigh.

Carli started to explain. "The birth certificate I had from my foster parents didn't have a birth father listed and I was afraid to ask. You don't know how many times I wondered and thought about it, and as the years passed it didn't seem that important. The one I found at my grandparents' house has his name penciled in."

Just then the barista interrupted with their orders.

"Nathan Olsen. Aren't you a sight for sore eyes? How've you been?"

She set the coffees down and flipped her hair back over one shoulder. Carli watched the pretty blonde girl in tight jeans and Tee-shirt with the shop's logo lay a manicured hand on Nathan's shoulder as she flashed him a high-watt smile.

"Uh, just fine. How 'bout you?" Nathan's eyes were fixed on his beverage.

"Oh, c'mon now. You're not blanking out on my name, are you? It's Christy. High school? Cheerleader? Remember? I was a freshman when you were the senior quarterback."

"Uh, uh, sure. I remember you. It's been a long time." The words came from his lips, but Carli noticed there was no recognition in his eyes as he barely looked in Christy's direction.

"Surely you haven't forgotten that homecoming party behind the bleachers, have you?" She winked.

Carli watched them. Please don't ask her what she's been up to. Definitely rude, but Carli wasn't in the mood to hear a long-winded life story.

"Where's Belinda?" Carli asked to save Nathan from a jam. She had become fast friends with the co-owner of the coffee shop, Belinda, the "B" in B & R. This place had soon become one of her sanctuaries where she could relax and unwind, plus Belinda was a good listener. Carli had become her official taste-tester and willingly tried every new coffee concoction Belinda could invent.

Christy glanced at Carli with a slight frown, as if suddenly realizing there was another customer in the shop besides Nathan. "She's staying home with a sick kid. I'm helping her out this week." She answered Carli's question, but kept her gaze on Nathan. "Normally you can find me at the Chamber office. I'm in charge of community events."

Nathan gave her a half-smile before turning his attention back to his coffee. He cleared his throat and looked at Carli. "You were saying?"

She grinned at the blush on his cheeks. She'd definitely have to ask him about that party behind the bleachers some other time, but right now she had more important things on her mind.

"I know my birth father's name." Carli had never said that out loud to anyone. It felt strange and made her heart beat faster. To actually have a name and now, to be sharing it with someone. She completely forgot about her latte, instead stared into Nathan's eyes.

"That's big."

"No kidding. I don't know if he's still alive or maybe dead. I don't know if I want to meet him. Maybe he hates me or maybe he doesn't even know anything about me. Do I want to meet him? Does he look like me? Is he nice or a creep? So, I'm thinking of looking into one of those heritage websites. Who knows? Maybe send my DNA in and look for a match. What do you think, Nate? Would you do it?"

"Whoa, now. I need to process."

"This is what swirls around in my brain all the time since I found the certificate." Actually she had wondered about her family history for most of her life, but never told anyone. This was the first time she was ever this close to knowing the truth before. In the past few months, she had learned more about her Jameson side. It was like she was on a fast-moving genealogy train and there was no way to slow it down. She'd either come out of this wiser for it or it would end with a crash and burn.

"Have you told Buck and Lola? That you want to find your birth father?"

"No, not yet. I will. I just want to look into it myself. Lola and Buck started working at the Wild Cow as young newlyweds for my grandparents. Of course, they remember my mother, Michelle, before she ran away. Do you think my birth father might've been a local boy?" Emotion filled her eyes with tears, and it surprised her. Even though she had stared at his name on paper numerous times, she couldn't bring herself to say it out loud...until now. She swallowed the tears and cleared her throat.

Nathan covered her hand with his. "Carli, I'm sorry for the pain of your past. We don't always understand why people do the things they do. I don't know what was going on in your mom's mind when she found out she was pregnant. Did that guy know he was the father? Did he abandon her? Maybe he knew nothing about a baby. Maybe she ran away, and he never saw her again. If you're curious, do the research. But take it slow."

"Thanks, Nate. It means a lot to have someone I can talk to about this stuff."

"What about Lank? Have you told him?"

Carli paused in surprise as she looked at Nathan. "What has this got to do with Lank? No. I have to be careful of that situation."

"No reason. Just wondering. I think that's smart, Carli, to keep this information close to the vest for a while until you can find out more."

"I'm his boss. He's my ranch hand. Why would I talk to him about my personal life?" Carli looked at Nathan in surprise. Where was he going with this conversation and why did he bring up Lank? No doubt she felt a spark when Lank was around, but it never crossed her mind that anyone else might notice. Was Nathan that interested in her that he sensed there might be something between her and the ranch hand?

"I don't want to bad-mouth anyone. Lank was a little wild in the past. String of girlfriends, typical for a guy on the rodeo circuit. Not the most stable kind of guy in case you're thinking of taking him into your confidence."

"I appreciate your friendship, Nate. This isn't something I feel comfortable sharing with Lank or anybody else right now." She leaned forward and put her hands on his. "Thanks for listening. I really mean it."

Carli looked at Nathan but didn't say anything more. What a change of topic from her birth father to Lank and his many dates. She tried not to let the surprise show in her eyes. Since when had Nathan Olsen become concerned about what she tells her ranch hand, Lank Torres?

Chapter Three

"Hey, I wanted to ask you about next weekend." Nathan Olsen shrugged out of his Carhartt® ranch jacket and let it hang over the back of his chair.

Carli studied the handsome face of her neighbor and friend and considered if there might be anything more besides friendship between them. He was so easy to talk to as evidenced by the fact they were still sitting at a tall metal table in the B &R Beanery in downtown Dixon. Talking with Nathan was like being with an old friend. She glanced down at her coffee which had long since grown cold.

"What do you think about art galleries? An art museum in Amarillo is having an exhibit I'd like to see, if you want to go. Do you like that kind of stuff?"

One of her favorite pastimes had been wandering through museums and galleries. She smiled, "Sure, sounds like fun." It was comfortable being with Nathan, safe.

"They're featuring an artist's demonstration.

Bronze sculptures, kind of like Frederic Remington. I'd really like to see his work."

Carli smiled again to reassure him. "Sure, I said I'd go. Sounds great."

"How about another coffee?" Nathan stood.

"Yeah, thanks, Nate."

He leaned closer, his mouth just inches from her ear. "When I get back, I want to hear more about the birth certificate and what you found. I bet you were a cute baby." He winked.

Carli felt her cheeks grow warm and she couldn't suppress her laugh as he walked away. Turning her attention back to the paperwork, she tried to put some of it in order before folding and stuffing it back into her bag, as Nathan placed their order. She had so much more digging to do on the subject of her birth father yet was hesitant to share her secret with anyone else.

The overeager Christy at the register was shiny and big-smiled. She and Nathan shared a laugh about something.

"Who's your lady friend over there?" Christy whispered, but in the empty, cement floor shop, her voice carried over to Carli.

"That's Carli Jameson. She owns the Wild Cow Ranch."

"Ohhh, she inherited Jean and Ward's place?" She looked in Carli's direction with a straight face, but Carli managed to give her a little smile. Christy leaned closer to Nathan. "You guys dating?"

"Kinda. We're good friends." Nathan collected their order and thanked Christy. "Keep the change." When he returned to the table, he had two big carrot-applesauce muffins for them.

Nathan's answer of "kinda" raised Carli's inner antenna, and when she noticed Christy disappearing into the back, she couldn't resist teasing him a bit. "You Texas men sure do attract the girls, dontcha?"

"Her? She said we went to high school together." He leaned closer across the table, glanced over his shoulder, and whispered, "I don't remember her."

"Well, darn. I was anxious to hear about that homecoming party." Carli giggled when Nathan blushed and glared at her.

"Don't remember a thing and that's my story."

"You may not remember her, but I think she's giving you the eye and is definitely interested. You must have made an impression."

Nathan turned around just as Christy appeared from the back room and was immediately greeted with a wide toothy smile followed by a flip of her hair over one shoulder. He whipped his head back around to Carli. And his face turned scarlet.

"Nathan Olsen, you are blushing like a teenager." Carli giggled again.

"Carli, quit it. Maybe we should go." He squirmed in his chair. "Besides I might be interested in other pursuits."

"I'm just teasing. But you should be flattered. A cute girl hitting on you."

"She's not the cute girl I want." His comment hung in the air between them, uncertain, awkward, but full of promise.

Carli chose to ignore it. "All right, Nate. So, talk. What's up with you? You're not your jolly, carefree self today."

"I'm thinking about making a change."

"A change? Something is really bugging you, isn't it?"

Before he could answer, the door chimed softly and Carli watched a woman and two youngsters enter, a boy around thirteen and a girl maybe fifteen or sixteen. Nathan and Carli's conversation came to an abrupt end, interrupted by the clatter of chairs.

"You two sit here while I order," the lady instructed as she pointed the kids to a nearby couch. The boy sank into the soft sofa, but the girl sat at a table.

The boy was a typical young teen, with gawky legs and arms that the rest of him hadn't gotten used to yet. He seemed shy but eager and curious.

The girl's hair was dyed as black as gooey asphalt and shaped into a spiky, disheveled cut. She wore an oversized black Tee-shirt with a white skull on front, black leggings, and black combat boots with the tops spread wide and laces dragging on the floor. Her feet clumped when she walked. Numerous leather and cord bracelets climbed her wrist.

Through deep purple eyeshadow she peered at the woman who was probably her mother, and growled, "I want a coffee."

"Lexi, I told you. No coffee. It makes you jittery and gives you an upset stomach."

"I want a coffee and a muffin," the girl gritted her teeth.

"Brandon, do you want some hot chocolate?"

"Sure, Mom." The boy peered cautiously at his sister as though she might explode.

"Lexi, I'll get you hot chocolate too."

"I said I want a coffee and a muffin." The girl

pressed her lips tight, her voice rising in anger. She glanced at Carli to meet her stare.

As Carli and Nathan watched the family, she remembered a girl like this in school, always in trouble, always angry. She also remembered parts of her life when she had been that girl. Resentful of the mother who had given her away and hating the father she never knew. It's a wonder her guardians, the Fitzgeralds, hadn't tossed her back to wherever they had found her.

The mother carried a tray with drinks and food to their table and the boy happily took a chomp out of his muffin. The young girl stood and swiped at hers with one swing of her hand. It flew to the floor in Carli's direction.

"I'm sorry," the woman pleaded. She looked frazzled. "Lexi, why did you do that? I'm not buying you another one."

"I said I want a coffee, not a kid's hot chocolate."

Carli stood and Nathan gave her a frown. But she felt the anger and hopelessness this girl held inside. Carli had felt trapped before too. She picked up her plate holding the same kind of muffin Nathan just bought and approached the girl. "Hey, I'm not going to eat mine. I haven't touched it. Would you like to have it? My name's Carli, by the way."

The girl frowned, looked at her feet, and avoided Carli's eyes.

Carli put the plate down in front of her. "I like your boots. Pretty cool."

The mother acted as if she might say something, but then remained silent.

"They're Doc Martens."

"They look comfy, but also sturdy."

"Yeah." The girl peeked up to meet Carli's gaze. Then said in a monotone, "I like your bracelet."

"Thanks. It's from a horse's tail I braided. From my horse Beau's tail. He's honestly my best friend. Then, see here, I added a little clasp."

Drawn to the jewelry, the girl fingered Carli's bracelet lightly.

"That's pretty," said the mother. "We had to give up our horses because of the feed cost. The kids used to ride all the time."

"Hey, would you like to have it?" Carli kept her attention on the young girl. "I live on a ranch with lots of horses and they're always losing strands from their tails. I can make another one."

The girl didn't look at her mother, instead focused on Carli's arm, then tentatively looked to her face almost like a scared fawn in the woods.

"Really? You mean I can have it?"

"Sure. I make them for people when I have time." Carli unhooked the bracelet and started to place it on the girl's wrist. First, she looked to the mother. "Is it okay?"

"Yes, thank you very much. Lexi, what do you say?"

"Thanks," the girl mumbled under her breath while looking at her arm.

The boy piped up, mouth full of muffin, "Hey, I want one too."

"Brandon, don't be rude. And close your mouth when you're chewing, please." The mother frowned at him.

His sister gave him a hateful look. "Boys don't wear bracelets."

"Y'all will have to visit my ranch sometime.

Maybe you can find enough horse tail hairs to make your own." Carli blurted the invitation before she even thought twice about asking complete strangers to her home. It wasn't the wisest move, but she couldn't take it back now. Before Carli turned back to her table, she looked directly at Lexi. "It was nice meeting you."

The girl didn't glance up but she was eating the muffin.

"Where is your ranch?" the mother asked.

"The Wild Cow. I hope you and the kids will come to visit. Maybe ride horses if that'd be okay with you. Here's my number." Carli grabbed a pen from her purse and jotted her phone number on a napkin.

"Thank you. That's very kind. We know where the ranch is. We used to go there for Christmas cookies when the kids were little. I'll call you." She handed Carli a scrap of paper in return and said, "Here's my name and number."

"Great. Hope to see you out there." Carli turned to Nathan. "Are you ready?"

Carli gathered her bag and followed Nathan to his truck. "I really miss working with kids. Did I ever mention I was part owner of a horse training business back in Georgia? I gave lessons and took kids to horse shows. I'd like to start a riding school here. What do you think?"

"I gotta say, you were really good with that girl. I kinda wanted to mind my own business."

"Too many of us look the other way. It's easy to do. I am drawn to that girl, Nate. I completely understand what's going on in her head. Maybe I should start giving lessons again."

With a kind smile, he said, "You're right, of course. You just want to take on the world, don't ya? I'll help you with whatever program you want to start, but have you considered the liability of kids riding the ranch's horses? There's so much to consider. And thanks for having coffee with me, by the way."

"The coffee was good, but I'm gonna need something a bit more substantial for lunch, cowboy. Like a hamburger. Aren't you starving?"

He laughed. "Actually, I could eat. It's been a long morning already. I thought you were some kind of health nut, like protein powders and vegetables I've never heard of. Stuff like that."

"Not always. Today, give me some good Texas beef."

Nathan's phone buzzed. He glanced at it and then clicked it off.

"Answer that, if you need to," Carli offered.

"It's just Dad. Whatever it is can wait because I don't want to go back." With that he put his cell phone into the middle console of the pickup cab and closed the lid.

Nathan pulled into the Dixie Maid where they ordered greasy burgers and shared tater tots, hot and crispy.

Conversation during lunch was lighter, but still friendly. They drove back to the ranch in silence as Carli kept thinking about the troubled young girl. She wanted to do something to help that family, but was it too bold to butt into their business?

Just before Carli could open the door to step out of Nathan's pickup truck at the Olsen headquarters, he put his hand on hers. She thought for a moment he might lean in and kiss her. He wore a deep frown etched on his face with a look of concern.

"What if you find him, then what?"

"You mean my father? Then nothing. I haven't thought that far."

"This is huge, Carli. You have to take it slow."

"Yeah, I know. Thanks for the coffee and lunch, and for listening. It was a nice morning."

"You never told me his name."

"Miller. The family's name is Miller, and the name on my birth certificate is Taylor." She took a deep breath to still her heart. "My birth father's name is Taylor Miller."

Saying his name aloud caused a reaction. Was it nervousness? Scared anticipation? Eagerness? Fear of the unknown or sheer terror of opening this door into her past?

Never in a million years had she ever considered the possibility of knowing that name.

Chapter Four

At the back of her grandparents' ranch house was a small room with a corner fireplace and two walls lined with bookshelves. The other walls were covered with faded photographs of people smiling and laughing at various horse events, shadow boxes holding tarnished silver buckles, and award plaques from various rodeos. The framed artwork featured several black and white penciled sketches with original signatures, some autographed "To Jean and Ward". In this room Carli set up a home office.

She moved a small, solid oak table from the master bedroom and took the decorative chair covered in cowhide from its spot next to the fireplace in the front room. Surprisingly, her grandparents had a satellite and Internet connection at the headquarters, so she was in business. She liked the coziness of the room as logs crackled in the corner wood burning stove, and evidence of her grandparents' lives surrounding her on all four walls. This one room reminded her of her small home in Georgia, cozy. The sprawling ranch house she had inherited overwhelmed her at times.

Right now, she had a mission. After saying the name of her birth father out loud to Nathan, she was ready to dive deeper into finding him. Maybe God would guide her. Was this something she should pray about? Remembering what Lola had told her, to "pray without ceasing", Carli whispered a prayer, hoping she was doing the right thing. She was unsure in her newfound journey of faith, but she was trying to give her worries to God as Lola kept reminding her. Her ranch foreman's wife was not only a good cook, but she had turned into a valuable spiritual guide as well.

Carli couldn't deny the aching need to know more. Since she found the birth certificate and learned his name, the mystery surrounding the circumstance of her birth parents was on her mind constantly. She opened her laptop and clicked on the heritage website to begin the search. With a yellow pad and pen beside the computer, she felt organized and confident which gave her courage to learn more about her past.

The same questions kept swirling through her head. Who was Taylor Miller? Where had he gone? Alive or dead? There must've been tens of thousands of people in the United States with the surname Miller and first name Taylor, male and female. Carli would have to narrow it down. She knew the names of her birth mother's side but wasn't sure she could find the right Miller family.

"Okay. Male. Texas. Over forty years old," she said aloud, and with a deliberate gesture, hit Enter. There was no middle name on the birth certificate, maybe Michelle didn't know it.

The website's directions advised to formulate a family tree starting with herself. She felt strange looking at it, having been used to being on her own for so long. Now she had a family. Even if most of them were dead. She filled in what she knew.

Carlotta Jean Jameson
Mother: Michelle Jameson
Father: Taylor Miller
Grandparents (on Taylor's side): Unknown
Grandmother: Jean Jameson Kimball
Grandfather: Ward Kimball
Great-grandmother: Lottie Jameson
Great-grandfather: Norwood Jameson

The Miller grandparents were still an unknown blank. From her own family tree several hints popped up on her home page. She'd research those later. She didn't know anything about Taylor Miller's grandparents, but she wondered if his parents' names were on a census record. Were any of them still alive? Maybe she would discover even more family she never knew anything about. She figured he must be a local boy because Michelle wouldn't have had her driver's license yet.

Something at the back of her brain kept trying to surface but she couldn't remember what. Names and the town of Dixon. Something about the town. She yelled out when she remembered, "Phone books!" Strange how they were obsolete now. One end of the room had bookshelves to the ceiling, and the lower part of the shelves were cabinets. She dropped to her knees on the floor at one end and there they were. The cabinet was stuffed with stacks of old phone books. Maybe, just maybe, the dates went back far enough. She tugged on the first stack and they spilled across the floor next to her.

Carli did some quick math and figured out when her mother would have been around fifteen years old and in high school. She found the right phone book in the next stack. Scanning through the M's, she found it. There were two families of Millers living in Dixon during that time and she had their addresses. Of course, the kids in the family wouldn't be listed in the phone book, but she had two names and one of them would have been her grandpa.

Nathan's question suddenly came to mind. What would she say to her birth father if she ever found him? Would she be angry? Emotional? Hug him? What would he think of her? Did he even know she existed? Her brain whirled like a spinning top with all the what-ifs. She found a listing in the old phone book for Gene Miller and Patricia. That had to be her birth father's family. The address was 606 Maple Street in Dixon. Closer. She was getting closer.

A knock on the front door pulled her out of the many, mind-boggling scenarios.

"Carli. It's Lola."

"Come on in. I'm in the back room." Carli quickly clicked out of the genealogy website.

Carrying her ever-present food offerings, Lola set a tray of muffins on one corner of Carli's desk. Hands on hips, she whirled around. "I love what you've done with this room. Perfect spot for your computer."

Carli spun her chair towards Lola and studied

the dish. "Oat bran, cranberry and carrot, if I'm not mistaken."

Lola laughed. The Wild Cow Ranch's cook was all of one hundred pounds if that. She didn't eat any of the mouth-watering treats she baked, and she was baking all the time, so she pushed them off on Carli. Buck and Lank ate with gusto and both of them remained reed thin.

"Gee, Lola, between you and Nathan, I'm gonna end up eating a big muffin before the day's out. Hopefully, you've extracted all of the calories." Carli folded her arms across her chest in an effort to resist.

"And I brought herbal tea, because you never have any." Lola removed the plastic wrap from the plate of muffins.

"That does sound good. Thanks." Carli gave in with a heavy sigh and reached for the treat. She closed her eyes and took a big bite. At least it had vegetables in it.

Lola called from the kitchen. "You already had a muffin today?" She walked into the study with a big grin on her face. "With Nathan? He's easy on the eyes. Isn't he?" Her eyebrows raised when she said his name.

Carli was in the middle of a bite and looked over her muffin at Lola. Great. Now she'd have to explain about her and Nathan. Welcome to rural Texas where the new girl from Georgia had become the topic of everybody's conversation.

Chapter Five

Lola Wallace sank into the leather chair and plopped her trim ankles on the ottoman in Carli's office. "Buck and I started out our romance with many a burger at the Dixie Maid." She laughed.

"There's no romance between me and Nathan Olsen." Carli stared at Lola to make sure she was listening. "I went over to the Rafter O ranch this morning to eat lunch with Nathan. We started off at B&R Beanery and Buns and then went to the Dixie Maid to eat a burger. Nothing to it. We're just good friends."

"I can't believe Nathan's dad let him have the time off. He rarely leaves the ranch."

"Nathan does seem to be the main man who holds that place together. He's such a hard worker and always busy with something."

"Speaking of ranch work and since you have your home office set up, is it okay that you take over paying the bills? I'm not a bookkeeper and I am not the most organized person around."

"I can do that. No problem." In her mind Carli

began to think about buying a file cabinet. It's exactly the kind of work she did for the real estate agent in Georgia, but this time it would actually be for her own property.

"Since it's your ranch, I thought it might give you a better picture of what's going on around here as far as expenses and cash flow. Your grandpa has a great CPA that takes my spreadsheets and calculates the tax and all. I can keep doing it if you want, but since you have your office set up and all..."

"No, you make a good point. I'd learn more about the day-to-day operations."

"You're not working on anything special now, are you?"

"Not really. Why do you ask?" Her father's birth name was on the tip of her tongue and she almost told Lola. Did Lola and Buck know her birth certificate even existed?

"You looked really intent, like you were concentrating on something when I walked in. I'm sorry if I disturbed you."

Carli's heart pounded. She paused before answering, thinking about what she knew and what she wanted to share. She hadn't hesitated to tell Nathan because he had become such a good friend. But to spill the pain of her past with the people who worked for her wasn't something she felt comfortable doing. "It was nothing." She smiled and took another bite of muffin so she wouldn't have to talk any longer.

"Tell me more about this friendly date to the Dixie Maid." Lola tried to suppress her grin this time, but her eyes sparkled as she watched Carli.

"The weirdest thing happened at the coffee shop.

I gave my muffin away to a young girl there. You might know the family. Kids' names were Brandon and Lexi." Carli remembered the youngsters so vividly but had failed to even pay attention to the woman with them. "Their mother's name escapes me."

"Can you remember their last name?"

"No, but the girl was definitely unique."

"How's that?"

"Actually, she threw a little fit."

"Sounds like a lot of excitement for the B&R." The kettle screamed. "Be right back. You're gonna love this ginger and honeybush herbal mix."

Carli saved the grimace that covered her face until after Lola left the room. The herb tea combinations Lola found to buy were unique to say the least, and she always wanted Carli to taste them.

When Lola appeared carrying two steaming mugs, Carli continued. "Like I said, this woman walked in with her two kids. The girl is about sixteen, I guess, maybe fifteen. All dressed in black, nail polish too, skull shirt. Angry attitude. You know the typical emo type."

"What's emo?"

"It's a subculture. Dark, deep emotions, certain rock bands. Teens are overly sensitive, lots of angst, the common theme being black clothes, jewelry, hair. Like emo core, means emotional and hardcore. The girl flung her muffin on the floor, so I gave her mine. I felt bad for her but also for the mom trying to handle everything on her own. I don't know if there's a dad in the picture or not."

"You have a kind heart, Carli. What'd Nathan think of it all?"

"I think he wanted me to stay out of it. I told him that's what everybody does. Meanwhile, I couldn't help but think about the youth suicide rate which is through the roof. I wanted to help her. I used to be that girl. Not so much the outward appearance, but I do remember the hate and anger inside. And by the way, I invited the kids and their mom to the ranch."

"Great. I look forward to meeting them."

Carli blew gently and then took a sip from her mug. "That's not bad." She looked up at Lola and then stared in her cup.

"I was wondering when you'd admit it was good." They both laughed.

"Did I ever tell you I owned a riding school and horse training business in Georgia? I'd like to do something like that again, well, the school part. Do you think it would work here?"

"No, you didn't and yes, I think it would work. That's a splendid idea." Lola's eyes sparkled as she sat up straight in the chair. "No one in this area offers riding lessons."

"The mother of the young girl at the coffee shop mentioned she had to give their horses away. I hope those kids can come to ride at the ranch sometime." Carli's excitement grew from the look on Lola's face. "I know Beau is good with kids. I really miss working with young people."

"Also, our chestnut mare, Sally, has raised so many ranch kids in this area. The Wild Cow took her in for retirement, but she would be good in your program." Lola sprang to her feet and began pacing with a concentrated look on her face. "We need extra saddles, all sizes, and headstalls. I'm sure we can come up with enough riding tack."

Carli finished off her muffin, and as usual Lola resisted eating. "We'll have to find some other horses."

Lola shook her head in agreement. "Yes, because the ranch horses the guys use are bred too hot. They live for cow work and cutting. I'm not sure they would be suitable for lessons."

"The young girl in black keeps haunting me. I want to help her if I can." Carli really missed her clients in Georgia. She often wondered how their competition careers were progressing. "To see that first-time connection between a horse and rider. Their eyes light up and it makes me so happy. I miss that."

Lola stopped pacing. "I think you have a super idea. And I'm sure Buck will agree. We'd love to help in any way we can."

Another knock at the door cut their conversation short.

"Carli? Lola? Anybody home?"

"C'mon in," Carli called to him. "We're in the study. Want some herb tea and a muffin?"

Buck, her ranch foreman, appeared at the door. "Herb tea?" His face was pinched as if in pain. Carli chuckled. She understood his pain.

"Is it full of that healthy stuff you keep trying to feed me?" Buck frowned at his wife.

"It's only because I love you, dear." Lola held the plate out towards her husband. He waved it away. His wife went to his side, patted his belly a little, and said, "Uh huh, and we've got to watch it, don't we, honey? Remember what the doc said at your last checkup? Eat healthy, watch your sodium intake, and lower your blood pressure."

"Yes, dear. But no herb tea! Not part of my diet and that stuff would cause all kinds of problems for me." He rolled his eyes good-naturedly towards Carli. "You know, Jean..." They all froze and stared at each other. "Oh, sorry, you remind me so much of your grandma Jean. Maybe I should call you 'Little Jean' or something."

"It's okay, Buck. I'm flattered that you think of her when you look at me."

"Anyway, Car-li," he enunciated, "there are two magic words any husband needs to learn in order to keep his woman happy. 'Yes, dear' is the right answer for anything. Remember to tell your future husband that, Little Jean."

"I don't know anything about a future husband, Buck. But I'll remember those words of wisdom for sure."

They all chuckled.

"So, what're y'all working on? It seems pretty serious in here. Are y'all planning a party?" Buck smirked and looked at his wife.

"Carli wants to give riding lessons again, like she did in Georgia. She misses working with kids." Lola looked to Carli and smiled, nodding encouragement. Lola and Buck shared a glance as if they were the only two in the room.

Carli thought it must be nice to have a special someone in your life. Someone who knew everything about you, and loved unconditionally, no matter what. No more tension or questions as to whether you both should be together. You just knew it was the right thing. That it would last forever. Carli wondered if it was even possible. Or just a fairy tale? Sometimes she felt so cheated that she never got to be included in a family with loving parents. Sure, her guardians, the Fitzgeralds, were kind, but they were older, and she often felt like a third wheel. She had no idea how a family functioned together. She chased her riding dreams and horse business, and sure the Fitzgeralds were always there when she came home, but she still felt like something was missing. It suddenly dawned on her as to why she habitually ran from relationships. Just about the time things got serious, she hightailed it out of there. Except for the one guy back home who had torn apart her trust and stomped on her heart on the worst day of her life. She had finally given in, with her whole heart. She thought he was the one. But he made the decision that it was over, and let Carli know by kissing her biggest rival at the horse show. Right in front of her, no less. That image never goes away. Her heart still stings. But now here was how it was supposed to work, right in front of her eyes with Buck and Lola. Trusting someone completely had to be possible. That gave her some hope.

But she couldn't think about romance right now. Not without ruining the friendship she enjoyed with Nathan. Not by giving in to the attraction she felt for Lank. Or giving any notice to those other good-looking Texas cowboys that crossed her path. She had a ranch to run, a birth father to find, and a troubled young lady to help. Affairs of the heart were way down on her list. For the moment anyway.

Chapter Six

Saturday morning dawned crisp and cold, but the network meteorologist predicted a mild day over forty degrees, almost fifty. Of course, what the weatherman said in relation to the Texas Panhandle hardly carried any weight. Carli noticed the topic was continually of interest to everyone who lived here. After the predictions were discussed, conversation then turned to the dramatic difference between the forecast and the actual conditions on the days, weeks, even years prior. It seemed as though rural people could talk for hours about the weather. It wasn't just a topic to pass the time, rather more like a detailed recap of their favorite team sport. And they were serious about their sports, too.

Carli's step was light and hurried as she walked to the corral. She had just answered a text from Lexi's mother. They were on their way, and she needed to make a few preparations. Before she knew it, she heard tires crunching on the gravel drive.

An older model Ford SUV pulled slowly into headquarters, and the mother from the coffee shop got out of the car. As Carli walked closer, she could see the young girl in the backseat. The mom's frustrated face said it all. "Lexi doesn't want to get out. Said she'll wait in the car. She's just impossible. I don't know what to do with her anymore." The woman's head shook back and forth, and her hands fluttered like birds' wings. Luckily, the windows were up; Carli hoped Lexi didn't hear that.

Lexi's brother Brandon waved from the front seat and Carli waved back, and then she placed a hand on the mother's shoulder. "Let me try. I'll be right back."

Carli hurried to the pen where she had Sally tied to the fence rail. She took the halter rope and led her out, stopping next to Lexi's side of the vehicle. She leaned down and tapped on the glass until she got Lexi's attention, then smiled while making the motion to open the window.

After a few minutes, the window slowly slid down. "What?" Lexi added a scowl.

"Remember me? I'm Carli. This is Sally and she needs exercise. Thought you might like to help us out and ride her today."

Lexi grunted but couldn't hide the excitement reflected on her face as she looked at the bay-colored horse with the kind eyes. The car window immediately went back up.

"I completely forgot to introduce myself." The woman offered her hand to Carli before scratching Sally between the ears. "I'm Emily Brown. And you remember Brandon and Lexi."

"It's really nice to see you again. I'm so glad you brought Lexi to visit."

"I'd like to leave her here while I take Brandon

and run some errands. We need to find him some new jeans." She lowered her voice and turned her back to the car. "Honestly, I'm afraid to leave Lexi at home alone. She seems so out of sorts lately. I can't figure out what's going on in her head, and, of course, I'm the last person she'll ever talk to."

"She's welcome here any time. We'll do fine."

Emily turned her attention to her daughter, and with a deep frown said in a low voice just to Carli, "Now, if we can just get her out of the car."

"Will you come and meet Sally?" Carli looked at Lexi with pleading eyes.

Lexi ducked her head, pretending to ignore them both and then the door swung open. Her long, jet black hair sported bright pink highlights on the ends, spikes on top, and this time her nails were painted bright purple. Wearing almost the identical black outfit she had on at the coffee shop, she placed both hands on either side of Sally's face and drew the animal's nose into her belly. She closed her eyes and froze.

"You know your way around a horse, I see." Carli couldn't help but smile.

"Yes, we had several horses, but then my hours got cut at work and I just couldn't afford the feed any longer. They went to a local rescue and were adopted out." Emily answered before her daughter could reply. "If you're good here, I'll be back in about an hour."

While Lexi was distracted, Emily hurried around her car, jumped in, and was gone. Carli watched Lexi carefully for signs of a meltdown like she had witnessed over the muffin incident. So far, so good. Her mother did not say goodbye, and never really spoke directly to her daughter. Instead, she stepped on the gas and peeled out like there was a monster on her tail. Carli pushed away sadness and curiosity about the family's dynamics and turned her attention instead to the girl dressed in black.

"C'mon. Let's start with brushing her and then we'll get her saddled."

Lexi barely gave a nod. A motion of her head so slight Carli would have missed it if she hadn't been watching closely. They all walked into the corral and Carli handed the girl a brush.

Lexi did a good job, giving the right amount of pressure to get the dirt out of Sally's coat but at the same time she had a gentle touch.

"What was your horse's name?" Carli asked. Silence from her new friend. Carli only heard the twitter of a few birds high in the elm tree and one of the horses stomped a foot.

Buck passed through stopping to greet their visitor. "Mornin', girls."

"Hey Buck, this is my new friend Lexi."

The girl gave the ranch foreman a shy, half-smile for a split second before focusing back on the horse.

Buck rattled around in the tack room for a few minutes. "I'm headed to check the North Pasture fence line and scatter some mineral around, Miss Carli."

"Thanks, Buck." Carli turned her attention back to Lexi.

"The grass is greening up. I'm hoping for some rain soon. You girls have a nice ride." Buck tipped his hat brim before leaving.

It was most likely pouring sheets of rain in Georgia this time of year, but here the air was dusty and dry. She glanced at Lexi. Carli never was any good at small talk, and obviously Lexi wasn't interested in it either. Carli felt helpless, yet a million things waiting to be said ran through her mind. Lexi reminded her so much of her younger self. Angry at the world, frustration. The feeling of despondency, lack of control, like things will never change, never get any better. Futility. Carli understood the storm inside this girl, churning away until there's nothing left but defiance and rage...and loneliness.

Giving up on any efforts to have a conversation, Carli left Lexi brushing Sally while she saddled Beau. Then she helped Lexi saddle up, and they were off. "Let's go along the creek. It's a pretty ride, plus good exercise for the horses. Lots of logs to walk around or over."

Carli bit her lip as Lexi slipped her combat boots into the stirrups. Surprisingly, they fit. They started out in the round pen where the horses plodded along at a relaxed walk. Carli noticed Lexi patting the neck of her horse, which warmed her heart. She even wondered what it would be like to have a daughter, kind of an unlikely thought for her. Still young, not to mention her messed up family history.

"Itchy." Lexi's voice broke the silence.

"What?" Carli barely understood her, she spoke so softly. "Is something wrong?"

"My horse's name was Itchy."

"Hands down, the best horse name ever." Carli smiled and glanced at Lexi.

"She liked to be scratched." They both giggled.

A peace settled over them as they urged their horses through a gate out of the round pen and down a slope to a narrow stream of water. Lexi nudged Sally and passed Carli on a wide spot beneath the cottonwood trees, crossing the dry creek bed and up the other side.

Carli followed. That was the start of a conversation, but she was afraid to ask anything more. Lexi might clam up again. They rode in silence, circling the fishpond and returning to headquarters. Lexi didn't utter another word and neither did Carli. The young girl seemed to enjoy the freedom, the breeze on her face, not having to smile at anyone or answer, the warm, rhythmic feel of the horse. Twigs snapped and horse hooves plodding along the ground echoed around them. The camaraderie of riding with someone. They made quite a pair—one angry teen just starting out and an uncertain young woman trying to figure out the direction of her life.

When they returned to headquarters, Lexi's mother and brother were standing at the gate watching them ride up the hill into the pens.

"I see both of you are smiling. Did y'all have fun?" Emily called out.

"Yes, we did," said Carli. "I'll have her back to you in a minute after we unsaddle."

Without a word Lexi managed to pull Sally's saddle off, put everything back in its place in the tack room, then stopped to watch both horses rolling in the dirt before she headed to the SUV. Carli followed and before the girl got into the car, she touched her shoulder. "Lexi. I hope you'll come back. Put my number in your phone. You're welcome here anytime."

"I will," she said before hunkering down in the back seat and slamming the door.

It almost sounded like a mumbled "thanks" followed, but Carli wasn't sure she heard that.

"This is a first. A daughter without a deep scowl on her face," Emily said. "Thank you." Tears bubbled in her eyes and she looked at Carli as if to say more, but she bit her lip instead and got into the driver's seat.

Carli waved as they drove away and couldn't help but notice the carefree, smiling girl on the horse had suddenly transformed into the dark, morose teenager again. It was a start, but was it something Carli wanted to pursue? The kids in this area were not polished and moneyed like some of her clients in Atlanta. She hoped the Texas youth would be more down-to-earth and excited about coming to her ranch. Would she be able to teach them anything?

"God, put me on the right path. Will a riding school help anybody?" Carli whispered as she watched the taillights of the Brown family's car slow with a bump-de-bump over the cattle guard and then turn to disappear into a thicket of mesquite.

Chapter Seven

By the time Carli unsaddled Beau after her ride with Lexi and checked the horses' water, she felt energized. Just the short time with Lexi reminded her how much she missed working with young people. She still had some self-doubt about opening a riding school, about everything she did, actually, but the feeling in her gut was that it was what she truly wanted. Sharing her love of horses with others gave her so much joy.

While she was in the barn breaking off a flake of hay, Lank walked up behind her. Despite the early spring chill, he wore only a Tee-shirt. She tried not to notice his muscled arms, the glisten of sweat at the base of his throat, and black hair that had grown longer, just past his shirt collar. And then she made the mistake of lifting her gaze to stare into his smoky-gray eyes. Her heart fluttered. She forced herself to look away.

"Who was that?" he asked.

"A young girl I met at the B&R Beanery. She used to have a horse and I invited her out to ride." Carli's first instinct was to tell him everything. Her fears about unlocking whatever was going on inside Lexi. Riding lessons and working with kids again. Worries about finding clients. What if she put out the information and nobody came? So many things to talk about, yet she held back. Would it be appropriate? She didn't need any complications. He was her hired ranch hand. But she felt drawn to him. She couldn't deny that.

"What was with all the black? Somebody die?" He leaned against the pipe fence, draping one arm across the top rail, and rested a dusty boot on the bottom rail.

Carli stared again and he met her stare back. Annoyed by his arrogant confidence, never afraid to say just what was on his mind. She sighed. And then her pulse raced, and she knew at that moment she was in a heap of trouble and would not survive the fallout. Stop it, you idiot girl. Best keep this on a professional level.

"I think Lexi, that's her name, is having an identity crisis. But nothing a good horse ride can't fix." Carli laughed.

"Not sure if horses can fix teenagers, but I agree it's worth a try."

"Horses fixed me, and I had more troubles than you could ever imagine," Carli confessed. She noted the look of surprise on his face.

"So, you were an at-risk kid, were you?" Lank stepped closer, genuine concern emanating from those eyes of his.

"At-risk kid? What does that mean?" Carli ignored the look on his handsome face and didn't offer any more specifics about her own situation.

"My mom used to volunteer at a facility in Amarillo. It's for kids who come from horrible family situations. Maybe abandoned by their parents because of drugs, or whatever. The point is to help them before they end up in jail or become a druggie."

"At-risk," Carli repeated. She wanted to help those kinds of kids and she could do it right here at the Wild Cow. She wanted to ask Lank more about it but instead her tongue was tied as she looked at him, and then she took a step closer before she could stop her body from moving.

"Something on your mind?" he asked.

Carli needed a friend. She needed someone to listen. Someone who could be a sounding board for all of the ideas that were running through her head. Nathan was a great listener, but then there was Lank, too. He knew the ranch. Knew the horses. He wasn't Nathan. She took another step closer.

"I've been thinking a lot about Lexi and other kids like her. Maybe they need a place to come. Maybe horses would be something they could channel their energy into."

"That would be great. I've loved horses since I could walk and thank goodness my parents allowed me to join the high school rodeo team."

"You rodeoed?"

"Bare-back broncs. But then an injury shortened my career. Bad concussion and, for my mom's sake, I promised not to ride again. I was on my way to the National Finals, or so everybody told me." A sullen frown crossed his face and he suddenly stopped talking.

"Now that your mom is gone, are you going to rodeo again?"

"Naw, I'm too old now. This body has been through a lot of wrecks." He laughed.

"I'd like to hear about them sometime." Carli clamped her lips together and silently cursed herself. Why that came out of her mouth, she'd never know. She had to keep it professional between them. Boss and ranch hand. She had to keep reminding herself.

Lank didn't reply but clenched his jaw and looked at her with a sadness in his eyes that made her heart ache.

Carli wondered about the emotion that he usually hid, and if it was due to the memories of his rodeo days or of his mom that had suddenly turned him sullen.

Her phone buzzed in her pocket. She broke eye contact to look at the screen. "Sorry. I should take this." She spun around and walked towards the gate. "Nate. Hi." She glanced back at Lank, planning to wave goodbye but she couldn't help notice the frown still etched on his face and the deep sadness in his eyes as he watched her walk away.

"Why don't you just come over here? We can cook something at my house." Carli ended the call and turned to face Lank again. "I guess Nathan is coming for dinner. I'll see you around."

"Yeah. See ya," Lank mumbled, his eyes cold, "Boss."

The last word uttered hard, with a tinge of aggravation. She spun on her heel, turned her back to him, and walked out of the corral. Carli wanted more than anything to turn around and tell him she was sorry he had to give up something he loved. But she kept walking.

Chapter Eight

A rap on her front door reminded Carli she had invited Nathan over for dinner. In the middle of searching online newspapers for any mention of her birth father or his family, she quickly shut it down, jumped up from the laptop, and hurried to let him in.

"Time got away from me. What do you want to eat?"

Nathan laughed. "Well, what'a ya got?" He followed her into the kitchen. Stopping in his tracks, he turned around slowly. "I haven't been in here for a long time. Your grandmother Jean was a character."

"Tell me everything you can." Carli slid into a cowhide cushioned barstool and watched him intently. He took his time and looked around the kitchen, every detail, every dish behind the paned-glass cabinet, every picture on the wall. He chuckled. "I remember this."

Nathan removed a framed 8x10 photo from the nail and looked at it closer. "That's me." He pointed.

Carli squinted to see a little kid, all legs and a face in the shadows under a wide cowboy hat, hanging on the fence rail at a rodeo. Instead of staying behind the fence like everyone else, he was inside the arena. A crowd behind him bulged in the stands.

"That's your Grandpa Ward on the bronc. Somebody dared him to ride it, and darned if he didn't make it the eight seconds. He was a tough old coot. Your Grandma Jean met him at the gate, and she gave him an earful. I thought she was going to punch him. I'd never heard her cuss before that day." Nathan burst into a deep, belly laugh that echoed through the quiet house.

"I wish I could have known them." Carli wanted to hear stories, but she had to control her emotions too. Every time she learned something new about her grandparents, it added to her sadness and feeling of isolation as the resentment towards her mother grew.

"Go on." She smiled, trying to hide the conflicting emotions that raged inside.

"I like telling you about them, but I'm not one to stay buried in the past, Carli. Just the fact you're carrying on the legacy they left at the Wild Cow is a huge thing. You're here now and we need to make our own memories."

"It doesn't seem that big a deal. Which is why I want to talk to you about another idea I have." Nathan returned the picture to the nail. Carli followed him into the kitchen and watched as he dug around in the refrigerator. "You've got eggs, but no bacon. How about breakfast for dinner?"

"There's bacon over at the cookhouse and pancake mix too. Sounds like a good plan to me."

Chatting and laughing at more bronc stories involving her Grandpa Ward, they walked to the ranch cookhouse and found what they needed. It was nice being with Nathan. He always seemed so kind, willing to help with anything Carli needed. She felt safe with him, plus he was a good listener. But with Lank she felt exhilarated like her skin tingled and she was fully alive. He was so irritating at times. Why did she keep comparing them?

She remembered Lola had once told her how God intended humans to feel—living their dreams, enjoying life to the fullest, being everything He designed them to be, all for His glory ultimately. Lola and Buck had taught her so much. She was maturing in her faith, but she still was uncertain about who she was and why she was here in Texas. Why her young life had been such a mess and why her parents had abandoned her. There were so many unanswered questions.

As they walked back across the compound towards her house, Lank drifted into her mind again. She wondered what he was doing this evening. Secretly, she wished he was the one walking beside her now. *There I go again. Always wishing for something I'll never have. Parents. Grandparents.* Her old equine business in Georgia. She really missed the young girls she had been tutoring. She pushed the past from her mind and tried to focus on the here and now.

Nathan found several cast-iron skillets and set them on the cooktop with a clang. "If you'll get the coffee going, I can handle the rest."

"It's a deal, since I was the one who invited you over. I didn't mean for you to have to work for your supper." They both chuckled.

"Now tell me. How are the riding lessons coming along? Any clients yet?" asked Nathan as he lay bacon slices into a pan.

"Have you ever heard the term 'at-risk kids'?" Carli found the coffee beans and filled the grinder.

"Fresh ground?" Nathan's eyebrows shot up in surprise.

"Yep. I'm a coffee snob." She tilted her chin and gave him a wide grin and then opened the package and took in a deep breath. One of the best smells in the world. "Belinda has been coaching me."

"Belinda and Russell sure know how to roast some coffee berries for sure." Waiting until the grinder shut off, Nathan answered. "I've never worked with kids like that, but I've heard the term. Mainly used in schools, right?"

Carli returned to her barstool and watched Nathan crack eggs into a bowl. "Peppers and onions?" he asked. "Hopefully, you have some."

She paused for a moment to admire the starched Wrangler jeans, green paisley Western shirt, and polished boots that stood in her kitchen. But he didn't make her heart skip a beat like the grubby, infuriating cowhand who worked for her. She cleared her throat and found what he needed. "These are kids who have all the odds stacked against them. I've been thinking about how we can make a difference in their lives. I'm not a professional counselor, but from what I've read sometimes these kids need a distraction. They just need a piece of normal."

Nathan flipped over the bacon, walked closer, and put his hands on hers. "You were abandoned, weren't you?"

Carli felt tears bubble up in her eyes and she swallowed the lump in her throat. The question never bothered her before but being here on this ranch and knowing she had real flesh and blood grandparents who searched for her made her feel even more abandoned. So stupid it brought such emotion still. She was an adult, for gosh sakes.

"Yes, my mother Michelle had a long, troubled past and, consequently, so do I. Don't get me wrong. I wasn't abused or anything like that. The people who raised me were loving and kind, but they were older. Closer to the age of grandparents so I was basically on my own from the time I could drive. I never even knew any of their family. They were somewhat reclusive. But they willingly funded whatever I wanted to do, and that happened to be anything relating to horses."

"You showed horses?"

"Yes, hunter-jumper classes. Really, it was All Around. Western Pleasure. Horsemanship. We did everything. Except for driving a cart. I haven't learned that. Yet."

Nathan laughed. "That's one of the things I admire about you. Always willing to tackle something new. I saw you can ride. You have real skills." Nathan opened and shut several cabinet doors. "Plates?"

"I'll get them. Are we dining formal this evening or kitchen?"

They looked at each other for a minute, and at the same time said, "Kitchen." Carli smiled. She set up the bar with plates and silverware. "Cream or sugar?" she asked.

"Just black."

Carli poured their coffees into the largest mugs she could find. Nathan turned from the stove and scraped a heap of scrambled eggs onto her plate.

"Flapjacks coming up. Find the butter, would ya, please?"

Carli buttered the hot cakes right as they came off the griddle. She found syrup in the pantry.

They pulled their stools up to the bar and dug in. Best looking dinner she'd ever seen. Between mouthfuls of pancake, she said, "These kids need help right now. I think I can make a difference."

As they ate, Carli talked to Nathan about what she knew about programs using horses to help kids. She had spent the afternoon researching and learning as much as she could. A facility in Oklahoma had a wonderful program. Carli ordered books written by the founder and planned to send a donation and buy their annual calendar.

The stories were so touching, but tragic.

"Some of the kids are abused or abandoned and come to the ranch in a broken, non-communicative state. One facility I read about also rescues horses so sometimes the animals are in just as bad of shape as the kids. Somehow, miraculously, a child and horse end up helping each other heal. Most are faith-based operations."

"That makes sense," said Nathan. "It's obvious God would be involved in some of the seemingly impossible stories."

"Even some of the founders have their own tragedies to deal with, which led them to open their doors to others." Carli refilled the coffee mugs. "I read about a lady whose parents had died tragically when she was just a girl. Her faith in God and love for a horse saved her from being destroyed by the loss. When she married, she and her husband were so broke financially but managed to buy a barren piece of land no one else wanted. Their home and program started there. Beaten and broken horses were rescued from the hands of their abusers, and eventually, at-risk children began to interact with the horses. God blessed the founders' efforts and the land and program flourished. He brought beauty out of ashes."

"That's in the Bible, you know. Beauty out of ashes. It's in Isaiah 61."

"Yes, I learned it from Lola. I'm going to have to study the whole chapter." Carli stared at him and thought he was a good guy.

Nathan continued. "So, how many kids would you have in the program?"

"We'd have to start off small. The problem will be finding horses suitable for this kind of outreach."

"I can definitely help with that. I'll get the word out and be on the lookout. I can also help with training. Whatever you need, Carli. Count the Rafter O all in with whatever you want to do." Nathan pointed to the last piece of bacon and, when Carli shook her head, he polished it off. "Are you wanting to get into the rescue horse business too?"

"I don't know about that yet. Seems like a lot to manage. I need to do more research. Of course, if we hear about an abuse or neglect problem in our area, we can certainly help. But I think my main focus right now should be on the kids. I really miss my coaching business."

"This all started because of that girl in the coffee shop with the muffin, didn't it? What was her name? Do you think abuse is a factor in her life?"

"Lexi? I really don't know what her story is. Anger for some reason. Or teenage angst. I'm no shrink, but she came out to ride with me. I forgot to tell you. She sure loves horses."

"Have I ever mentioned how much I admire you?" Nathan carried their dirty plates to the sink. Carli watched him in surprise, frozen to her seat, and didn't even stand up to lend a hand.

He didn't turn to face her but instead filled the sink with sudsy water. "You gave up everything you had known to move here. That took some guts. I've lived here my whole life and I can't even imagine what that must be like. A stranger in a strange place. You fit in like you've been here forever."

"It wasn't that big of a deal. Once I made my mind up, there was no turning back. I tend to be like that. It takes me forever to decide, but once I stop doubting, I just bulldoze ahead. But look at you. Your destiny is decided. What a beautiful life and family. You have no decisions to make."

Nathan let out a heavy sigh, his head bent over the sink as he washed their plates. "I don't want to spend the rest of my life running our ranch." He froze at his task and stood silent for a minute. "I can't believe I told you that. I've never said it out loud to anyone."

Carli walked over to the sink and stood behind him. She placed a hand on his shoulder. "What do you want, Nate?"

"I want to be an artist."

"What kind of artist?"

"Everything. Working with metal, bronze, sculpting. I also like to draw and paint. But mostly I'm obsessed with learning about bronze sculptures. There, I said it. That's what I want to do."

"You should follow your dreams, Nate. If that's your passion, go for it."

"I wish someone would tell my dad that." He turned to look down into her eyes. "Are you following your dreams?"

Carli's heart fluttered as he leaned his face closer. She could tell he wanted to kiss her by the fire in his eyes. Yes. But no. How could this be the right thing when her heart said no? But she was drawn to him. At the last minute he pulled away.

"It's getting late. I should go."

Stunned out of the moment, it took Carli a while to still her heart and then to realize he already had his hat on. She followed him to the front door and clicked on the porch light. "Thanks for cooking dinner. It was fun. And thanks for listening."

"Any time, Carli. Are we still on for the art gallery opening? I'll call you." He walked halfway down the sidewalk, but suddenly turned. He stopped at the bottom step and, at eye level, looked intensely into her eyes. With no hesitation he kissed her. Soft at first, and then the second time firm and deep.

"I hope that's a new memory for you." He turned and strode to his truck. The only response she could manage was a wave at his taillights as he drove away.

Glancing up, she looked across the compound and saw the silhouette of a cowboy standing in the light of the saddle house door. Motionless and still, he didn't move from his spot. Carli stared back, watching Lank watching her.

Stupid men. Always making things so darn complicated. She spun on a heel and slammed the front door behind her.

Chapter Nine

At her desk in the back den of her grandparents' house Carli wrestled with names for her riding school. The business she had in Georgia, with her partner Mark, had been named for the road where it was located. Seemed like a lifetime ago, but in reality, just less than a year. Her life was so different now. In Georgia she had to work part-time for a realtor in order to pay her bills and spent every spare minute on the horse show circuit and training a few clients—high school girls. It was a daily struggle, a delicate balance, like juggling the puzzle pieces of her life, working so hard to stay afloat financially while chasing her passion for horses, but always feeling like something was missing.

Back in Georgia, she didn't have much of a social life or any close friends to speak of. And her cell phone now in Texas certainly wasn't blowing up from the acquaintances she had left behind. She always heard, "out of sight, out of mind" and now understood how people moved on with their own lives. The show competition had been rigid, and meaningful relationships on the circuit were hard to develop. Any kind of travel was always horse show related.

Carli often thought of her old life though. Georgia was green and beautiful, mountainous in some areas. Texas was dry and flat, yet a different kind of breathtaking emptiness with an endless sky that reminded her of an awesome Creator. Interesting that every day she was feeling more and more like this place was her true home.

She had found her family, where she belonged, but was still unsure about her purpose. Buck told her that God has a plan for everyone, but we need patience because He works by His timing, not ours. She had stopped questioning if she had made the right decision to move to Texas and live on the Wild Cow. There was no going back now. She left her life in Georgia behind. As Carli remembered, she wondered if maybe the struggles she had faced were hints from above of what was waiting for her, like a nudging whisper telling her she should move on.

In just a few short months she learned to love this place, the ranch of her ancestors, but she still felt there was something else she should be doing. Working with young riders again might fill the void, and she needed an eye-catching name that would attract students but also have special meaning. She didn't want to use the Wild Cow Ranch, although that name was well known around the area. The riding program would be separate from the cattle operation.

She dug around in a cabinet, looking for her yellow notepad. Nothing in the old file cabinet but old utility bills. Where had she put that pad? The ideas were coming fast into her brain, so she scribbled riding school names on the backs of invoices dated from ten years ago: Safe Haven, Horse Haven, Hope Horses, Dream Catchers. Should she use the word "horse" in the name and logo?

What did she like about riding horses? So many things—the freedom, solitude, it was almost like flying. The responsibility of taking care of another living creature, and the sense of accomplishment at mastering the partnership with a thousand-pound animal. Trust. And just the sheer love and bond between rider and horse. That's what she wanted the kids to experience. In addition to feeling safe as if in their own clubhouse, even if only temporarily for an hour or two, she wanted them to feel love and joy and to learn about horses and riding. That was it! LoveJoy Horseback Riding School.

After researching other riding programs in the state, she was glad to notice there were none in her immediate area. Next, she set up a Facebook public page with details about prices and times. She spent way too long fiddling with a logo, but it was fun work. Next, she designed a simple flyer to leave with Belinda at the coffee shop and ordered a box of business cards. Also set a regular day and time so that everyone, from volunteers to parents, could mark their calendars. The first Saturday of April seemed like a good date to start. In Georgia this time of year, there could be sporadic showers. She thought of the expression, "April showers bring May flowers." She wasn't sure about Texas spring rains, but if the weather was bad, the kids could brush horses and learn how to put halters on inside the barn. Excitement urged her onward. She couldn't wait for the program to start. She had a few short weeks to get ready.

Carli thought long and hard about ages. Should she offer it to smaller kids as well? Teens and tweens were the group that most sparked her interest, probably because that had been such a tumultuous time for her. She decided on ages between twelve and sixteen, and really didn't want to deal with older kids. With the riding school naming and other details off her list, she turned to the genealogy website.

Thousands of Taylor Millers in the state of Texas. It sounded kind of crazy to Carli. But she had to start somewhere.

Carli saw that some searches even produced photos. What would it feel like if she recognized facial features similar to her own? Everyone kept telling her how much she looked like her mother, Michelle, but surely, she had some things from her dad too? It was rather strange to imagine coming face to face with the man who gave her life. For some reason, she just knew he was alive. But where? Did he still live in Texas? Or did he leave a long time ago? He could be anywhere.

She'd been at it all morning, as was her habit lately, before the day got away from her. Late at night her brain was too tired for research, but his name never left her head. Right now, she needed a fresh pot of coffee. Just as she finished setting it up, a knock at the door resulted in Lola's familiar voice.

"C'mon in. It's open."

Lola walked into the kitchen surrounded by a buzz of energy and a bright smile. Definitely a morning person. "I am so ready for yoga classes to begin again. I'm thinking about holding them in the cookhouse until we can go back outside. Want to join us?"

"Thanks, Lola. I think I want to stay on track with my research. Don't want to lose the momentum. How does LoveJoy Horses sound for the name of a riding school?"

"I like it! And I completely forgot to tell Buck about your idea. I'm gonna call him right now."

"No. Lola, wait. Don't bother him. I'm sure he has plenty to do today."

But Lola had already reached her husband. Ignoring Carli's pleas, she said, "Hey, sweetie. Could you take a break and come to Carli's? We could use your help." Lola pressed the red End Call button on her phone. "He'll be here in a second."

Carli rolled her eyes but did appreciate Lola's support. She hated to disturb the ranch foreman with her silly ideas. He must have more important issues to deal with.

Buck knocked on the door and opened it at the same time. As usual, he took a second to stomp any dirt from his boots.

"What's up, ladies?" He found them in the back den where Carli had set up her office.

Lola gave him a peck on the cheek. "Hon, Carli has a new project for the ranch. I think you'll like it."

"Oh," was all he said as he took his cowboy hat off, rubbed his fingers through his graying hair, and set the hat upside down on an end table.

Carli read the worry in his lined face and was embarrassed that Lola had disturbed him. "I'm not bothering you, am I? If this is a bad time, we can talk later."

Lola handed him a mug of coffee. He smiled at her, set the cup down, and paced a little to look out the window. He wasn't a man to sit still for very long, just like Lank, Carli noticed.

"And let me say it isn't anything you'll have to add to your To Do list. Nathan is lending me a hand with this." Carli stared at him and swallowed.

"Spring is a busy time around the ranch with calving season, but I'll always make time for you, Miss Carli." He laughed. "So, let's hear it." Buck eased into a leather chair and stretched his long legs on the ottoman. He lifted his mug again.

"I'll leave you two at it. I need to make some phone calls to my yogis, move tables, and get the cookhouse set up." Lola gave Carli a pat on the shoulder. "Tell him about the girl in the coffee shop."

"Lexi Brown is her name. Do you know the family?" Carli gave a quick wave to Lola and turned her attention to Buck.

He shook his head and Carli continued. "I want to start offering riding lessons at the ranch." She told him about the incident in the coffee shop and about the first ride with Lexi. Buck stood and looked over her shoulder at the computer screen as she showed him the public page for LoveJoy. He offered ideas on horse-related activities for the kids should the weather be too cold or rainy for riding.

"What kinds of kids are we looking for?" Buck asked.

"All kinds. Kids who want to learn how to ride, and at-risk kids too, which covers teen alcoholism, domestic abuse, violence, and crime. Maybe their parents are incarcerated. Kids who just need an escape from their reality. And kids with mental health issues like autism. If we can offer several hours of something they love, it would be a step in the right direction." Saying it out loud made Carli realize just how much more she needed to know. Working with disciplined show horses and young riders from affluent families in Georgia, to rural Texas kids with deep emotional issues would be a big transition.

"Your grandparents would be so proud that you're here," Buck said.

"I've heard that from several people, but I didn't know them, so I don't feel any kind of connection, but I am learning to love this ranch. I hear what you're saying, but I haven't grasped the family thing. Maybe in time. I hope to leave my own mark on the Wild Cow. Tell me about my grandparents. When were you hired? Did you know my mother?"

He sat down, a look of concentration and a frown deepened on his face. He shrugged out of his jacket and tugged to loosen the black silk wild rag around his neck.

"If you'd rather not talk about it, Buck, I understand. The past can be painful." Carli couldn't help but hold her breath.

He hesitated, took another sip of coffee, and then looked at her. "I don't know where to begin."

Carli froze, the half-smile set on a face of stone but inside her stomach jumped into her throat. She had never asked him direct questions about the past before, particularly involving her mother, Michelle.

Chapter Ten

"It was such a time of turmoil at the Wild Cow after your mother ran away." Carli's ranch foreman Buck looked at her intently for several seconds before saying anything more. He settled back in the overstuffed chair and swung his lanky legs onto the ottoman, balancing his mug on the chair arm. Carli turned her desk chair around to face him.

Buck's voice was soft, very controlled. He looked at ease sitting in her grandparents' study, now her office, but he hesitated before saying anything more as if weighing what he should or should not say. "I like to remember some of those times. It wasn't all bad. Your grandparents, Ward and Jean, were my best friends as well as my employers. Lola and I came here as newlyweds, and I wasn't exactly a Christian back then, still sowing my wild oats as they say. My dad was a tough guy, not the most loving. I couldn't wait to get out from under his iron fist. I left to do my time for our country in Nam, but then came back to the Wild Cow and I've been here ever since. Ward and Jean gave me a home as well as a start on my faith walk. I learned a great deal from them."

"What do you remember about my mother?" Carli leaned forward, listening to every word. He set his empty coffee cup on the side table, but she didn't offer to refill it. Afraid to break the moment, she wanted him to keep talking.

"Jean and Ward were older when they started their family. When Jean gave birth to your mom, Michelle, it was a happy time on the Wild Cow. We had just hired on because Ward bought a neighbor's place and he lost his best hand, Jean. Your mom was a newborn then. I guess little kids bring joy with them from heaven. Michelle used to climb on my shoulders, and I ran around with her as she giggled like crazy, and Jean and Ward beamed with ear-to-ear smiles. They taught her to ride a pony almost as soon as she could walk. A bundle of energy, that kid had to stay busy all the time. We had many years during her childhood that were so memorable. Just like any young family, I guess. Lola and I were unable to have kids, so we readily adopted your mom. She called us 'Annie' or 'Tía' for Aunt Lola and 'Unky Buck' or 'Tío' for me."

"What happened to change everything?" Carli asked.

"She became a teenager?" He shrugged and frowned, as if dark thoughts clouded his mind. "When Michelle was around fourteen or fifteen, the boys were really noticing her. She was a pretty girl, big eyes, long silky hair. You do look just like her, you know. As much as Jean and Ward loved her, they also had a lot of ranch responsibilities as well as the rodeo circuit. Maybe Michelle felt pushed to the back of their attention. They had lots of money tied up in roping horses back then. They hauled Michelle around with them since she was a little tyke. I guess she got tired of it and thought boys were a whole lot more exciting than ranch work and the rodeo circuit. She was always independent and wanted her freedom." He looked at her, his eyes cool and steady. A frown creased his forehead.

"Go on," Carli prodded.

"So, more and more, she fought with her parents and whined about the chores, and then started lying, too. Michelle would concoct some story about girls at school having a weekend sleepover. She was very dramatic and told her parents it would 'ruin her life' if she missed out on events with her friends. Of course, it'd be a weekend Jean and Ward had commitments to travel to the rodeo. So, they believed her and let her stay home. Lola and I knew she was lying."

Carli wanted more than anything to understand what made her mother do the things she did. Why did Michelle have this incessant need for constant fun and lies to her parents? For as long as Carli could remember she had been the exact opposite, always seeming older than her years. Honestly, the popular party crowd always bored her. Carli couldn't help but wonder what her life might have been like if her mother had raised her instead of the Fitzgeralds.

"Michelle loved people and parties. We saw her around town, and we heard rumors, but we were caught between a rock and a hard place. Was it our place to rat her out? Now, I wish we had. We were so young and in love, and I just kept my nose buried in the ranch work. If we had said something, it might have stopped her from running away, but then again, she was so darn stubborn. If you tried to rein her in, it just made it worse. Nobody could control the runaway train wreck that was Michelle."

Carli's heart raced. She wanted to tell him about the birth certificate she found with the name of her birth father, but she was afraid. Of what, she didn't know. For some reason it was her secret still. She wanted to hang on to the knowledge for a few days more. "Do you know any of the guys she might have dated?"

"Michelle had many boyfriends, if the rumors were true. I hate to speak of the deceased in a bad way, but you're asking. I don't mean to be disrespectful. Your mother was so full of life. Her smile lit up a room the minute she walked in and she never knew a stranger. Everyone claimed to be her friend. Everyone wanted to be her friend."

"What did my grandparents do?" Carli finally stood, walked into the kitchen to get the coffee pot and refill their mugs.

"It was the classic pushing and pulling between parent and child for dominance, for authority. They grounded her or took her car keys away, forbade her from riding her horse, but she'd rebel and lie about her whereabouts, then things kept getting worse. Coming home late, red eyes or the smell of alcohol, until finally she didn't come home until the next day or even second day. She talked back to them. Harsh, ugly words were said. Words that can never be taken back. And your Grandma Jean cried. It was becoming an impossible situation. On nights she didn't come home, they hated to bring the sheriff into it because rumors were already going around. Jean and Ward hated the gossip and attention it brought to the Wild Cow."

"And then what?" Carli was on the edge of her seat.

"And then she became pregnant with you."

"Oh." Carli let out a sigh and rose. "What happened then? Were they upset?"

"I think they were really sad. But I gotta say, neither Ward nor Jean ever yelled at Michelle after that. They showed her love. Unconditional love. And said they would help her raise the baby. You."

Buck turned quiet, staring into his mug. Lost in the past. "And then she was gone," he mumbled under his breath. "Vanished. All I remember was the sound of a motorcycle one night. I thought it was someone riding through headquarters really slow but now I know he was parked out by the corral, waiting. The roar when he gunned it was ear splitting and then the sound grew fainter and fainter. I didn't even look out. Now I know Michelle left with him."

"My grandparents must have been devastated." Carli's heart hurt.

"And she left a scrap of a note," Buck continued. "If I can remember right, it read something like, 'I'm leaving. Can't stay. Don't worry. I'll be fine.' Pretty much broke their hearts. Not only was Michelle gone. But she took you, too. Their only grandchild."

"What did they do?" Carli leaned in closer and scooted to the edge of her chair.

"They called the sheriff this time. We never found out who she rode off with. The sheriff questioned all her friends, but turned up nothing, so we think the guy must have been from another town. Michelle covered up her tracks well, but she had to have had help. If anyone knew who took her away that night, they weren't talking."

Carli let out a whoosh of air, though she hadn't realized she was holding her breath. She paced over to the windows, her back to Buck. Was the man on the motorcycle that night her birth father? A sadness crept over Carli as she listened. She might never know the truth. "When did they find out I was born?"

"Jean and Ward figured approximately when you'd be born. They asked all over Texas it seemed. Contacted Michelle's school friends again, asked everybody they knew at rodeos if they'd seen her. Someone kept her hidden, but we never found out who. As for your grandparents, it's as though the joy was sucked out of them. They kept hitting dead ends until finally they hired a private detective. After that, he gave them the sad report. He tracked your mother to Los Angeles, interviewed a few of her new party-going friends out there who didn't really want to talk to him until he slipped them a little cash. Ward and Jean spent a fortune trying to find her. Once again Michelle was able to stay hidden. She had slipped through their fingers."

A sadness jolted her heart. "Was she an addict by then?"

"Some of the crowd she hung with were, as far as I can recollect from what Ward and Jean told me. Others were just free spirits—artists, street musicians, homeless vagabonds. You know the type. Michelle was probably a little of both. But you know what? During all that time she never gave up her one passion, horses. But even then, her parents could never find her. They heard about the men she'd taken up with and the shows she competed in, but it seemed like they were always one step behind. She probably changed her name many times."

Carli quietly listened to Buck. The story fit her mother so well based on the one time Carli met her when she was around fifteen. Her adoptive guardians hadn't objected. Carli remembered her beautiful smile, but definitely her lifestyle had taken its toll. She looked worn and tired, older than her years with dull hair and eyes. Carli never told anyone before, but she followed the horse show circuit results. Sometimes Michelle used her real name, Jameson, and Carli dreamed about finding her. And then one day she was older with a job and didn't care as much.

"What about you? Where were you all this time?" asked Buck.

Carli shrugged. "I was born in Amarillo and given to the Fitzgeralds, my guardians, as a newborn. They never legally adopted me which is why I still use the name Jameson. All they told me is that they learned about me from some of their cousins. Michelle signed me over and went on her merry way, and the Fitzgeralds took me back to Florida. Then Georgia. End of story." Just saying it out loud created an ache in her heart. Why couldn't she have been a part of her grandparents' life? The stupid decisions Michelle made had cheated them all.

He swung his legs off the ottoman, hunched his shoulders and looked down. "I guess Michelle hit rock bottom in California."

"Yes, the attorney told me she overdosed just a few months before my grandpa Ward died."

"I don't think Jean and Ward were ever the same after Michelle ran away. It seemed as though the joy evaporated from their life. Then they put all their efforts into finding you, but they were too late. Michelle had given you up and they lost track of her too. It pains my heart to think what her life might have been like, surviving from one fix to the next. Such a waste. She was a beautiful girl. And your grandparents came so close to finding you both. Ward was alive one month before you got here."

Carli struggled to swallow the lump in her throat. Stupid and careless decisions can affect so many lives in ways people have no understanding of the outcomes. Her mother had chosen drugs over her. It didn't seem fair.

Buck stood and put a hand on her shoulder. "But it's not the end of your story. You're home now. And I believe God had something to do with that. It's an answer to Jean and Ward's prayers, but not in their timing. We don't know why. You're here now and that's the most important thing."

"Out of the blue, Michelle sent Jean and Ward a short letter saying she had put you up for adoption. It was the last they heard from her. So, they had some little clues. A little closure if you can call it that."

Still so many unanswered questions, but Carli learned more about her mother in this one conversation with Buck than she had during her entire life. Her heart ached at the suffering her grandparents had endured.

"What's all that?" Buck pointed to a stack of papers on the floor.

"Just some old invoices and bank statements. I'm gradually cleaning out cabinets." Carli looked at him intently for a few seconds and then asked, "You ever hear of a man named Taylor Miller?"

"Yeah. J.T., we called him. Hired him one summer to build fence. Why?"

Her heart thudded in her chest. She was certain Buck could hear it. Carli cleared her throat and looked into her mug. "No reason. Just noticed his name on some papers, is all. Why J.T.?" Obviously, he didn't know about her birth certificate since there didn't seem to be any concern as to why she was asking about the kid named J.T.

Buck chuckled. "His first name was John. He was the star quarterback his junior and senior years for the Dixon Wildcats. Sure did enjoy watching them play. They went to District playoffs and made it to State the next year when J.T. was a senior. J.T. threw the winning pass but the receiver dropped it. They still talk about that game around here."

"So, what happened to him?" Carli tried to ask as though she didn't really care if he answered or not, but she felt as though Buck noticed her sudden interest. She didn't want to point out the connection between J.T. and her mother yet.

"There's one person who might know J.T.'s whereabouts. And if he's still alive."

"Who's that?" Dread hit Carli the minute the question escaped her lips.

"The man who grew up here and thought he would inherit the Wild Cow Ranch before the attorneys located you. Billy Broderick. He and J.T. were best friends in high school."

Carli thought Billy Broderick was out of her life since his now ex-wife had set fire to the barn soon after the judge ruled in Carli's favor to inherit the Wild Cow. She remembered the brash temper-fit Billy had pitched at the hearing when she was declared the rightful heir. If his behavior was considered normal with the kind of men he hung out with, then she definitely did not want anything to do with his best friend—and her birth father—Taylor Miller. Were they alike? Overbearing jerks? Asking anything of Billy Broderick would be an impossibility. The man hated her and would probably go to his grave cursing the day she was born. How ironic the one person who prevented Billy Broderick from owning the ranch was actually the long-lost heir fathered by his childhood friend, J.T.

Chapter Eleven

When Nathan pulled to a stop in front of Carli's house, she looked like a young schoolgirl rocking in an oversized porch chair and scrolling through her phone. Her head raised and he couldn't wipe the grin off his face. He'd been looking forward to spending the day with her all week. In one smooth motion, she stood, slung a huge tote bag on to one shoulder, skipped over the porch steps, and jogged to his pickup truck.

"Hey," she said, bringing with her a radiant smile of sunshine, eyes sparkling with laughter, and the smell of something sweet mixed with musk. She wore her Grandma Jean's turquoise boots with her pants tucked in the high tops. Fringe swung from the sleeves of a brown suede jacket as she stepped up into his pickup truck.

"We need to talk." The smile suddenly disappeared, and the tone of her voice dashed any hopes he had of the day ending with kisses.

Nathan hesitated for a moment. There was something he needed to tell her too. "Yes, we do. I have something to ask you."

She settled into the seat beside him. Dug in her oversized leather bag and swiped her lips with gloss before placing the tote in the back seat because it wouldn't fit in the floorboard next to her feet. Why in the world would she need to bring a purse that big for an afternoon in Amarillo? Before stepping on the accelerator, he looked over at her. She turned to face him, pulling one leg onto the seat.

"Don't tell anyone…" They said in unison and then laughed.

"Ladies first," Nathan said.

"Okay." Carli looked down at her lap and cleared her throat. "Have you told anybody about my birth father?"

Nathan slowly let out the breath he'd been holding. At least this wasn't going to be a "let's be friends" talk. "I meant to ask Dad, but honestly I forgot about it."

"Good. Don't say anything. I'm doing the research on my own and you're the only one who knows the name. I want to keep it to myself for a while."

"Not a problem. I can keep your secret."

"Now you." Carli turned her full attention on him, piercing him with those hazel eyes, making him forget what they were even talking about. He studied her face for several moments.

"You had something you wanted to say?" she reminded him.

Nathan put the car in drive and slowly accelerated. "I haven't told Dad about my interest in taking my metal work to the next level. Actually, no one in my family knows how important it is to me. Don't mention it to anyone. I'd never hear the end of it, if they all knew we were spending the afternoon in a gallery. And, by the way if anybody asks, this was your idea."

The sound of her laughter filled the pickup cab and made him smile despite the seriousness of his request. His father had his future already mapped out. As the oldest of five kids, Nathan never wanted to disappoint his father, but the responsibilities of being an Olsen sometimes felt like an anchor around his neck. She nodded her head and spun around to face forward in her seat. "Don't worry, if anybody asks, I've got your back. This reminds me of a Country song. That's your story and you're sticking to it."

"Good to know I can rely on you, Carli." Nathan wanted to say they could be even more but didn't. He was afraid to push her away before they'd even begun. "I'm impressed you know the words to a Country song." They both chuckled. He could get used to the sound of her laugh.

"How can life be so simple and so complicated at the same time?" she added.

Nathan agreed. "That's an understatement." He knew what was tossing his insides into such a jumble. Nothing new. He'd been walking a tightrope his whole life. He knew his dad expected him to do the ranch business, take it over, be the head of the family when his parents were gone, and carry on the Olsen legacy. But Nathan wanted to do other things. Pursue his own dreams. The ranch was his dad's dream. More and more he noticed that every minute he spent at the Rafter O made him even more resentful, but this was his lot in life. The only solution he could see was to keep his thoughts to himself and do the work expected of him.

Driving to the Art Museum of the Texas Plains, Nathan felt her watching him.

"You're like a kid on Christmas morning," she said.

It was true. He'd been waiting months for this event. "Some of my favorite artists may be there." He told her about the different sculptors he followed, how they started out in their careers, the obstacles they faced, and the success they eventually achieved. Even though he had never met any of them, he felt they were his kindred spirits.

Nathan glanced at her face for any signs he might be blowing his chance to spend many more dates like this with her. But Carli's occasional nods and questions encouraged him to keep going. Once he started talking about his passion for metal work, he couldn't stop. Most girls could care less, but Carli genuinely seemed interested.

"Sorry if I'm boring you, Carli. Thanks for coming with me." After talking her ear off for the first hour of their drive, he finally asked, "How are things at the Wild Cow?"

"Things are good. Which reminds me, opening day of the riding school is the first Saturday of April. You should be there. Did I tell you I spread the word through social media? I've had some great response. Even got a few release forms filled out and spots reserved."

"This all began with the crazy girl in the coffee shop, didn't it?" he commented as he exited off the interstate and stopped at a red light.

"It may have planted the idea, but I gave riding lessons in Georgia. The show horse ring was intense though. This will be more fun, I think. And don't call her crazy. I know just how she feels."

"Sorry. I'll try to be there." His voice sounded hollow because he knew his father would have other plans for him, especially if he found out there was something Nathan wanted to do. He pushed his irritation away and focused on the day ahead. "This is the place. I hope you're not too bored."

"Nate, why would I be bored? Don't apologize for talking about something you love. I told you I love art, too. I used to always visit one bronze sculpture of a cowgirl at the Booth Western Art Museum in Georgia. I've never told anybody this, but I couldn't afford anything for my house, so I used to hang the ads from a magazine on my wall and pretend I actually owned the original artwork the ad promoted. Take a deep breath and let's go in. I'm thrilled to be here and I'm glad you asked me."

"As a ranch owner, art is a smart investment. You should consider buying some new pieces for headquarters. You can afford it."

"There is hardly an inch of wall space left in my grandparents' house, but I have to admit it would be nice to add to their collection. I'll think about it."

Nathan parked and hopped out of the truck. Carli called out to him. "Nate! Your keys! Don't leave them in the ignition."

"Darn. I'm a little distracted." He reached back into the vehicle and shoved the keys into his pocket.

"C'mon, Nate, it'll be okay." They both laughed. She grabbed his hand and tugged him towards the front entrance, and he willingly followed, hoping she'd never let go.

Chapter Twelve

Nathan and Carli walked into the cool air of the Art Museum of the Texas Plains. Nathan breathed in the space. A faint smell of floral air freshener mixed with the quiet and beauty. There really wasn't any atmosphere like that of creativity and history. High quality treasures, artwork by talented masters, created by unexplained gifts no other human possesses or by an obsession that is impossible to understand.

"I like it here," he said. "I feel like I'm walking into an institute of higher learning or Carnegie Hall to hear a famous musician. Artists can create such works from nothing. They didn't exist before."

"I've never thought of it that way," Carli said. "The power to make something of unbelievable beauty must be intoxicating. I don't have a creative bone in my body."

The front-desk receptionist handed Nathan a brochure that showed a numbered map for the museum sections—photography, paintings, prints, Native American art, pioneer artifacts, drawings, sculptures, Asian art, and a collection of Tibetan miniature paintings, all housed in three stories. There would be a lot to see.

Flashing his best smile at the young lady near the front door, Nathan asked, "I heard there might be a sculpting demonstration. Could you please tell me where that's located?"

The twenty-something volunteer with orange hair behind the desk was rather exuberant. "Outside there are some really cool abstract sculptures. Kinda funky. I think you'll like them. They're welded steel and painted. The sculpting demonstration area is in the main hall to your right on the second floor." She pointed to the map.

"That's exactly what we want to see. Is there a demonstration today?"

"Some of the artists are supposed to be here. One was doing a presentation yesterday. I'm not sure what's on the schedule for today's event. They come and go as they have time. Some of them conduct workshops at their own studios by appointment. You might want to look into that."

He turned to Carli. "Do we need to rent a stroller for that purse?"

Carli laughed. The receptionist hid her smile behind a hand.

"Funny guy. C'mon, Nate." She looped her bag over one shoulder and tossed a big smile back at him. He chuckled and followed her to the elevator.

As the doors closed Nathan couldn't hide his disappointment. "I thought for sure one of the sculptors was supposed to be here today."

"Well, maybe there will be. Just hang on until we get up there."

The glass doors opened to show an expansive room, polished hardwood floors. A few people slowly glided from one artwork to the next in quiet appreciation.

Nathan walked closer to a small replica of a larger bronze by a cowboy artist whose career he had followed for several years. The sculptor was well known for creating a fifteen-foot bronze of a world champion bucking horse. This piece stood about three feet and showed a cowboy hanging on for dear life. The detail of the horse's muscles and tack, the look of sheer determination on the cowboy's face, was surreal. Next to the replica was a plaque with words by an unknown writer:

"Be fearless in the pursuit of what sets your soul on fire."

Perhaps the quote was meant for bronc riders, but Nathan wondered if this was true of his life. Somedays his insides tossed around in a constant jumble. He knew his dad wanted him to commit to the Rafter O, take it over, be the head of the family enterprise when his parents retired. But Nathan wanted to do other things. Pursue his own dreams. The Olsen ranch was his dad's dream, and the culmination of dedicated work by his great-grandfather and grandfather. Was it wrong he didn't feel the same? If he lived someone else's dream, what kind of life would that be? It would be like throwing his own away. But how could he tell his father? How could he disappoint him? Nathan stood frozen in place staring at the bucking bronc until Carli broke through his thoughts.

"Let's go this way." She grabbed his hand again.

Shaking the worries from his brain, Nathan led

the way as they continued to stroll through the exhibit, stare at the sculptures, and read the descriptions next to each. He was in art heaven.

Nathan read aloud about how bronze sculpting dated back to ancient civilizations. And how the "lost-wax" casting and section molding techniques were used to make larger sculptures. He wondered if he sounded like a reference library, but it felt so good to have someone at his side who he could share his passion with. Carli stood close, listening. They still held hands and she didn't pull away.

"I want to learn everything about this," he told Carli as he looked at the bronze carefully, taking note of every contour, wrinkle, and detail.

A slight, tanned-faced man with a handlebar mustache was suddenly behind them and quietly asked, "Are you an artist?"

Without turning around Nathan answered, "I try to be."

"That's one of my pieces you're looking at."

Nathan gasped and turned. The man's face was wrinkled and weathered, obviously from time spent outdoors, and probably in the saddle from the looks of him. No one could put that much detail in bronze to depict an animal's power unless he'd been involved personally. Crow's feet and wrinkled neck and hands were evidence of his years. A starched white, Western-styled shirt with pearlized snap-buttons finished off his gentleman's attire, complete with leather bolo tie fastened by a hunk of turquoise stone and silver clasp. Caiman-belly, handmade Lucchese boots were shined like mahogany.

The man smiled at Nathan. "'I try to be' is not

the right answer to my question, Son. You either are or you ain't. What's it gonna be?"

Nathan found his tongue tied. He stood there. No one had asked him that question before. Unsure, Nathan couldn't answer so the man spoke again. "I apologize. Don't mean to be nosy. Just wanted to know if you were one of us."

"One of you?" Nathan was a bit perplexed.

"Artists. Are you one of us?"

Nathan chuckled. "I guess I am, sir. I work with metal and other things, but I have a lot to learn. How did you know?"

"I thought as much by the way you were studying that sculpture. Only artists can look at something so intently." The stranger tipped his cowboy hat and said in a real friendly tone, "Ma'am. I'm Brad Travers, artist. I'm gonna be doing a little demo about working with bronze here in a bit, if y'all would like to stay."

Carli and Nathan both shook the hand extended to them. Nathan couldn't hide his surprise. "I'm Nathan and this is Carli. It's great to meet you. You're Brad Travers? I really admire your work."

"That's me. In the flesh. And thank you kindly, young man, for your high praise."

Mr. Travers commenced to pin a microphone on his lapel, with the help of a museum employee. Carli and Nathan sat on the first row of a semi-circle of chairs.

"Ladies and gentlemen, please gather 'round, get yorselves comfortable. There are some benches at the edge of the chairs if you need to sit. Thanks for coming out today. I won't actually be able to pour bronze here. After all, this ain't a foundry, right?"

His mustache spread as he smiled at the people.

The museum worker stepped forward. "I need to introduce you first," she whispered. The small group of art patrons chuckled. Brad removed his hat and took a bow.

"Brad Travers is a world-renown sculptor," the lady started. "He has won many prestigious designations including the American Art Awards, the National Academy of Western Art awards in Oklahoma City, and is an honorary member of The Royal Society of Sculptors in the U.K., just to name a few. His monumental sculptures are displayed in many art museums, colleges, and other public buildings around the country. He lives right here in our area with his wife and family. Please help me welcome master artist, Mr. Brad Travers."

"First, to start things off proper like, I am Brad Travers and I am an artist." He looked directly at Nathan who froze. He'd never said those words aloud in his life and Nathan wondered if he'd ever consider himself worthy enough to introduce himself that way.

"I've been an artist for some fifty years. Although I must admit, for many of those years I was a starving artist. And had to take some other jobs like ranch hand, high school art teacher, even janitor. I've spent lots of time in the saddle pushing cows because ya gotta do whatcha gotta do to pay the bills, especially if you have a wife and kids to feed." As Travers talked more, people wandered closer, filling the seats. He paused to let a handful sit down.

The artist continued, "I've been doing art things my whole life. Sometimes painting, sometimes mixed media, woodwork, metal art, and finally bronze sculptures. It's my passion, almost my reason for being on this earth. Although I must give credit where credit is due. If I wasn't able to do art, for whatever reason, I'm certain the Good Lord would have given me some other wonderful job to do. He always has the best plan, and He wants us to have the desires of our hearts. But for me, I couldn't deny the tug to create. I'd like to show y'all a video about the process and I'll be happy to answer any questions you might have."

Nathan had to keep a check on his tongue while the video played. A million and one questions came to mind. At the end, several people politely raised their hands. Nathan's gut burned with impatience. He knew this was his calling. But how do you create something so complicated? Where could he even begin?

As the video rolled, Travers narrated through all the steps: sculpting in clay, making a mold, pouring the wax, the "lost wax" casting method which dates back to early Egyptian dynasties, he explained, pouring the bronze, patina. Nathan couldn't take his eyes away from the video. He watched with total concentration.

"It was good meeting you both." Travers walked over to Nathan and Carli after the crowd had thinned. He placed a hand on Nathan's shoulder. "I see the passion burning in your eyes. Follow your art, Son. I hope one day I'll come to visit your sculptures in a museum like this. Here's my card. You should come out to the studio. I'll give you the dollar tour."

They shook hands. Nathan couldn't ignore the

excitement inside. All his dreams, things he wanted to do, and this artist just reminded him of them. But his dad had different plans for his life based solely on a birth order and nobody ever asked him what he wanted.

After meeting Travers, he felt driven again. Now he just had to tell his father that managing their family's cattle ranch would never be a part of his future. He glanced over at Carli. She made a huge change in her life, so why couldn't he? Follow your art, Travers had said. Follow your heart, Nathan thought. Grabbing Carli's hand, he led her towards the stairs. They still had another floor to explore and the outside exhibits. Time to focus on the here and now, and for one day stop worrying about the Rafter O. He'd have to leave his future in more capable hands instead of driving himself crazy with worry.

Show me what I'm supposed to do, Lord.

Chapter Thirteen

Carli followed Nathan towards the courtyard at the Art Museum of the Texas Plains. He insisted on looking over the sculptures that stood outside. She willingly tagged along behind him all day, enjoying his excitement to show her everything there was to see. She liked that he wanted to share this place with her. They were laughing about something as he reached past her to hold the door open. They stepped outside and he immediately turned to grip her upper arm. "I'm not here," he whispered through gritted teeth.

Before she could ask him what he meant, the exit door slammed. Carli stood alone facing a beautifully trimmed outdoor stone-paved patio with vendor booths and colored flags. She turned to face a closed door. Nathan had disappeared inside. She tugged the door open and stepped inside. "Nate?"

He was nowhere to be found. Vanished. The last thing he muttered was, "I'm not here." What had come over him? Probably some ex-girlfriend he spotted. But then how would Carli know any of his past love interests? The boy must have a string of them just like Lank. Another reason she didn't need the complication right now. Things get messy when you go beyond friendship.

Confused, she turned away from her search. Nathan could find her later, whatever was going on with him. She didn't want to spend time wandering through the art museum looking for him. Instead, she'd rather explore the arts and crafts booths. Carli stepped back outside and suddenly came face-to-face with the cause for his strange behavior.

"Carli. I thought that was you." Nathan's sister called across the courtyard and made a beeline towards her.

"Angie. Hello." Carli gave her a tentative smile, confusion and caution still rumbling in her mind.

"I just love arts and crafts, so I drug my momma and a few friends up here with me today. Are you by yourself?"

Carli let out a gush of air. Angie must not have seen her brother and obviously, Nathan did not want his sister to know he was on a date. Why would he be so ashamed of being seen with her? Anger and hurt burned inside for a split second, yet she hesitated to rat him out.

"Any unusual booths I should check out?" Carli decided to ignore Angie's question.

"Definitely look at the woodcarver's booth at the far end. He does some amazing work. And one of my favorite local jewelry makers is here. Just bought this." Angie held out her arm to show off several delicate silver wire bracelets with chunks of turquoise.

"Those are nice. I'm going to that booth first."

They both giggled. "It was so great seeing you."

"When I find everybody, we're heading out for a late lunch. You should come with us." Angie stepped closer and gave her a hug.

Angry seemed such a small, insignificant word to define her feelings at this moment. The longer she'd been thinking about it, the more her blood boiled. She hated losing his friendship, but how could she be friends with someone who obviously was ashamed to be seen out in public with her? And if this was an actual date, she had seriously considered taking their relationship to the next level. But not anymore. His behavior made no sense. She'd been over to his house several times and met all of his family. And to think she was even considering kissing him again. What a great way to start a relationship.

Nathan took her by the elbow. "Let's get out of here. I can explain."

She decided against the wood carving and instead allowed Nathan to take her hand and guide her around the building to the parking lot.

An awkward silence surrounded them as they climbed into the pickup truck. As he pulled into traffic, windows of the truck open to the sunshiny breeze, Carli leaned her arm out the door, took in a deep cleansing breath, and looked over at her neighbor. "It's been a great day. Thanks, Nate, but I'm not sure what happened back there."

"I just didn't want to see my sister."

"You didn't want to be seen with me." Carli stared ahead and crossed her arms over her chest. She'd give him a few minutes to explain and then she'd demand he take her home.

"No. That's not it." Nathan jerked his head over with surprise on his face. "That's what you thought?"

"What else would I think? You left me hanging there by myself. Obviously, you didn't want Angie to know we were on a date." She turned to glare at him.

"Really? You agree this is a date?" He didn't try to hide the silly grin that spread across his handsome face, and then his tone turned serious. "This has nothing to do with you, Carli. Honestly, I didn't want to explain to my sister why I was at an art gallery. It would have been a thirty-minute discussion. Okay, maybe it was a little about you. I'd have to explain why we were there together. Angie is relentless. You have no idea at her talent for interrogation."

Carli laughed, a lightness settling over her heart. "I totally misread that entire situation then."

"Forget about my family. I'm glad you're here. Wasn't it great meeting Brad Travers? I've read articles about him and followed his career for years. He gave me his card and told me to contact him! Even invited me to his studio! I want you to come with me."

Carli listened as Nathan spoke about his encounter with Travers. It was easy to see his heartfelt enthusiasm about pursuing his passion for sculpting. She looked at him and smiled. "You know you have a glow about you that wasn't there before."

"What're you talking about? Are you teasing me?"

"You're glowing, literally glowing like a light bulb. When you talk about art, your face lights up and your eyes sparkle. You're gushing like a toddler at Christmas."

"That's ridiculous. Men do not glow, and they

absolutely do not get giddy," Nathan said. "And I hope you're hungry because you're about to meet the best steak in your life."

"Bring it on," she said. He might deny it out loud, but Carli saw the way he hung on every word Travers said. Nathan still had a wide, silly grin on his face. It was impossible for him to stop smiling. Carli's heart burst with hope and pride for him. She wished she felt the same about the choices she had made in her life. As they picked up speed, the air suddenly turned cool. She rolled up her window.

Nathan exited the interstate and drove to the north side of Amarillo, past the stockyards and a ballpark. Carli had never been in this part of the city before.

"Where are we going?" she asked.

"Some place my sister and her friends would never have lunch." He laughed.

"Your mother was with them too."

"Oh, great. That would have really been a scene."

He parked the truck in front of a bright yellow building with a covered porch that stretched across the front and down one side. "The Outpost Steakhouse" read the sign. Carli's stomach growled and she decided she didn't want to go home yet.

Nathan turned in his seat to look at her. "Are you still mad?"

Carli hesitated for a minute, trying not to grin at the look of concern on his face. "I'll give you one more chance, cowboy. Only because you mentioned steak."

Chapter Fourteen

Nathan Olsen held the door of the steakhouse open for Carli and she blinked as her eyes adjusted to the dark interior. She found herself in the middle of an eatery with a Texas theme on steroids. Stuffed deer heads with impressive antlers were scattered over the dark paneling that surrounded the dining room. Every empty wall space was covered. Holding court on one wall was a massive stone fireplace with a bobcat sitting on the mantel, one paw raised, his mouth open showing fangs. Carli had never seen so many preserved animals in her life. Around the top of the room was a balcony which was where the hostess led them.

As Carli walked up the stairs, she looked down on the dining room below. People sat at long tables; diners were evenly spaced around the room. Waitresses scurried to and fro wearing wide cowboy hats, red bandannas, white Western shirts, and short blue jean skirts.

Carli and Nathan were shown to a cozy, corner booth. An ornate brass chandelier hung over their table, and Nathan had to remove his cowboy hat to slide into the bench. When she sat down the noise of the first floor faded and she couldn't help but notice the waitress eyeing Nathan. The girl handed Carli a menu but opened Nathan's for him and leaned closer. "May I tell you our specials for today?" She smiled. With model-perfect teeth, her eyes sparkled full of promise meant only for him.

Nathan never glanced up. "No thanks. Bring us a mug of your house ale to start with, please." He glanced at Carli. "They make their own beer here. Their dark ale tastes like pecans. If you don't like it, you can order something different and I'll drink your glass too."

She giggled. "All right. I'm game." Carli realized she had laughed a lot today, until the episode with Angie. Her ego still stung a bit, but food would help her mood. She gazed at Nathan's strong chin, sporting the shadow of a beard. His eyes, the color of a blue Texas sky, glanced up from the menu and met her gaze with a sweet smile. His hair brushed the top of his shirt collar, proof of the slight rejection he had for that clean cut, cowboy image. After today, she realized the conflict that churned within him. He hid so much inside. They both harbored many secrets.

Nathan was comfortable to be with, like a summer day, all warm and fun. It would be so easy to fall for him. As she glanced from her menu, he watched her, and their eyes met again. Unsure and questioning, he waited. Wanting something more. She wasn't sure if she could give it to him. Avoiding his glance, she studied the menu.

After their order was taken, Nathan watched Carli take a long drink of her ale.

"What'd ya think?"

"About what?" Carli took a second sip. Not bad.

"About everything. The day. The art. Brad Travers. The ale."

"Well, that's a lot. I need another drink." She chuckled. "First of all, this is tasty. You can't drink mine."

"I'm glad you're here." He reached across the table and laid his hand on hers. "I mean it."

"I never realized how much this meant to you until I saw you talking to that artist. I had no idea how passionate you were about this sort of thing. So passionate in fact you go to great lengths to hide it from your family." Carli watched a sadness reflect in his eyes.

"I make sketches sometimes so I can figure out an art piece that's in my head. I love working with metal and wood, or the idea of it anyway. Sculpting, painting, I love all kinds of art."

"That's great, Nate. Do you have a collection at the Rafter O?"

"A few oil paintings of horses, but nothing significant. I can't turn this off inside my head. I see beauty in nature, the colors, the textures. Don't get me wrong. I'm proud of this land and the legacy my family has built on the Rafter O. I just don't want to push cows for the rest of my life. Is that a bad thing?"

"No, not at all. And you don't think your dad will understand?"

Before he could answer, the waitress brought their plates of food, and Nathan asked for another round of ale. Carli ordered the smallest steak on the menu, but it was still huge.

After the waitress left, Nathan continued, "My father is practical, all business. I'm the oldest son. He needs someone to take over the ranch when he's gone. To tell you the truth, I think Angie would be better at the ranching business. She's in the middle, third in line. When my sister Janie returns from the military, maybe the two of them would like to partner in it."

"I admire you for thinking of them and the obligation you feel towards the Rafter O. It is a new era—women's empowerment and all that." Carli raised her eyebrows.

"My sisters love everything about the ranch. Both of them ran barrels, and the youngest, my little brother, Travis, is more focused on girls right now. It's always been a given I'd step into Dad's footsteps, just like he did and my grandpa and great-grandpa did before that. We have a long legacy of ranching that runs through the Olsen family."

"You know some of my story, Nate, and I'm certainly not one to give advice. I put up walls and hide my true feelings from others and, ultimately, bury my own dreams from myself. I still don't know what I want. I rejected the idea that I had any family, but then one day I discovered a family I never knew existed. And that's when it hit me. I wanted to make this my home. Texas. And I always wanted family. As it turns out, I have ancestors who lived here for generations before me. They might be dead and gone now, but I've found a new family with dear friends."

"I've told you this before, what you've done is admirable. It's pretty incredible really, how things turned out for you. Buck and Lola love you like a daughter. And you don't have to put up walls with me, Carli."

"You can think that, but on the inside I'm a mess—unsure, scared, alone. I wish God would send me a sign to tell me I'm on the right path. I made the move to Texas, but now what? Should I open a riding school or not? With cattle prices holding steady, maybe I should buy more grass. Or not. I doubt every decision now, and I've never been that way before."

"He doesn't send you some giant-sized message like a lightning bolt, but little signs if you look for them. Small things that just work out to let you know you're on the right path." Nathan scooped up a buttery bite of baked potato on his fork and stabbed into a chunk of steak.

Carli studied him. On the outside he looked like the typical polished Texas cowboy, but now she understood that on the inside he was just as conflicted as she felt. "If I can do it, you can too. I guess what I'm saying, Nate, is that we should live our lives for ourselves. I don't mean in a selfish way. We need to be true to ourselves, authentic people. We can't live and act like some different person with likes, dislikes, and dreams that are opposite from what we truly feel down deep in our soul. You've got to follow your dream, your heart. Even if it sounds wild to other people."

Nathan took a swig of ale. "You talk big, but have you contacted your birth father?"

Carli gasped and looked up at him in surprise.

"That's kind of a low blow. I'm working on it, for your information." She looked at her plate, pushing food around instead of eating. Truthfully, she wasn't sure if she really wanted to meet the man face-to-face. She directed the focus back to Nathan. "You should be honest with your dad. I believe once he listens and understands, he'll still be proud of you and one of your biggest supporters."

"Thanks, Carli, that means a lot. Where do I start? It seems like I've been keeping my secret for so long. I do some metal work at the ranch, but I keep it hidden in one back corner of the shop and work late at night. What am I afraid of?"

"Start small. Let's go visit that artist's studio. Yes, I'll go with you."

"I've been thinking about working somewhere for the experience. I might be able to get a part-time gig teaching drawing or something at one of the local junior colleges."

"Well, there you go. It's complicated, I know. But it's a step in the right direction."

"A former art professor of mine has reached out to me about it. Even though I got my degree in agricultural business, she always encouraged my love of art."

"You should pursue it. Now, when are you gonna talk to your folks?"

"I don't know. They have a lot on their mind. You know, with Janie in the military and all. There's always something going on with the ranch. And Libby. She's my youngest sister. Then Travis is the baby. Libby's talking marriage and my folks don't think she's ready. Seems like there's always a crisis in the Olsen household."

"But Nate, you can't keep putting your life on hold. If you wait for the right time, it'll never be the right time."

"You know, I'm approaching thirty fast. Maybe I should make ranching my life, like my dad says. Why am I fighting it so much? I should probably get married, have some kids. A ranch is a great place to raise a family."

He paused and stared intensely into her eyes, but Carli pretended she didn't get his meaning. She didn't know where this thing with Nathan was going. Starting a family was not in her future. She didn't see herself as being the motherly type.

"Nate, you can't throw all your dreams away. You can't live someone else's life. We should make a pact. You tell your folks about your plans to become a world-famous bronze sculptor. And I'll start the research to get serious about tracking my birth father down. Deal?"

"I'll think about it," was all he said before turning his attention back to his lunch.

Carli sighed. They were such a pathetic pair.

Chapter Fifteen

The drive home from the art museum was quiet, Nathan and Carli both lost in their own thoughts. Carli understood the turmoil that must be going on in his head. She had felt the same way trying to decide about giving up her life in Georgia and moving halfway across the country to claim an inheritance.

Spending the day with Nathan made her realize how much she missed having a close friend. Her previous business partner, Mark, had been her sounding board. It never got too intimate, but they talked every day about the Georgia riding school, their boarders, and their shared passion for horses. She missed that companionship. Despite people being around at the ranch, she still felt totally alone in Texas. Sure, she considered Buck and Lola family, but she was their employer after all. They worked for her. And Carli kept walls up against everyone she met. She knew that, but she had done it her whole life. Maybe because her mother had left; it was self-preservation. If you don't get too close, then nobody can ever disappoint you.

Today with Nathan, she talked more than ever before. She didn't remember sharing that much with anyone, even her former business partner and good friend, Mark.

Nathan glanced over at her. A moment of surprise showed on his face as if suddenly realizing she was still in the pickup.

"Where is Brad's studio?" she asked, in hopes of getting Nathan to talk again. The silence made her think about the past and she didn't want to linger there anymore.

"I do plan to call him and set up a date to visit. I'll let you know."

"And you're going to talk to your parents. Right? After watching you today, Nate, you have to follow your passion. You'll be miserable if you don't."

They were on a dirt road, almost to her ranch, when Nathan suddenly pulled the truck over to the side and shut off the engine.

"What's the matter?" she asked.

Slowly, quietly, he turned and leaned to her, putting one hand on her shoulder. "You've always been so encouraging, Carli. I have a lot to think about after today. You mean a lot to me and I'm sorry if I hurt your feelings at the museum."

She knew he was moving in for a kiss and her heart pattered in anticipation. Part of her wanted to just let go and see what happened, but then her radar or gut feeling or whatever it was, signaled some sort of an alarm inside her. She placed a hand on his chest but found him immovable. "Nate, we're friends. I really like you. But I'm not sure about this. Let's go slow. Okay?"

His expression showed disappointment as he regrouped, leaned back in the driver's seat, and cleared his throat. "Sure, Carli. Sorry. I guess I got caught up in the excitement of the day."

"It's okay, Nate. It was a super day. And I like you. But my feelings are a little mixed up so I think we should go slow."

"What's his name?"

"Who?" A flash of Lank's face hit her brain. Surely, she wasn't that transparent.

"The guy in Georgia you decided to leave."

She chuckled with relief. "Yes. There was a guy in Georgia. I thought he was the one but turned out he had his eyes set on someone else."

"All right, Carli. Just know I really care about you and I'd like us to be more than just friends. But I'll go slow and hope you catch up soon."

She placed her hand on his forearm for a second and smiled as he started the truck and pulled onto the dirt road.

As they got closer to the Wild Cow Ranch headquarters, Carli snapped back to reality. She knew paperwork was waiting in her office, and she'd been wanting to ride Beau. She also wanted to give the other ranch horses a go in the round pen to determine if any of them might work for the riding school. Maybe she'd have more time tomorrow. Right now, she'd better be careful of Nathan's feelings. Should she invite him in? Would it send a mixed message?

As usual, he hurried around to open the truck door for her. She stepped down, and he blocked her path, holding his arms out wide. "We're still friends. So how about a friendly hug?"

She looked up to his eyes and they shared a smile. "Of course, we are, silly. We'll always be friends." She walked into his strong arms, warm and solid. Part of her was annoyed she hadn't let him kiss her, but another part just couldn't be that trusting. She wasn't ready for anything serious yet.

Abruptly, she heard Lank's voice and twisted loose from Nathan's tight hug.

"If you two are done foolin' around, I need to see you, boss lady. We have a problem in the barn."

Glaring at him, Carli bitingly said, "We're not fooling around!"

"Looks like it to me."

"You'd best be careful what you say, Lank. Don't be disrespectful." Nathan puffed up his chest and stepped closer to Lank.

"What's it to you, man?"

Nathan moved in a step closer. They were nose to nose. "Don't be a jerk, Torres."

Carli knew she needed to step in before things got out of hand.

"Just a minute, you two. Lank, I'll see you in the barn. Nate, thank you for a nice day. Now both of you get back to your own business. That's enough."

"Yes, ma'am, boss lady. Whatever you say, boss lady." Contempt shadowed Lank's voice. He saluted and grumbled as he walked away. But not without first staring daggers into Nathan's hide. Nathan glared back.

"I thought you two were friends."

"Used to love him like a brother. Not anymore," came the curt reply as Nathan climbed into his truck. "I'll talk to you later, Carli."

"Sounds good. And thanks again, Nate. I had fun today." She set her tote down on the front porch and then spun on her heels to follow Lank to the barn. She gave a quick wave to Nathan as he drove away. She couldn't help but smile to herself. It had been a fun date. She glanced up to see Lank watching her with a deep scowl on his face. Her smile faded. He turned his back to her and kept walking towards the corral.

"Are you two a thing now?" Lank flung the question over his shoulder, his voice hard and mocking.

"Is it any of your business?" Carli wasn't going to let him annoy her. She finally found a friend she could go places with, if she could keep him at bay about the kissing for a while longer, and she wasn't going to let some smart-aleck cowpuncher ruin her mood. She glared at his back, broad shoulders, and lean muscles defined through his pearl-snap shirt. Despite the late afternoon chill, he wore no jacket.

"Looked like you have something going on is all. Seems like the Olsen family has welcomed you with open arms." He shrugged his shoulders as he opened the corral fence and stepped aside for her to go through the gate. She stumbled and her shoulder glazed his outstretched arm. She ignored the churning that grew in her belly.

"What's the problem?" Carli stopped in the middle of the pen and placed her hands on her hips. She looked around and saw nothing out of place. Returning from her date with Nathan who was all inspired, she had planned to work on the genealogy research tonight. But instead, she was standing in the middle of a horse pen.

With one fluid motion Lank skirted past her and then was up and over the pipe rail fence. "This is the problem." He stood next to her horse. "Beau has been acting strange. Almost colicky. I thought you should know."

"I'll see if he wants some grain."

"I already fed your horse, while you were out partying with your boyfriend. He didn't eat much at all."

She faced him and jammed a finger in his chest. "For your information, we were at an art gallery event and then we went to eat. We're friends. Not that it's any of your concern."

"Appears you're settling into your new life in Texas just fine. Good for you. And that hug was way more than friendly." He glared at her and she glared back.

How this guy had the power to irritate her was beyond reason. Carli decided he was annoyed at something, but she couldn't figure out what. Maybe even past the point of being a mild annoyance, as anger glinted in his eyes. She turned her back on him and walked to the tack room.

"I told you, I've already fed him this evening." Lank stayed close on her heels.

"I have some extra supplements. And maybe a little mineral oil." She stomped to the saddle house and flipped on the light switch. The outside light slowly faded as the setting sun disappeared from the horizon.

"When's the last time you rode Beau, by the way?" Lank was like her shadow, too close.

"I plan to start riding him again tomorrow. What is wrong with you?" She turned to face Lank, staring directly at his face. In the beam cast from the one dim bulb, a darkness of a beard lined his square jaw making her heart flutter. His eyes still shined mean.

It was a long moment before he said, "If you're not happy with my work, just say so."

"I have never, ever said anything about your work."

He looked at her with defiant eyes, his jaw clenched. "If you keep coming behind me and doing my job over, then I guess I'm not up to your standards."

"What are you talking about?" Carli felt drained. She had no idea why Lank was confronting her on something that obviously had nothing to do with what he was saying.

"Me doing your work and then you doing it again." He grabbed a broom and began sweeping.

"Can you be still for just a minute?" She placed a hand on his arm. "What work?"

"Me feeding Beau, your horse," he growled with a hard emphasis. There was that mocking tone again.

Carli decided to end the conversation. "Correct me if I'm wrong, but you are an employee at this ranch. You will do whatever work is required of you and whatever work needs doing. Why the attitude?"

"I'm tired of being at your beck and call. You think you know all about cows. Now you're in tight with the Olsen family. Big money. Ranching legacy. You're somebody now!"

"Good grief. That's crazy."

"Think you're some highfalutin ranch owner.

Too good to even feed your own horse. Don't lower yourself by speaking to me. I'm just the stupid ranch hand."

"If you don't want to work here with me as your boss, Lank, just say so. Ranch hands are a dime a dozen."

"Really? Well, then I quit," he yelled.

"You can't quit because I'm firing you first," Carli yelled back. "I want you off my property." She turned her back to him so he couldn't see the tears in her eyes and half-ran back to her house.

At her desk, Carli tried to sit at the computer and focus, but her blood was boiling. The nerve of that guy. Questioning her time with Nathan. Accusing her of abandoning her horse. With a heavy sigh she clicked off the computer and got ready for bed. She thought about how she would tell Buck that she had fired his only ranch hand.

As she lay in bed, she played the conversation with Lank over and over in her mind. Nothing made any sense. What a stupid way to end a perfect day. He just made her so dang mad. She should have let Nathan kiss her. At least she could have ended the day on a more positive note. That was a moment she'd never get back. And then Nathan's comment came to mind: "Used to love him like a brother."

Suddenly she sat bolt upright in bed. She was the problem. Her moving to Texas had caused a rift between two friends.

Lank was jealous.

Maybe the attraction she felt for him wasn't just one-sided. She remembered the time Lank found her in the snowstorm. He was afraid for her and so attentive. He acted as if he wanted to say something, but he never spoke. Could he have feelings for her too? Stop it. She did not need or want to get involved with anybody.

Carli's thoughts were reeling. She was curious about the missed kiss from Nathan, but it was Lank's face that floated in her mind. He looked so darn cute when he was furious, and she hated how his glance made her heart flutter. And now she had fired him. What in the world had she done?

Chapter Sixteen

Seemed like there were always a pile of dirty jeans waiting to be washed around a ranch. Carli didn't mind as she stuffed laundry in her washer before dawn. She couldn't help but be energized this morning, except her stomach fluttered with nerves, and then to discover there were no clean pants to wear. In her excitement and work to prepare for riders, she had forgotten to do laundry. She sipped on coffee but did not find food appealing.

After the dryer buzzed, she pulled on the warm pants, tucked the ends into her grandma's turquoise boots, and found a fairly wrinkle-free, red-paisley, pearl snap shirt. So much for being a highfalutin ranch owner, as Lank had accused. She wanted to make a good impression with the parents and kids. No matter, she would always be just Carli. No diamonds or turquoise jewelry and fancy duds for her. She pulled unbrushed hair into a ponytail and shoved a brown felt hat on her head. Slamming the front door behind, she half-jogged to the corral.

The kids were coming to LoveJoy Riding School today, her new equine program.

She squinted at the sun and said a prayer of thanks for the Saturday in April without wind. So far, the morning was calm. The temperature was jacket worthy, but bearable. It was a good day for riding.

According to the response from the online registrations made through her public page, she would have four kids. Two girls and two boys, one of the girls being Lexi. Carli was happy she wanted to come back.

Lexi was the first to arrive. Carli said hello to the mother and while they chatted, a second car pulled to a stop next to the dining hall. Carli walked over and introduced herself. A young girl about the same age as Lexi, with board-straight red hair and a freckled face gave Carli a shy smile as her mother made the introductions.

"We're glad to have you here, Bianca."

Carli waited a few moments to give the others more time to arrive. The girls stood awkwardly apart in the pen, without smiles and not looking at each other. Both were dressed in black, with the exception of pink highlights that now streaked Lexi's hair. A fluorescent pink chain dangled from one ear. Lexi showed interest as Sally followed Carli into the pen. The girl obviously loved horses. Lola brought in another horse for Bianca.

After a few more minutes, Carli decided the boys must not be coming. Nathan hadn't shown up either. Lank wandered to the fence rail and crossed his arms along the top. He waved at Lola but paid no attention to Carli.

Even though she had fired him several days ago, Buck rehired him the very next morning before she could explain what happened between them. The best thing for her was to have as little to do with Mr. Torres as possible. It seemed they couldn't even be civil to each other anymore. The riding school took up her time, with little energy left to analyze what could possibly be going on in the crazy mind of a Texas cowboy. She made the decision to only go to Buck with any ranch business and ignore Lank as best she could.

It didn't appear the two boys who had pre-registered would be arriving any time soon. Maybe running late?

"I think we should get started, don't you?" Carli turned to Lola. She was thankful for Lola's willingness to help and for her support from the very first. It meant a lot that Lola and Buck were supportive of her ideas.

"Hello, I'm Carli and this is Lola. If you're here, then you probably love horses as much as I do, so welcome to LoveJoy Riding School. We're so glad to have you here today. I want you to know this is a safe place and I hope it will be a fun place for all of you. We'll learn about horses and I think you'll have a good time. So, please relax, breathe in the fresh air, and let's get started. We have a few rules—"

"Great. Here it comes," Bianca murmured, as she crossed her hands over her chest and rested one boot on the fence behind her.

If Carli handled this right, these girls might become fast friends before the day was over. She glowed at the thought of doing some good and changing lives. Nathan had told her to watch for little signs from God which indicated she was on the right path. She'd be on the lookout.

Based on Carli's experience from working with clients in Georgia, she knew about establishing rules the very first day. She wasn't intimidated by teenagers. She walked closer to Bianca. "A lot of times, rules keep us safe and help us to get along with others. So here goes: No cursing. No yelling or loud voices around the horses. No walking directly behind the horses. Be respectful of other riders. Listen to your instructors. The two-story building over there has restroom facilities. That's pretty much it. Other than that, we are here to have fun and learn about horses."

Already, Carli noticed the eye rolling from both of her new clients. "Come with us. We're going to clean some tack first, brush the horses, and then saddle up for a quick ride," she said. The response wasn't any better.

Bianca shuffled her feet and mumbled, "I didn't come here to be nobody's servant or maid."

Carli studied the red-haired girl with the big attitude. She was going to be a challenge. "Around a ranch, everyone pitches in. Equipment like saddles and bridles have to be kept in good condition. We don't want a bridle or reins to break in two while someone's riding because the tack was dirty, dry, and cracked. So, we clean it, oil it, and keep it like new."

"I don't know how to do any of that. My mom says I have to be here, but I don't have to do a thing you say," Bianca grumbled. "Besides, I don't want to break my nails." She held her hands out, fingers spread, admiring fluorescent orange polish.

It was Lexi's turn to roll her eyes and smirk. Luckily, she didn't say any words, but the snort of escaping air, "Hmph," was what set Bianca off.

Bianca spun on her heels and faced Lexi. "You got somethin' to say to me?"

Before any words could be exchanged, Lola stepped between them and led the way to the saddle house where all the tack was stored. "Come this way, girls."

As Lexi passed by Sally, she stopped and gave the horse a scratch behind one ear. Sally buried her nose in Lexi's stomach and snorted.

"She remembers you." Carli smiled at her.

Lexi couldn't stifle the grin that appeared on her face.

Carli draped an arm across Sally's neck. "It's not easy being in a bad mood around horses. They'll settle your spirit every time. Ready to get started?"

Lola opened the door of the building and stepped to one side. "C'mon, girls. We'll give you both gloves if you want. No muss, no fuss."

Carli hoped that Lola's firm, but kind, mothering would penetrate their tough shells. She didn't know their situations, but felt she could relate to being independent, rebellious, trying to survive on her own in life. She didn't have a real mother since Michelle had abandoned her, and she'd been angry about it for a lot of years. Maybe that's why she was drawn to these girls and the secret turmoil they buried deep inside.

Carli had already laid out the supplies they'd need on a wooden counter—rags, saddle soap, leather conditioner. And gloves to protect Bianca's new manicure. Carli brought over a few bridles and reins. Chairs and stools were already arranged around a metal work bench so they could all sit in a circle as they worked. Carli smiled to herself and thought maybe this was how old-time quilting bees were—older women teaching the young ones. Except in this day and age the girls had taken over the saddle house instead of staying inside to sew.

Lola started with instructions. "Now take your sponge, wipe it in the container of saddle soap. Give the leather a good rub. We'll soak the bits in hot water to get rid of any grass, spit, grime—you name it. We want to keep the leather supple, so it doesn't dry out, crack, and break. And we'll make sure the stitching is secure and the buckles are working. Okay?"

Lexi said, "Yes."

Bianca huffed some as the side of her mouth stretched in a smirk. She scrunched her eyes and stood up from her seat. "I don't have to do this, and you can't make me."

Carli opened her mouth to reprimand the young girl, but Lola's eyes told her to be still. It was kind of strange. Even though Carli was ready to chastise Bianca for talking disrespectfully to them, it was as though a voice inside her said, "Help her." Over and over again. "Help her." Was that Carli's mind talking? Was God nudging her? She had heard people say that God spoke to them and Nathan reminded her to be aware of signs from God.

"No cleaning. No riding." Carli was firm. "Taking care of your tack and taking care of your horse is a big part of horsemanship. We want to teach you all of it if you'll let us."

"How 'bout we keep working and I'll tell you a story." Lola's suggestion was met with smirks, but hands stayed busy on the task.

Carli pulled out her phone to take a few pictures she would add to her social media pages later, with the parents' permission. She glanced at the time. Only fifteen minutes had passed. This was going to be a long morning.

Chapter Seventeen

As Carli set a bridle down in front of the only two riders who had showed up for opening day of her new LoveJoy Riding School, she cast a glance at the girl who refused to participate. Carli ignored Bianca's outburst wondering what she should say. After several long moments, Bianca shrugged one shoulder and fiddled with a set of reins, brushing saddle soap on them with her sponge.

In a low, soothing voice, Lola started. "This story comes from the Bible in the book of Luke. There once was a father who had two sons. But for our story I'm going to make it a father with two daughters."

Carli showed Lexi how to take a bridle apart, unbuckle the parts, then they both started cleaning the strips of leather.

Bianca smirked and rolled her eyes but didn't say anything.

Lola continued. "One day one of the daughters came to the father and said, 'I want my inheritance and I'm going to leave home.' That sure made her parents sad.

"The father loved both daughters and he only wanted the best for them. He agreed and the daughter left. At first the girl had a great time, traveling the world and partying with friends. The people she hung out with liked her as long as she was paying for everything. Unfortunately, her good times didn't last forever. Eventually, the money ran out. Then those friends started disappearing, one after the other. She had no place to live and nothing to eat."

Carli stood to hang up several of the cleaned bridles on pegs that lined one wall. She glanced at the girls and noticed that Lola held their attention. They were not distracted or rolling their eyes, but instead listened intently. Another sign? Thank you, God.

Lola's soothing voice was easy to listen to. Even though Carli remembered the Prodigal Son story from Luke 15, she was just as enthralled as the girls. Lola continued. "The young girl, now hungry and homeless, abandoned by her wealthy friends, begged for work at a family farm. 'I can do any work you have,' she said. The owner agreed to hire her and in exchange for her help with the chores, she could have a place to stay.

"The first chore on her list was to feed the pigs. You might know that pigs love mud. They like to wallow in it because it protects their skin from sunburn and parasites."

"Do you have pigs at the Wild Cow?"

Carli was surprised that Lexi finally spoke. "No, we don't. Have we ever had pigs on the ranch, Lola?"

"I can't say we have. Cows and chickens, and of course many ranch horses. One year we kept two

Texas Longhorns at the headquarters. Ward took an interest in alpacas, but thankfully we didn't have to learn about them. But I can't remember having any pigs. They like garbage. A bunch of leftovers, veggies, and a soupy mixture of scraps called slop. That's why they call it 'slopping the pigs'."

Both Bianca and Lexi scrunched up their noses and mouths. "Eww."

"Gross."

"You're right," Lola said. "It was gross. And it got worse. The girl was so hungry she even thought about eating a little food from the scraps she fed the pigs. The hollowness in her stomach reminded her she had finally hit rock bottom. She recalled the wonderful places she had seen and the abundant food and friends that were now gone. She cried and cried and thought of how mean she had treated her mother and father. It was a stupid idea to leave home and spend all of her money. Now she had nothing. What was she going to do? Where was she going to live?"

Lexi spoke up again, quietly, "Couldn't she go back home?"

"Do you think her father would let her come home?" Lola asked.

"This story is so lame," Bianca chimed in, all smart-mouthed and puffed up. "Her father would probably call the cops on her."

"The girl did think about going home," Lola continued. "Her parents owned a business. The girl wished that maybe she could be one of the workers. She would do everything asked of her, all the things she'd been asked to do before but had rebelled against. And they might pay her a small wage and give her some food. It had to be better than stealing scraps from pigs. She wondered if her father would be angry, maybe even turn her away. But she had to try. She didn't know what else to do. So, she borrowed enough money for a bus ticket, with a promise to pay it back as soon as she could and left to go back home."

Carli and the girls stopped cleaning the leather to listen as Lola proceeded with the story.

"When the girl reached her home, she hesitated. Would she be forgiven? Or would she be turned away again for squandering her inheritance?

"To her surprise, her parents came bounding out and wrapped their arms around their daughter. The father said, 'You're alive! You're home! We love you!' The mother called out. 'We missed you. We'll make a big dinner with cake and ice cream!' To the other daughter, she said, 'Let's celebrate your sister's return!'

"The girl cried in her mother's arms and said she was sorry for leaving. She promised her father to work hard. 'I want to help you now. What can I do for you?' she told them. But the second daughter who had stayed behind wasn't as excited. Do you know why?"

Bianca spoke up, tough as usual and flipping her red hair behind one shoulder. "Yeah. Because the sister who stayed home didn't have all the fun, did all the work, and nobody was giving her a party. It sucks if you ask me."

"What do you think, Lexi?" Lola asked.

She remained quiet for a moment, looked down, then a little side glance towards Bianca. But Lexi finally spoke up, "Maybe they just forgave her. They really missed her. And loved her."

"That's exactly right," said Lola. "Of course, the parents loved both daughters equally, but they forgave. You know girls, in this life people are always going to do bad or stupid things. And sometimes people change. They might do something dumb or mean this year or this day, but then at a later time, they've changed into a nicer person. Everyone makes mistakes. It's up to us to forgive. Don't we want to be forgiven when we mess up?"

Both girls remained silent. Carli nodded. "Boy, have I made some doozies along the way. Sometimes I've had friends forgive and sometimes not, but we all work hard to do better next time, I think." Except for her mother. Carli would never have a chance to mend that bridge. Would Michelle have ever changed? Carli needed to stop dwelling on the past.

"And the most important thing," Lola continued, "the real meaning of this story is that Jesus already forgave us for everything—our past, our present, even our future mistakes. All we have to do is talk to Him about what is bothering us, tell Him we're sorry, and He'll be there with open arms. He wants to welcome us home. So, it's up to you. I think God sends people into our lives to help us sort out our troubles. That's what Carli and I want too. If we can help you girls with anything, we hope you'll feel safe in coming to us."

"We all share a love of horses, and we want you to know this is a safe place. We hope to become friends." Carli added, "Thank you, Lola, for that great story. What did you girls think?"

"It's all a dumb fairy tale," Bianca spouted. "People hurt you and they're out for what they can get.

There's no knight in shining armor. There's no God on his white horse to rescue you. And I'm sick of this cleaning. I want to go home."

With that, she threw her sponge into the soapy bucket and the dirty water splashed all over the other three. She jumped up and ran out of the saddle house.

Carli stood to follow her outside. If this was a sign from God, she had no idea how to react or what she should do. Maybe her riding school idea was destined to fail before they even got through the first day.

Chapter Eighteen

Carli grabbed a lead rope and brush and hurried out of the saddle house to follow Bianca. Something about the Prodigal Son story had upset her. Seemed there was no lack for drama on the riding school's opening day. But Carli wasn't giving up yet. These girls were going to ride a horse before they went home, if it was the last thing she could do.

"Have you met Mouse?" Carli called out to Bianca who stood in the pen. She hadn't walked into the road yet and didn't have her cell phone out, so she wasn't calling her mother.

Carli slipped a lead rope over the gray gelding and led him closer to Bianca. "Now that we have our riding gear in ship-shape condition, it's time to brush your horse. Wanna give it a try?"

Bianca glanced at Carli and then watched Lexi and Lola emerge from the saddle house. Lexi gave Sally a scratch and began to brush her back with firm, short strokes creating puffs of dust as she worked.

Without a word, Bianca took the brush from

Carli. Her frown decreased as she concentrated on her work. Carli worked on Mouse's mane as Bianca brushed his neck.

Carli's heart swelled as she watched the transformation on the young girl's face. Stress was leaving her, even if only in little bits. All was at peace again, at least for the moment. The power of horses to calm and soothe is a mighty thing.

Bianca suddenly jerked her head around to watch Lexi.

"Hey, I want to brush that horse." She walked over to Lexi and Sally. "Move!"

Lexi didn't back down. "Just wait. I was here first and I always work with this horse. You've got Mouse."

Bianca shoved her shoulder against Lexi. "You can't hog everything."

Lola watched with her mouth open. So much for peace. Carli froze in place with a curry comb in hand, trying to figure out what was happening.

Lexi stood her ground. That set Bianca off and she took both hands and shoved her. Lexi stumbled back, regained her footing, and charged.

In seconds they were rolling on the ground, pushing and grabbing each other's hair. Profanities and name-calling spewed from both girl's mouths.

As they were spinning and tumbling around, Lola and Carli dove to separate them. "Now, just a minute, girls. Stop that! Get up," Carli said.

"You'll spook the horses." Lola wrapped her arms around Lexi's waist and pulled her back.

When both girls scrambled to their feet, held back by Lola and Carli from taking another swipe at each other, their clothes were dirty as well as their faces. But no blood as far as Carli could see.

"She started it!" Lexi hollered. "I was just minding my own business brushing Sally. I knew I shouldn't come to this thing. Y'all are just a bunch of losers."

"You're a poser. You don't know a thing about horses," Bianca said. "Think you're so cool in those combat boots and all. You're just a wimpy b----!"

"Hold on," Carli stepped in. "No cursing. One of our rules, remember?"

"You can go to h-e-double-el with your rules," spouted Bianca. "I told you I didn't want to be here."

Carli took a deep calming breath. "We're not going to ruin the time we have left today because of this disruption."

"Let's get you girls dusted off and then Carli can take you on a short ride. We have time before your moms get back." Lola led the way to the cookhouse. Carli nodded in agreement to Lola and mouthed a thank you. It was obvious someone needed to teach these girls how to act, but Carli decided they'd spent enough time talking. She wanted to end on a positive note, give the girls a good memory to take home with them.

Maybe a short ride would calm the situation. After their faces were washed and clothes dusted off, Carli instructed both girls to follow her into the saddle house and pointed to the saddles.

"This is heavy," said Lexi. "I can't do it."

"Just a poser, like I said," mumbled Bianca.

Carli was at her wits' end with both girls. Together, she helped Lexi lift the saddle over Sally's back.

With boots in stirrups and everyone ready, Carli led Beau to the gate, and leaned down to open for all to pass through. Bianca kicked her horse, Mouse, and trotted off leaving the others behind. Carli's mind was abuzz. With all the excitement she completely forgot about the riding tips she had planned to review today.

As they worked their way through the pen down to the creek bottom, Carli took in a deep breath. Towering cottonwoods were sprouting small buds as they reached towards a brilliant blue sky dotted with puffs of white. She inhaled again trying to shake off the tension caused by the girls' earlier scuffle.

Lexi trotted a few short strides to catch up with Carli, head down, eyes fixed on her horse.

"Looking good, Lexi."

"That's not what Bianca would say," she mumbled.

They both watched Bianca ahead of them trotting too fast, Carli thought, her flaming hair flying free.

"Lexi, we're all at different levels with everything in our lives, whether it's education, physical gifts, even our spiritual walk. We're all on our own journey. Some of us might have more riding experience. I think your mom said you used to have horses. Did you ever get lessons or was it just for fun? Did you and Brandon get on them once in a while?"

"I used to ride almost every day after school, and then my mom got rid of them. We couldn't afford their feed." She looked so sad.

"I'm sorry about that, Lexi. I can imagine you miss Itchy a lot. Animals give us so much love. It really hurts when we lose them."

"It sucks. Nothing ever stays the same."

"You know, Lexi, sometimes we look at others and think they have it all together or that their life is easier than ours. But you know what? Oftentimes they have it just as rough, or rougher, but we can't see what's happening to them on the inside. Does that make sense?"

"Sorta."

"I know Bianca gave you a hard time before when you two ended up thrashing around. We'll all have to talk about it next time you come out. That's gotta be one of our rules, no fighting. We want this to be a safe place for everyone."

"She started it." Still, Lexi's head was down.

"I know. But I'm going to give you two tips for today. One is when someone starts a fight, sometimes you have to be the one to walk away. If you don't add to it, like fuel on a fire, the fight can't escalate. Tip two is a riding tip instead of a life tip." Carli laughed. "Keep your head up when riding. Look up, in the direction of where you want to go. Head up, shoulders back, your whole body follows, and then your horse follows. If your eyes and head are down, you slump, your body leans forward. It could convey to your horse that you want to stop. Got it?"

"Yeah, thanks."

"You're welcome. To be a good rider, you just have to learn the right things to do. Kinda like in life."

Just as Carli started to enjoy the ride and felt

calmer, Bianca came fast loping up to them. Aiming for Lexi, she jerked back on the reins to bring her horse to an abrupt stop. Lexi's horse startled and sidestepped. "Watch it!" she snapped.

Carli saw the apprehension on Lexi's face. "Sally's okay, Lexi. Just tell her 'whoa'."

Turning to Bianca, she had to reprimand her. "I don't want you riding like that on my horses. Don't jerk on his mouth. And don't upset other riders or horses. Our number one goal is to keep everyone safe."

Bianca's mouth smirked and her eyes rolled skyward. "If little Miss Poser can't control her horse, she shouldn't be on one. I've been riding since before I could walk. I know what I'm doing. And I'm sick of your rules. You take all the fun out of everything. I'm outta here."

With that, Bianca yanked her horse around and jabbed both heels to kick Mouse into a gallop straight for the barn.

"Bianca! Walk him back to the barn, please. No one is to race a horse back..."

But it was too late. Bianca couldn't hear her anymore. Or maybe she just had tuned Carli out.

"Sorry, Miss Carli."

"It's not your fault, Lexi. Let's just get these horses back to the barn and unsaddle them. We're all going to have to talk before I can take students out on a ride again. That behavior is just too dangerous and it's unkind to the horse. It's not what LoveJoy Riding School is all about."

Good Lord, what have I got myself into?

Chapter Nineteen

Carli forced a smile and waved at Lexi's mother as the girl climbed into the back seat. She watched brake lights move slowly out of ranch headquarters until their vehicle rattled the cattle guard at the top of the hill, and then vanish around the turn. As their car disappeared, another one came into view and drove slowly down the hill.

"Bianca, your mom's here," said Carli.

The red-haired spitfire emerged from the saddle house with a big smile. A total transformation from the angry young girl who had been rolling around in the dirt hours before, or so it seemed. Carli was suspicious of this youngster.

Carli opened the corral gate for her. "Thanks for coming today, Bianca. It was nice meeting you. Next time we'll ride in the arena and go over some ground rules."

The girl let out an "Hmph".

The second car pulled to a stop and a woman with fire-engine red hair like Bianca's stepped out. "How'd you girls do today?"

"Pretty good, for the first day," said Carli. "Thanks for bringing her out. Looks like Bianca knows how to ride."

Bianca glared at Carli. "We had to listen to a stupid Bible story, Mom." Bianca grumbled as she walked towards the car.

Bianca's mother looked at Carli, concern showing across her face. "Your public page doesn't say anything about Bible study."

"LoveJoy is a Christian-based school. It's mentioned in the 'About Us'," Carli explained. "My plan is to bring kids together who love horses. I'm learning new things about the Bible and I thought others might enjoy it too. Today's discussion was on the Prodigal Son. The girls seemed pretty interested."

"I don't think Bianca will be coming back. You can't force religion on her. She's had enough of that from her grandmother." Without another word the young girl and her mother got in their car and drove away. Carli stood stunned, watching their car until they were out of sight.

Lola walked out of the cookhouse. "Are the girls gone?"

"That's it. I'm closing the riding school. This must be a sign from God!" Carli slid down against the pipe fence on the outside of the corral and collapsed on the dead grass. Her body felt like it'd been run over by one of their registered Angus bulls.

"What are you talking about?" Lola pretended concern but couldn't stifle the giggle that followed.

"I am so wiped out. My feet hurt, my back hurts, my head hurts." Carli cradled her face in shaky hands, her voice choked with tears. "Those girls! What in the world caused them to roll around in the dirt and try to beat up on each other? That was a total disaster. And the way Bianca rode like a wild woman not paying any attention to me. And now Bianca's mother says I'm forcing religion on them and she's not bringing her daughter back. I can't do this, Lola." Carli yanked off her cowboy hat and wiped her face with the sleeve of her shirt. What a stupid morning.

"Believe me, this is no sign from God. This is dealing with teenagers." Lola eased down to the dirt next to her. "You're not really that much older than they are. Well, maybe ten years. But you can relate better than I can. Maybe it was my Prodigal Son story that got everyone stirred up?"

Carli turned to look at Lola and when their eyes met, they burst into giggles.

"I may not be a parent, but I have nieces and nephews, and I've taught Sunday School for most of my life. You have to be patient."

"Patient? This was like a war zone," said Carli. "I wasn't prepared for that."

Lola patted Carli's leg. "How about I rustle us up some lunch? I have cherry cobbler from last night."

"Thanks, Lola, but I think I'll go home and sit in the quiet. Thanks for your help this morning. I really appreciate it."

"It was my pleasure. I had fun." Lola stood, but before walking away she turned. "Your school is a good idea, Carli. Don't give up on the kids yet."

"I don't know how to handle emotional outbursts. What should we do?" Carli couldn't find enough energy to even get up from the ground.

"Just be kind and love them. That's all we can do." Lola patted Carli on her shoulder. "You'll do just fine."

What exactly should she be looking for to know if she was on the right path or not? God had a funny way of showing her which way to go. One thing for sure, she needed to read every article she could find on dealing with difficult teens. She was absolutely unprepared for today. She didn't exactly have huge expectations for opening day of the riding school, but this was definitely not what she had envisioned.

All she wanted to do was offer a chance for kids to be around horses, enjoy a nice ride, and teach them a little bit about the most amazing animals on the planet. She had loved horses her whole life, and she wanted to give others the same opportunity.

Is that too much to ask, God?

Wearily, she put her hat back on, stood, and brushed her hands off on her jeans.

"Y'all had some excitement today. Anybody hurt?"

Carli looked up to see Lank leaning in the saddle house door, his thumbs hooked in his belt, a wide grin covering his face. She ignored the flutter in her stomach. Glad he was here and didn't take her firing him seriously, but also annoyed he always looked so decked out and "Texas ranchy". He was the real deal all right. Cowboy hats got to her every time.

"No one was hurt. Some hair pulling and mild shirt ripping. Rowdy teenage girls. I wish it hadn't happened, but I guess it's all part of the process."

"Buck said to brush some horses and clean the tack room. I got my job back."

"Yes, I see you got your job back, Mr. Torres." His eyebrows raised at the use of his last name. It made Carli feel empowered, that she could get to him however slight.

"I'm happy to help with your riding school any time, Carli. By the way, where was your boyfriend?"

Oh, brother. Here we go.

"We can't all take the morning off for this program. Nathan was supposed to be here but must have gotten held up. He's just being neighborly."

"A little more than that, I'd say."

"What is that supposed to mean?"

"Well, you go on dates, don't you? That's more than just being neighbors, if you ask me."

"No one asked you, so please keep your opinions to yourself." She didn't want to talk about this with him. It was her personal life. She was his boss. He was a ranch hand. They'd all been through a lot what with the fire, then the snowstorm, but now she had to get serious and run her ranch. Guys like Lank only complicated things. After this morning, it was more than she could handle.

"I guess that's right, Miss Jameson. No one asked me."

"I've got to get cleaned up. And I'm sure you've got work to do."

"Sure thing, boss lady. Whatever you say."

She glared at him for a moment, trying to decide if she should yell and scream, or just ignore him. He met her gaze, his eyes cool and steady, which annoyed her even more. She spun on her heels and walked to the house.

What a day. And Lank just added the cherry on top. She had a lot of thinking to do about her plans for the LoveJoy Riding School. She asked for a sign. She got a sign all right, but was it a sign from God or the Devil himself? She had no idea how to know the difference.

Chapter Twenty

A bright flame-burst lit up the barn, and then an air compressor clicking on filled the quiet. Nathan Olsen looked like a Star Wars stormtrooper in his white welder's helmet as he operated the acetylene torch. The shop was peaceful, and he worked surrounded by darkness except for the task light hanging directly overhead. He liked welding late at night or early morning before dawn when he was less likely to be bothered. He had automatically assumed the job of ranch welder after his grandfather passed, but not before he learned everything he could from the old man. Building gates, repairing cattle guards destroyed by distracted drivers, and anything else that needed repair. Today he took a bold step to make something a little different. Probably inspired by the day with Carli at the art gallery. After lying awake for several nights thinking about the design, he woke up this morning eager to give it a try but didn't make it to the shop until after dark this evening.

Carli stayed on his mind as well. He gave her

credit for leaving a life in Georgia to move to the Texas ranch she had inherited from a grandfather she never knew. He wanted to know more about her, yet he felt her holding back. Maybe something happened in Georgia? Maybe it had to do with her being raised by guardians and never knowing her family? She was a mysterious puzzle, that's for sure, but he wasn't giving up hope. He was drawn to her, more than he'd ever been before to anyone else.

As he bent over his work in deep concentration, he didn't know anyone was in the shop until he felt a hand on his back. Nathan flipped the welding hood up and turned to look over his shoulder.

Skip Olsen raised his voice over the equipment sounds. "Whatcha up to, Son?"

"Making a copper rose for Mom's birthday. She loves roses. Take a look. I'm almost done."

"When did you learn to do that?" He glanced at the piece for a split second.

Now's your chance. Say something. Tell him. Nathan's heart thudded in his chest, but before he could open his mouth, his dad began listing chores. "We're gettin' a load of mineral block delivered tomorrow. Could you meet the truck with the skid loader and stack them in the hay barn? Haul a couple of round bales out to the big pen for the horses. The vet's coming, around ten, to take a look at a couple of the broodmares, just routine. Then I have a bunch of paychecks you can hand out to the boys. And make sure your brother drags that arena next to the barn. It's muddier than a pig pen."

Nathan's shoulders dropped in defeat. "Maybe Angie could do it? I'd like to finish this up for Mother." The minute the words left his mouth, he knew he should have kept it shut. His father's face took on a brighter shade of red and his expression grew hard.

"I gave you time off in the middle of the week to eat lunch in town. And then you were gone all day long last weekend, but you never said where." His booming voice echoed in the concrete shop building and drowned out the welder. "I think I've been more than generous. No more lollygagging. This ranch doesn't run itself."

Nathan turned the welder off. "Yes, sir," he said quietly. Then Nathan looked to his dad and asked, "Where you gonna be?" It was a risky question, but once again it slipped from his mouth before he thought to not speak.

"I've got a Honey Do list to tackle with your Mom in town. Need groceries and I don't know what else. I think she invited half the county to celebrate her birthday and Mother's Day. And of course, her greatest joy is cooking a big meal. You should invite Carli."

"Sure, Dad. Hey listen, I'd like to talk to you about something."

Ignoring Nathan's comment, he kept talking. "Oh! Almost forgot. Can you get someone to follow you and drop my truck off to Lamar's? Needs an oil change and tires rotated. Sometimes they can deliver it back to us. Or you could wait for it. We'll take Mom's car to town."

With a heavy sigh, Nathan replied, "Sure, Dad." There was no way he could get through all that in one day. The other Olsen kids went about their business, while the entire operation fell on his shoulders. He'd gone so many years without saying anything, it was next to impossible to argue now. His breath came raggedly in frustration and anger, but he choked down his words and remained silent.

Before he flipped his face mask down again, he focused on the copper rose. The thin sheets of metal were bending exactly like he had pictured, slowly taking shape into an open flower.

Nathan heard his father mumble as he walked to the door. "Now get to bed. We have a long day tomorrow. Don't know why you fool with that kind of stuff. It's not like you got any real talent for that sort of thing."

The words stung and Nathan was surprised by that. He wanted to be a full-time artist and knew if he had the chance to work at his craft and study more, he might actually be able to make a living at it. He always loved making things since he was a little kid—Lego cities, wooden furniture, and his grandfather Olsen encouraged his interest. To Nathan it was a passion, not some passing phase; it was something he had to do to feel that his life mattered. It was as though he was given a mission, a gift, a special talent no one else possessed. If he didn't work with it, if he just let it waste away and go dormant, he felt it would die, that maybe his life and dreams would die. But he never told anyone about his desire to become an artist until he met Carli. She inspired him to be better.

His mother thought it was a nice hobby and often praised his efforts when he'd been a young boy. She never knew about the burning desire he kept hidden though. But he didn't have much time to work on his ideas, and he knew no one realized how deeply he felt it in his soul. He couldn't imagine his parents, particularly his father, understanding him wanting to "do art" for his life's work. Naturally, they thought he'd take over the magnificent Rafter O Ranch, a place he couldn't figure out how to get away from. The idea left him with a bitter taste in his mouth. What if he didn't want to oversee the towering legacy of the Olsen family? As the first born, it had always been assumed he would take over, but no one ever asked his opinion.

How could he explain it to them? How could he make them understand he was sick of ranch work and didn't want to do it every day for the rest of his life? Instead, he wanted to get up in the morning, happy to be alive, excited to work on a piece of his own creation, his art. He wanted to live out his passion.

Carli understood. He could talk to her about things like this. She listened. She encouraged him to talk to his dad. And said we all had to be true to our own dreams, that we couldn't live someone else's life. She was right. He'd tell his parents soon. He just had to.

But right now, he stayed lost in the flame of the torch. His secret place. It was where he could go to feel at peace. Watching the metal change shape and turn red with heat held him spellbound, like watching volcanos being created, lava flowing in a river out of a mountain. Then he would bend and shape the soft metal into an object that had never existed before—like a rose for his mother. He made other larger things—a barn sign for a neighbor and a few decorative pieces another neighbor took to be sold at a craft fair, just for fun. His father never knew about any of them.

What he really wanted to work on were life-sized, bronze sculptures. But he had to learn more about that.

He shut off the torch, removed his helmet, and pressed Carli's number on his phone contact list. "Hey, how ya doing?"

"Is everything okay, Nate? You sound troubled."

"I'm working on a metal project. Needed to take a break. I wanted to ask you about Sunday lunch with the family. We're celebrating Mom's birthday and Mother's Day."

"Sure, Nate, that'd be fun, thanks for asking."

"My dad was the one who reminded me to ask you over." He smiled when he heard her laughter at the other end.

"Sounds nice, Nate. You said the magic word—food. I do like a good burger."

They both chuckled.

"And Carli," his voice grew serious, "thanks again for going with me to the art gallery."

"Don't mention it. It was a fun day. See you Sunday. I'll just drive over."

He disconnected the call, slipped his phone back into his pocket, and opened the cooler. He took out a water bottle and set it on the metal workbench he had made a few years back. As he looked around the shop, he began thinking about taking his art to the next level.

Nathan took a sip of water and thought about what his grandpa used to say in an effort to get him to hurry up and make a decision on what kind of milkshake he wanted from the Dixie Maid Drive-in. Grandpa Olsen was an ornery old cuss who spoke in plain cowboy lingo. He could be crude sometimes, but you always knew where he stood on things.

"Do your business or get off the pot, boy." Saying those words out loud made Nathan laugh. "I hear ya, Grandpa."

It was time to get serious about this so-called "hobby" of his. He needed to own it or just forget about it. More than anything, he wanted to give it a try. There'd be hell to pay around the Olsen family ranch though. For that, he was certain.

Chapter Twenty-One

Nathan Olsen waited patiently for the old drip coffee pot to finish as he studied the layout of the shop building that took up one side of the Rafter O Ranch headquarters compound. It wasn't sunup yet. Unable to sleep because the copper rose kept tugging at his mind, he finally stopped fighting the covers, got dressed, and came out to the shop. He contemplated a new arrangement, one that would allow him room to set up a metal working area. If he moved that pile of old trailer tires from the far corner and stacked them outside, he might be out of everybody's way. Wooden pallets rose almost to the ceiling. Those could go somewhere else too.

His parents had raised him and his brother and sisters in the local church, but more than that, they taught them about the Bible. And sometimes when weather or livestock issues kept them from getting to church, the family read the Good Book together. As the kids found their way through the teen years, some were more interested in youthful pursuits and pranks. But Nathan believed they would always have faith rooted in their being.

Nathan believed in God but didn't run around like a fanatic or get into other people's business. His faith was personal, but he did share with others if the opportunity presented itself about how it made a difference in his life. He would be the first to admit he wasn't a perfect man and sometimes went for days without what he called "scheduled" study or prayer. But he always felt that God had an eye on his life and cared about him.

So now in his time of unrest he thought he would search in what his grandfather had frequently called "Life's Instruction Manual". His hardback Bible was in the house. Seemed like a lot of people used their "devices" nowadays to look up scripture, and he also had given in to the convenience. He searched about the "desires of our hearts".

Nathan was familiar with the scripture Jeremiah 29:11: "For I know the plans I have for you, declares the Lord, plans for good and not for evil, to give you a future and a hope."

Reading that filled Nathan with peace. God really does care about me. Okay, Lord, what's my future? Cows? Or art?

He clicked on the link to Proverbs 16:3: "Commit your work to the Lord, and your plans will be established." Okay, Lord, this art's for You. Please bless it. I thank You for giving me the talent. You know I love to do it. Please use it for Your good, to make people happy. I feel this is the path for me deep in my soul. Give me your peace, Lord. Help me talk to my folks. Give them an open mind. Thank you.

As he raised his head and opened his eyes, Nathan saw his mother standing in the doorway waiting, watching him. A bit of panic hit when he thought of the copper rose on his worktable.

He hopped down from the bench and walked over to the torch area, discreetly slipping a cloth over the rose, and said, "Hey, Mom. Whatcha doin'?"

"Checking on my favorite oldest son. I have four other kids ya know, so I have to be careful about favoritism. And I'm bringing you something for breakfast. I heard you leave the house before dawn." She placed a plate of homemade oatmeal bars on a table nearby.

She loved repeating that joke about favorite kids for as long as he could remember, probably said the same thing to them all. He often watched his mother in wonder, trying to imagine how she did it with five kids, especially when they were little. Must've been a challenge to corral them all.

"Thanks, Mom." He barely glanced up before digging in.

"What are you working on?" She walked towards his bench, curiosity showing on her face.

He was closer and intercepted quickly. Moving the cloth-wrapped rose out of sight, he brought forth a small metal cross he had dabbled with for fun.

"That is very nice. I love it, Nathan. What are you going to do with it?"

While she admired the cross, he picked up another oat bar.

"Maybe sell it at the farmer's market this summer?" He shrugged, answering between bites. "Belinda handles them for me at the coffee shop booth."

"I didn't know you made these. You really are talented, Nathan. And you enjoy it, don't you?" She beamed with pride in her eyes as she ran her hand over the polished metal.

"Yes, ma'am, I do."

"Looked like you were praying when I came in. Hope I didn't interrupt your time. Is anything troubling you, Son?"

Here was another opportunity. Should he say anything or wait until both his parents were together?

Before he could decide what to say, his mother said, "You know, Nathan, your father and I love you and your brother and sisters more than anything in this world. We are blessed to have all of you and thank God for each of you every day. And we only want the best for you. We want you to be happy and safe. You can always talk to us about anything that's troubling you."

He couldn't believe this opening. Running the words through his brain first, now would be the perfect time to bring the subject up, but he felt unprepared. Even if his dad wasn't there, maybe it was the right time to get the ball rolling.

"Mom...I need to tell you something."

"If you want to wait till your father is here."

Nathan jumped in quick. "No, I need to get it out or I'll go crazy." He smiled a little, only to hide his racing heart. Why did he hesitate?

"Go ahead." Her eyes were sharp and assessing, giving him her full attention.

"Mom, you know I love you guys. But the truth is I don't want to do ranching the rest of my life. I want to pursue my art. I'm not sure Dad will understand."

"What won't I understand?" Suddenly his father

appeared in the doorway and Nathan felt a stab of sickness in the pit of his stomach.

His mother went over to her husband and patted his arm. "Hon, let's listen to Nathan. He was just about to tell me some things that have been on his mind." She was still holding the metal cross in her hands.

The Olsens sat together on a wooden bench across from Nathan who leaned against the metal workbench, his dad's face set in a stern expression.

Nathan cleared his throat, hesitating for a few moments. "I'm going to clean out that corner of the shop and have a place to do some metal work." No reaction. So far so good. He continued.

"I can make a living doing this. I feel strongly about it." He told them about taking Carli to the art museum, meeting Brad Travers, and how he wanted to learn about making life-sized bronze sculptures. He took a deep breath; his palms were clammy but now was as good a time as any. "I don't want to run the Rafter O."

That last revelation was met with stony silence from both his mother and father. His dad frowned with cold fury glowing in his eyes, then looked around the barn, seemingly processing what Nathan had just said.

His mother took hold of her husband's hand as if to calm his nerves before he said something they'd all regret, and looked at her son. "Nathan, we want you to be happy. We want all of our kids to be happy. That's the bottom line."

After several long moments his father cleared his throat and finally spoke. "Son, we want the best for you. But this little hobby of yours is not going to pay the bills or support a family. You have an obligation to this ranch and to the legacy your great-grandfathers began. I took over for my dad. You're the fifth generation of Olsens on this land. I'm not going to allow you to throw away everything you have here to make little metal doo-dads." His father looked at him with a mixture of confusion and anger glinting in his eyes. Nathan's heart clenched with pain.

"Angie could run the ranch with you, Dad. She's a natural."

His father stood, walked closer, and pointed a finger in his face. "Your sister is not the oldest. The Rafter O always goes to the oldest boy. It's been like that for generations."

Nathan thought about asking what about families that don't have any boys, what then? But he didn't want to make his father's head explode.

It was out now, so he might as well go for broke. "I want to be an artist."

Skip Olsen's face turned a bright shade of red as he stared at his oldest son. "What are you doing to this family?"

There was that phrase again—"desires of your heart". Oh, Lord. You really do care about us. Please help my dad understand and let him not be disappointed in me. The scripture flashed through Nathan's mind again. He was overcome with emotion, but he couldn't see how he could make them understand. This wasn't a hobby. This was a lifetime commitment. He needed to study and learn and devote every waking hour to pursuing his dream. A cattle ranch did not play into his plans.

Chapter Twenty-Two

Carli stepped out her front door to join Lola's early morning yoga class and tripped over a bouquet of flowers. Big yellow sunflowers surrounded by daisies and delicate baby's breath with blue cornflowers, red, pink, and orange mums, all tied together in a vivid jumble with a red and white checkered bow. She bent to pick them up and found a card.

"Carli, Thanks for listening. You are very special to me. Fondly, Nathan."

Carli glanced up to see Lola walking towards her and waved before turning to take the flowers inside and find a vase and water.

"Wow aren't those pretty! Secret admirer?" Lola asked as she followed Carli into the kitchen.

"They're from Nathan," said Carli in a serious, quiet tone.

"Nathan did good. He's so thoughtful and such a nice young fella." Then with a twinkle in her eye, she asked, "You think there's something there?"

"Lola, it's just a thank you. He took me to an art museum in Amarillo. That's all it is."

"Maybe for you, Carli. I think that boy...er, man... has a lot more on his mind. He's had his eyes on you since the first time you met. He comes from good stock. You could do a lot worse."

"You know I have so much going on in my life now—the equine program for the kids, plus trying to learn everything I can about running this ranch. I don't have time for a boyfriend."

"But one day, don't you want a husband and a family of your own? Pretty soon you'll have to start thinking along those lines. That's all I'm saying." Lola got a vase down and filled it with water. Carli didn't mind Lola knowing her way around the kitchen.

"Yes, Mom," Carli teased, and arranged the flowers into the container. "You know, not everyone gets married and has kids. This is the twenty-first century after all. Women have more choices nowadays."

"You gonna call and thank Nathan?"

"Yeah, I should do that right now. I might be a little late for yoga class."

"And, Carli, speaking of families." Lola laid a warm hand on Carli's shoulder. "You know. if you ever want to research the Jamesons, I'm always here to help. I'm not trying to rush you, it's just that I'm sure there are tons of family papers stashed all over this house. Your Grandma Jean never threw anything away. I can help. Just whenever you're ready."

Carli swallowed the lump in her throat and pulled away from Lola's touch. She focused on arranging the flowers in the vase to avoid eye contact. Maybe Lola didn't know about the birth certificate. Maybe Jean or Ward never told anyone about the identity of her birth father, if they knew. It was her secret for now, and she trusted Nathan to keep it to himself. She wanted to do the research on her own for a while and wasn't ready to tell Lola just yet. From what she had recently learned about small communities, any bit of gossip relating to the Wild Cow Ranch and her heritage would ignite like a prairie fire all over the county, and she'd be in desperate need of a team of smoke jumpers to extinguish it.

"Thanks, Lola. I'll be there in a minute."

"Come whenever you can. I'm sure you'll feel good after stretching, maybe get rid of some stress. I'd better get going. The ladies should be arriving any time."

Carli pressed Nathan's name on her phone.

"Mornin', Carli. How are you?" His deep, cheerful voice lightened her mood. Was the guy ever discouraged or down about anything? Such a contrast from grumpy Lank who seemed to be annoyed with everything she did.

"Good morning, Nate. What's up?"

"About to saddle up. It's such a nice morning, and I need to check the late birthing heifers. I've only had to help deliver a handful. We're almost done with this year's crop. Did you need something?"

"I just called to thank you for the lovely flowers. That was really sweet of you."

"So, you like them?"

"How did you get on my porch without me hearing you?"

He chuckled. "That's a secret I'll never tell. If you were my girl, I'd give you flowers every day."

She gulped hard. What? He was getting bolder

and moving faster all the time. She wasn't ready and wasn't sure how to answer.

"Uh..." she stammered and then cleared her throat.

"I don't mean to freak you out, Carli. Just speaking my mind. Already told you how special you are to me."

"I'm flattered but remember I said to go slow?"

He chuckled again. "They're just flowers, Carli. No biggie. I wanted to let you know I had a great time. Hey, you want to bring Beau and go for a ride? I'm trying to put some miles on a colt for a guy. Or I could come to you."

She was tempted. If the prediction held true it should be a mild day with minimal wind and it wasn't all that cold. She hadn't taken Beau out for a while. Would it encourage Nathan even more if she kept spending time with him? She always had a lot of work waiting for her in the office. Couldn't just go off galivanting when she had a ranch to run. But she really needed a friend and he was so easy to be with.

"I dunno, Nate. I've got a lot to do here. Plus, I was just about to join Lola's yoga class. I think they're starting soon."

"Seriously? Bend your body in unnatural ways like a pretzel? Or ride Beau across the pasture on a beautiful morning? When was the last time you had him out anyway? Think of him. Horses need to run. And it would be more exercise for you than yoga stretches."

He was a hard one to argue with. "All right, Nate, you win. I'll load up Beau, tell Lola I can't stay for her class, and head your way in a few minutes."

"Sounds like a deal. I'll give you the two-cent tour of the Rafter O by horseback. See you in...say, a half hour?"

"Okay, half hour."

As she was saddling Beau, Lank came around the corner with a hammer in his hand, nails between his teeth, surprise reflected on his face when he saw her. Shoving the nails into one pocket, he asked, "What're you up to? Taking Beau for a ride? Want some company?" His stare was bold and the look on his face hopeful.

Carli's stomach did a flip flop, which caused her to grit her teeth and ignore his eyes. She'd actually love to go out for the day with Lank. But she'd just fired the guy only a few days before and promised herself she would try to act more professional, distance herself because of the employer/employee relationship.

Concentrating on brushing Beau, she remained quiet, staring at the horse's side to give herself time to think of a reply. Lank waited.

She swung the saddle blanket in place. Finally, Carli said, in her employer voice, "Actually, I'm meeting Nathan." Why did she even tell him that? It was none of his business what she did or who she did it with.

Lank lowered his head a bit, then looked up through dark lashes. She almost melted when she saw the disappointment on his handsome face.

"I don't want to create any problems between you and your boyfriend, boss. I've got work to do." With that, he turned and walked away.

Carli's chest ached. Darn, she hated when he called her "boss" and Nathan wasn't her boyfriend.

The man was intolerable. He could wipe away her calm spirit with just one encounter. She pursed her lips with annoyance. Would they ever figure this out and feel comfortable with each other? She had to let it go for now because she was running late to meet Nathan.

"C'mon, Beau, let's go." She looped his lead rope around the fence rail and left to hitch the trailer. Within minutes she was on her way to the Rafter O and then remembered she forgot to bid her apologies to Lola for ditching class. But as Nathan had pointed out, why would she want to be cooped up in a class bending her body in strange contortions when she could be riding her horse across the Texas Plains? It really was a no-brainer.

Chapter Twenty-Three

Wearing a ballcap, her honey-colored braid trailing down her back, Carli loved the warm sun on her face. It had been a hard winter. And that snowstorm! Ugh, she didn't want to remember how cold she had been. She could've died really. But today she would put those bad memories out of her head. And she flat refused to think about Lank. Instead, she focused on the cowboy riding along with her as they made their way across a pasture on the Rafter O ranch.

Nathan and his horse came loping behind her. He looked good, but then he always dressed with all the necessary Texas cowboy gear. Western hat, tan hide chaps, boots, and spurs. Which reminded Carli, she needed to find a leather worker who could make her a pair of chaps. Nathan wore a blue wool vest with the Rafter O brand. She couldn't help but notice his tanned face, broad shoulders. What woman wouldn't go for him? Plus, he was a genuinely nice guy. *Why do I always make things so difficult? Just pick the nice guy.* For some reason, she couldn't. Her mind grappled for a second. It wasn't that Lank wasn't a nice guy. It was just that every time he opened his mouth, he was so aggravating and then when he looked at her...

"I'm glad you're here, Carli."

"Thanks for the invite." She tipped her face to the sun and willed her thoughts to quiet. "I didn't realize how long it's been since Beau and I were out of the corral."

Within minutes they were in the saddle and Nathan was leading her through Rafter O headquarters towards the gate on the far end.

He smiled. And kept staring at her. She swiped at the wispy strands over her face that had come loose from under the ballcap.

"It's not far." Through the gate into the next pasture, he ignored the dirt road and took off across the grass.

Carli didn't know if the wind ever really stilled here, only changing from forceful gales to gentle breezes. For the present, at least, it felt soft on her face. The vastness of the sky and prairie always surprised her—the openness with no shelter, no trees. An infinite emptiness swarming with life, but you had to know where to look. Maybe she was still nervous from being stranded in a barn during a snowstorm. It was one of the scariest times of her life.

At the top of the next rise a group of antelope stood stone still, watching the riders before suddenly coming alive and bounding away. Meadowlark calls provided stereo surround sound, their eerie screeches coming from every direction. In the wide and shallow valley, new calves watched with curious eyes from behind cautious mothers. Several of the momma cows raised their heads, nostrils to the air before turning and lumbering off with their babies following close behind.

"What about Sunday? You have a few weeks to decide, but there's always a place for you at our table," Nathan asked. "It's my mother's birthday."

"Hey, you haven't told me yet about talking with your folks about your art. What'd they say?" Carli found it interesting that Nathan exuded charm and self-confidence sitting astride a horse, but he couldn't tell his parents about his burning desire to create things out of metal. She realized the expectations of being the oldest Olsen must be a huge burden to bear.

Nearing a clump of shade trees, Nathan lifted the reins slightly and asked his horse to walk. Carli followed.

"It was one of the hardest things I've ever had to do. I knew my dad would be furious. And he was but tried not to show it. I think because my mom was there, he didn't explode and tell me all that was on his mind. She's always supportive of any of us kids, no matter what we want to do."

"I think she'd be supportive of me too, and I'm not her kid." Carli laughed. "She's just that kind of sweet soul."

"Thanks, Carli. She really likes you, ya know. Anyway, after hemming and hawing on my part, I told them. The conversation is far from over with my father. But I felt inspired after meeting Brad Travers. I've been working on a copper rose for Mom's birthday present."

Nathan dismounted and looped his reins over a tree branch. Carli handed him a Gatorade from her saddlebag.

"You think we should just ground-tie them so they can munch on some grass?"

"I'm putting some hours on this horse for a family friend before he gives it to his daughter," Nathan said, "and I'll feel better if they at least think they're tied to the tree. This is only the second time I've ridden him. You never know what might spook a horse, and I, for one, don't feel like hoofin' it back. Besides, Beau probably wouldn't want to haul both of us home."

"What was it you wanted to show me?"

"This is the largest cottonwood on the place and

the perfect spot for a picnic. Mom made us turkey sandwiches. I would never think to bring food along, but that's my mom for ya." Nathan stood under the tree and placed his hand on the trunk. He beamed with pride like a little boy with a new puppy.

Carli leaned back to study the bark. Half of the trunk lay to one side as big as a car, the other part towered above them. Several smaller trees provided a deep shade. "It's beautiful."

Nathan spread a blanket in the center of the grove. They found comfy spots and opened their sandwiches and drinks. Carli was surprised she was hungry, but then remembered all she had that morning was coffee. She had intended to do yoga first thing. Pulling off the ballcap she let the soft breeze glide through her damp bangs and tried to rearrange them with her fingers. Thank goodness for braids. She'd never be able to see for riding with hair whipping across her face.

"You're really pretty, Carli."

She couldn't deny there was a gleam of interest in his eyes as he watched her. "Yeah, right. I'm sweaty. This is exercise, you were right."

"You always change the subject when I pay you a compliment."

"Do I? Maybe I'm not used to them. And it is true, I am sweaty." She smiled.

"You might have to get used to compliments, Carli. I would tell you every day that you're a pretty lady."

She rolled her eyes and smiled but didn't answer. Instead, she stuffed a big bite of sandwich in her mouth, hoping he'd get off the compliments and move on to something else.

"Been wanting to ask you, Carli, how 'bout we go on a real dinner date to a fancy restaurant?"

"Why?"

"Why? Because I want to spend time with you, and we can get to know each other better. You can pick the restaurant."

"I don't know of any fancy restaurants around here, Nate. And I'm not so much into getting dressed up. Jeans, Tee-shirt, boots are fine with me."

An easy grin played at the corners of his mouth. "Carli Jameson, as I have several sisters, I happen to know girls like to get dressed up sometimes. What about when I first met you at our barbecue? You wore a black dress, turquoise necklace, and, I believe, your grandmother's turquoise boots. You were the prettiest girl there."

Gulping her Gatorade in a couple big swigs, Carli felt a mild panic that he remembered what she was wearing the first time they met. She was suddenly anxious to escape. We've gotta get going. Any minute, he's gonna try for another kiss. Time to go.

"I'm done, Nate. Let's ride." Carli stood and began gathering up their trash and stuffing things into his saddlebag as fast as she could.

"All work and no play then. Let's go." The grin he gave her was almost irresistible. Almost.

They mounted and rode on, stopping to fill their canteens with fresh, clean water at a windmill.

As they walked the horses, Beau's ears perked and he became stiff legged, didn't want to move. He was definitely spooked. The other horse picked up on it and then both were listening to something over the rise. They started dancing, their feet skipping up and down.

"Oh, great, what now?" Carli said.

"Just keep him steady. Maybe it's nothing."

No sooner had the words left Nathan's mouth when they spotted a couple of coyotes looking down at them. It surprised Carli that the mangy animals showed more curiosity than fear. About that time the horses got their scent. Beau's head jerked up.

In a split second, Nathan's horse reared and then came down hard on his front hooves. He bucked a couple of times. Try as he might, and he was a good rider, Nathan's body jostled around like a lumpy feed sack full of apples, and then one boot came out of the stirrups.

At that point, Carli knew he was in terrible trouble.

Chapter Twenty-Four

Carli and Nathan's peaceful ride suddenly took a turn for the worst. She watched the muscles in his forearms strain against his shirt sleeves as he gripped the reins. He tried to bring the horse's head around to one side, but with ears pinned back the powerful animal lunged high. All four hooves came back to earth with teeth-chattering force. Nathan's balance was off since he'd lost one stirrup. Carli saw daylight between his butt and the saddle, his face set in grim determination. Nathan launched from his horse to one side, hitting the ground with a dreadful thud. The horse spun several times and then took off, disappearing out of sight over the next rise.

As much as Beau might've considered following the other horse home, Carli was glad he listened to her and settled down from his dance steps.

Nathan landed on his whole right side, from boot to head. He was covered with dust and some blood trickled on the side of his forehead. His shirt was torn at the elbow.

Carli held tight to Beau's reins but swung her leg over the saddle and knelt next to Nathan. "Are you all right? That happened so fast."

With eyes a bit crossed, he looked up at her with a silly grin. "Is this the only way I'm gonna get your attention?"

"Nate, be serious. What hurts? There's blood on your head. I'll get you some water."

"Just don't let go of Beau. We need him."

"Can you stand? I'll help you. Give me a second."

Keeping a death grip on Beau's reins, she poured a bit of water from her canteen onto her hand and leaned down to wipe the blood away from the side of Nathan's face. It looked like a minor cut. "Take a sip of water. Is anything broken?"

He swiped her hand away. "I'm not thirsty, but I can't move my shoulder." He groaned as he rolled over to sit up, cradling his right arm.

"Are there more coyotes somewhere, like a pack? Will they try to attack us?" Carli couldn't help but look nervously over her shoulder.

"They usually hunt alone, maybe with one other. They don't run in large packs like wolves. And it's super rare for them to attack humans. They're shy. They'll leave us alone." Another groan escaped his lips.

"Wait. Let me help you." Carli secured Beau's reins to a tree limb before bending over to help Nathan to his feet. "All right. Can you get up on Beau? I'll hold him."

Luckily, if there was any silver lining involved in this incident, Nathan had fallen on his right side. His left leg was still strong, although his whole body was wobbly from the fall, and he was able to place his foot in the stirrup and haul himself up onto Beau's back.

"Good boy, Beau, stand still. Aren't you getting on behind me?" Nathan took the reins in his good hand. Beau shuffled a bit before Carli could climb on.

"This isn't working," he said through gritted teeth. He let go of the reins to hold his arm again.

"Too much pain? I guess every step Beau takes jars your shoulder. Let me help you climb down," said Carli.

Nathan could only nod, his face pale. After several minutes he spoke. "I'll call somebody to come get us. Mom and Dad are in Amarillo, but Travis should be home." He took a sharp intake of breath and sat still for a minute. "Would you get my phone out of my vest pocket?"

"It's not there, Nate."

He mumbled something under his breath. Carli used her phone to punch in his number and they followed the buzz. It had landed in the middle of a pile of limbs and dead leaves. She punched Travis' name and handed the phone to Nathan.

"We had a wreck. Bring a trailer. We're under the big cottonwood in P2. Thanks, little brother."

"What is P2?" asked Carli.

"Pasture 2, as opposed to pastures 1, 3, 4, or 5." Nathan froze again and squinted his eyes shut to a shooting pain.

Carli laughed at the original names, but suddenly felt concern. "Your face has no color. You're as gray as a ghost. Should we keep walking or do you need to sit?"

"Let's start walking. He'll see us." Nathan grew

quiet for a moment as he clutched his arm. "Apparently, that horse needs more rides on him. He's still green."

"You couldn't tell it from where you were, but that horse crow-hopped at least five feet in the air. No one could hold on to that."

"I may not have had a good view, but I knew I was pitching. I sure felt it at the end. As my grandpa used to say, 'Don't worry, the ground will catch ya.' All I know is, that dang horse sure did blow up on me."

Beau followed behind Carli and Nathan as they bantered back and forth side-by-side a while, chuckling at the crazy mishap of their day so far. Some riding date. Carli smiled to herself.

At the top of the hill, they stopped and were about to let out a collective sigh when Beau scampered again, his whole body tensing, and the hairs on his back stood straight up.

"Beau got a whiff of something. That coyote must be around close."

"Or it's that crazy horse. No telling which direction he went. I don't know that he could find his way back to the barn. I've only ridden him in the round pen until today."

Within half an hour or so, Carli looked up to see a truck pulling a livestock trailer bouncing across the pasture and heading straight towards them. But as they got closer, she noticed it was Lank driving with Nathan's brother in the passenger seat.

"You two need a lift?" Lank called out as they got closer.

"Looks like a cowboy without his horse to me," Travis yelled.

He and Travis laughed, but Carli failed to see any humor in their situation. Nathan glared at them with his jaw clenched and unspoken pain reflected in his eyes.

"That buggery horse dump you, bro?" asked Travis.

"Coyotes. They surprised us," said Carli. "Thanks for coming to get us."

"It wasn't any trouble," said Lank. "Travis and I were fixin' to load up and go to a ropin' when you called."

Nathan climbed into the passenger seat and Travis moved out of the way, took his hat off, and leaned back against the headrest. He shut his eyes, beads of sweat covered his forehead.

"You probably should go to a hospital." Carli walked closer and put her hand on Nathan's shoulder.

"Carli, put your horse in the trailer." Travis walked to the back and swung open the latch gate with a creak.

"I've got a better idea. Carli, why don't we make a wide sweep and see if we can locate Nathan's horse. We'll meet y'all back at headquarters." Lank looked at her matter-of-factly with those blue-gray eyes. He turned to unload his horse and led it over to stand next to Beau.

"Let me drop off my big brother, and then I'll head out from headquarters to meet you." Travis shut Nathan's door and walked around to the driver's side. "Between the three of us, we should be able to locate that horse." Lank nodded his head in agreement to the plan.

Carli stood still. She looked at Beau and then

at Nathan, avoiding Lank. She wondered if she should go with him. But why not? Maybe she wasn't thinking clearly because of the coyote and Nathan getting hurt. It would be helping them out, but it would also be time alone with Lank. She didn't have enough energy to argue and fire him again.

So, when Lank held out his hand to take Beau's reins from her, she let him and then put her foot in the stirrup.

"I'll call to check on you later," she said to Nathan.

"You guys have fun, and Lank keep your mouth shut. Try not to get fired." Travis busted out laughing. Carli couldn't help but laugh too. Nathan's little brother always seemed to keep everyone in stiches.

Lank urged his horse into a lope and Carli followed. She had no idea how to begin looking for a scared and frightened horse in a strange pasture. And then she remembered, Nathan hadn't even told her goodbye.

**

Travis glanced over at his brother. "You don't look well, man."

"I've been better," Nathan said.

"Taking Carli out to the big cottonwood, huh? What's that all about?"

"It seemed like a good idea at the time." Nathan gazed out the window at Carli and Lank as they rode side by side towards the far windmill on the horizon. He swallowed hard. He couldn't ignore the feeling of dread as he watched them. This day didn't turn out as he had hoped.

Chapter Twenty-Five

"How's Nathan doing?"

Carli sat on a stool in the ranch cookhouse watching Lola make breakfast for Buck and Lank. She sipped on her coffee and felt a contentment like never before as she breathed in the aroma of the place she wanted so badly to call home. And truthfully, it was becoming more and more like home and Georgia seemed more and more like a lifetime away.

"He's doing pretty good." Carli stood and took the spatula from her to stir eggs while Lola opened the oven to remove the biscuits. "The doc checked him out yesterday. Said the fall gave him a mild concussion and his shoulder was out of place, but they fixed that. The doc said Nathan should still be careful with his activities. But he's stubborn and doesn't always keep his arm in the sling like he should."

"Men, right?" Lola smiled and set a mixture of strawberries and blueberries on the bar before Carli.

Dumping the eggs into a serving bowl, Carli turned her attention to the fruit and scooped up a bite before talking. "Nathan invited me to go with him today to the studio of that artist guy we met at the museum. I think it's near the town of Canadian."

"You gonna go?"

Lola set a small plate down with warm biscuits and slathered them with butter, honey, and brown sugar. Carli shook her head. "I'll stick with the fruit. Thank you though. And yes, I'm going with him."

Lola shrugged and pushed the plate a little closer. "You know you want it."

"Oh, good grief." Carli rolled her eyes and took a biscuit. It was their never-ending, tug-of-war over portion control and food choices.

"Nathan can't drive yet so I'm picking him up soon."

"Nothing going on here. Don't worry. Go off and enjoy your day."

Carli stood in the doorway to the kitchen as Lank and Buck were coming in. Lank stopped, his eyes widened in surprise as he surveyed her from head to toe, and then he met her gaze. "Morning, boss."

"Morning," was all she said.

Buck tipped his hat and gave her a wide grin. "You sure clean up nice."

"Thank you very much, Mr. Wallace." Carli smiled and curtsied, then called out, "You guys have a great day. Bye, Lola."

Taking extra time with her makeup this morning, she chose a tan fringe dress with the turquoise boots. She found one of Grandma Jean's award buckles, which she attached to her old belt, added silver dangle earrings and a few silver bracelets. Just maybe she'd pass for a Texan. Not to give Nathan any more ideas that their relationship should advance to the next level, but because she'd worn mostly jeans since moving to the ranch. It felt good to be girly for a change, curl her hair and put on mascara.

As Carli drove to the Rafter O, she thought about the riding school. Actually, she had thought about working with kids again every day since that first disaster with Lexi and Bianca. She'd never been afraid to take a chance before. Taking a chance in Georgia and committing to her business partner Mark had been one of the scariest things she'd ever done in her life. But once she had made her mind up, she focused her full attention on it. Everything was zapping her strength, mentally and physically, but she also felt invigorated by the new project. Was this part of God's plan? She still felt confused. Both Nathan and Lola talked about signs from God that might tell her she was on the right track. Two teenaged girls rolling around in the dirt, pulling each other's hair out hardly felt like a sign from above.

Nathan was pacing back and forth in front of the Rafter O headquarters when she stopped. He tossed her the keys to his truck. "We can take mine."

***

As they got closer to the river valley that dissects the Texas Panhandle, Nathan admired the flat, treeless ranchland turning to rolling hills. The scenery suddenly included trees on either side of them, the leafy green of new spring shading the two-lane blacktop. It was so different from the rolling pastures of the Rafter O Ranch. When Carli and Nathan drove up to the Travers home, a stone ranch building, Brad was in the side yard with a younger man throwing a rope loop around the horns of a dummy steer.

"He sure has a lot of energy for an old guy," Nathan said.

Brad waved to Carli and Nathan as they got out of the truck.

"Hey, guys, glad you made it. I see you had no problem with my directions?"

"Well," said Carli, "except for back there about a mile where you said there'd be a black horse in a corral. No black horse. We weren't sure whether to turn or not."

Brad let out a hearty laugh. "Oh, yeah, sorry, I forgot. About this time every day, they bring him in for some feed. At least the rest of the directions worked."

They all chuckled. The young man stepped forward with his hand outstretched. "Hey, I'm Tad. Theodore actually. Nice to meet you both."

"My grandson. We're Brad and Tad."

Carli was polite, her lips still, but her eyes darted from one man to the other. Then her mouth erupted with laughter.

"Grandpa loves to say that. I've been called Tad since I was little. Tadpole. Also short for Theodore."

"I know something about nicknames. I was never crazy about my real first name," Carli said to the tall, lean, young man who looked like a younger version of his grandfather.

"Oh, yeah, what's that?"

"Can't tell you. I never say the name out loud, ever."

Again, more laughter all around. Then Brad noticed Nathan holding his shoulder.

"Hey, how're you doin', man? You said on the phone that a green horse throwed ya. Dontcha know you're supposed to stay on those things?"

"He punched the breeze all right. When there's a crazy coyote around, horses tend to act a bit spooky. I'll be okay in a few days. Dislocated my shoulder and a little muscle sore is all."

"I hope you get better soon," Brad said smiling.

A petite woman with a long gray braid pulled to one side appeared at the door and called out, "Brad, bring our guests inside. Or do you want me to set up refreshments out there?"

Nathan noticed her silver crutch with elbow support.

"Tilly, we'll come in, so it'll be easier. I'll help." Then to Nathan and Carli, he said, "She's the love of my life. C'mon, I want to introduce y'all."

For lunch, his wife had made some beef and bean tamales, salad, cornbread, and iced tea. Apple pie for dessert. Carli tried to offer to help, but Tilly would have none of it.

"Please, sit. You're our guests. It's no trouble. I just made us a little lunch."

They all gathered around a long, wooden table that looked like it belonged in a castle—heavy, solid, immovable. Nicks and scratches marred the surface, but they only gave it personality. Nathan watched Carli run her fingers along the outside where there were intricate, carved scrolls. "This table is amazing. What kind of wood is it?" she asked.

Brad smiled with an understated look of pride. "Mesquite. I made it right after we first married. It's practically a member of the family."

His wife chimed in. "He made it with his own two hands."

All he said was, "Tilly," with a tilt of his head, but not really a chastisement.

"What? I'm proud of you. You worked hours on this table. It's a work of art."

"That's for sure." Nathan was mesmerized. "Look at the variety of colors in this wood. It really is amazing work." Leaning sideways in his chair he ran his fingers along the gleaming varnished surface and patterns and grooves along the sides. "These aren't just for decoration. They're people! Men with rifles."

Quietly Brad said, "It's the Battle of the Alamo."

Nathan pushed his chair back some and looked at the carved scenes on the sides of the table near him. "Wow. I didn't know you also did woodwork."

"An artist can dabble in many mediums. Art is all around us. It's part of life, a reflection of our thoughts and emotions. An artist has no choice sometimes. It drives him...or her." He winked at his wife. "If we don't create art, we'll dry up. We need to let our creativity come forth, express what's inside of us. Or else, we'll go crazy. You know what I'm talking about, Nathan, don't you?"

Nathan looked down at his hands and was a little embarrassed to have the spotlight on himself, but at the same time it was as though only he and Brad were in the room. Brad was speaking his language, right to Nathan's heart, and he so badly needed to talk about it. For a few minutes, he hesitated. He had never revealed this part of himself before.

"I know exactly what you mean. For years I've wanted to do my art full-time. But with the Rafter O and my responsibilities..." He hesitated, but then just admitted it. "My dad has high expectations and none of them include art. He doesn't see how I could ever support myself, let alone a family." He glanced at Carli.

Tilly passed around the large salad bowl and her grandson almost started to dig in, but she touched his arm and said, "Let's say the blessing. Brad?"

"Yes, hon." He smiled and took her hand and looked to everyone to join hands.

"Or do you want Ryan to say it?" his wife asked.

"Ryan's not here, sweetie. I'll say the blessing."

Grandson Tad glanced at Nathan and then looked down at his plate.

Tilly's voice filled the quiet kitchen. "Ryan's not here. Ryan's not here. Ryan, come back. Ryan, come back."

Nathan realized something was amiss as he noticed the empty place setting and looked at Carli who returned his glance, a smile frozen on his face. Always confident and sure, this was one time in his life Nathan had no idea what to do or say.

Chapter Twenty-Six

Ignoring his wife's chant, Brad Travers bowed his head. "Let us pray." Tilly immediately turned silent.

Nathan's strong fist engulfed Carli's petite hand as they all bowed their heads around the Travers' dining room table. Then Brad started. "Dear Lord, thank you kindly for bringing Nathan and Miss Carli to our home. We thank you for this bounty and for the blessings you bestow upon our family every day. We ask you to watch over Nathan and Carli and please give them the desires of their hearts. Let them also strive to stay in your good graces and use their gifts and talents for your glory. Bless this food and the hands that prepared it. Amen."

Carli smiled at Nathan as he released her hand.

Brad dished out portions of beef brisket and passed plates. There were tamale fixings for those who wanted to wrap the meat in corn-based dough. Nathan helped himself to potato salad and pinto beans. The flavorful, tender beef touched his tongue and after he swallowed, he couldn't help but say, "This is delicious. Thank you for inviting us."

Brad stuck a basket full of warm yeast rolls under his nose. "Take one. Nathan, to follow up on what you were telling me, sometimes you've got to own your destiny. Do what you feel is right for you—come hell or high water." Looking to his wife, he said, "I'm blessed to have the support of my family."

"You can call me Nate, and I admire you for your commitment to the arts." Nathan helped himself to another roll and passed the basket to Carli.

"You've got to make a stand, Nate. I'm not saying to disobey or disrespect your father. But be honest with him, with everyone, with yourself. This is your life. Your dad is living his."

Nathan felt Brad's words pierce his heart as the others politely listened. He never denied the drive to learn all he could about sculpting to himself but admitting that desire to others was the problem. He never imagined the possibility of actually being good enough to earn a living as an artist. It was easier to ignore any thoughts of a different life. The days were much more pleasant if he kept his mouth shut and followed along the Olsen family life's pathway. It had proved successful to many generations before he came along.

"Eat up, everyone. Tilly made some good grub here. Nate, after lunch I want to show you something in the barn. We can talk more, and I can answer any questions you might have."

"Yes, sir."

Silence descended on the diners for a few moments. Carli glanced cautiously at Tilly, smiled, and then asked, "How many kids do you have Mr. Travers?"

"We've got two daughters and a son—all married and all have given us wonderful grandkids."

"Two sons," Tilly interrupted.

"Yes, dear, two sons." He touched her hand. "Ryan is in heaven with Jesus, right hon?"

She didn't answe, but stared blankly at the food on the table as though in her own dream state. Then she said, "Ryan is a decorated war hero. Served in Afghanistan. I still pray he'll walk through that door one day." She sounded perfectly lucid and alert. Nothing like the chanting from before.

Brad held his wife's hand and continued. "One daughter is a nurse, one is a teacher, and our son, Chad, is a rancher. Nate, there's another case of a father wanting his son to follow him into the family business. Only, with me, I wanted my son to be an artist. He does have some natural talent at drawing. It soon became obvious though that he had other interests, so I turned over the cow and horse operation to him and I became a sculptor full-time. As life would have it, his son...our grandson, Tad, here, loves to paint and want to learn about sculpting. We couldn't be prouder of all our kids and grands. God has surely blessed us."

Although it was a somewhat serious moment, his wife giggled and then in a sing-song, breathless chant, she said, "Brad, Chad, and Tad. Brad, Chad, and Tad. Brad, Chad, and Tad."

Nathan wasn't sure what to do so he looked to each face for help with a proper response. Carli's smile froze in place again.

Despite the momentary awkward silence, everyone broke out in laughter. Brad cupped his wife's cheek. "Oh, Tilly, you're so cute." She giggled like a teenaged girl.

Nathan felt more comfortable and at home with Brad than with his own family. At least here he didn't have to guard his every word or feel that his dad was watching and judging his work. It may not have been his father's intention, but it was how Nathan felt. Here, with Brad, Nathan was connected as though he had finally found a kindred spirit.

When lunch was over, Carli insisted helping Tilly clear the table and carry the dishes to the sink. Mrs. Travers was quite agile despite her limp and having to maneuver around the table and chairs using her crutch.

"Let's go to the barn, Nate. I've got something to show you," Brad said.

Nathan looked to Carli, and Brad added, "Miss Carli, you're welcome to join us, too."

"It's fine." Carlie smiled. "I'll visit with your wife and wash dishes if she doesn't mind. I can catch up with you guys in a while."

Nathan touched her arm. "Thanks, Carli. See you in a minute."

The red barn wasn't home to any animals. Instead, it was Brad's studio. And when Nathan walked in, he couldn't help his mouth from gaping open. Surveying the large, spacious room, he saw sculptures of all sizes and varying degrees of completion. Some were under tarps. There was also metal work, copper, black wrought iron, and steel. Tables and shelves held different tools. An acetylene torch was on one table along with the protective face mask and gloves. Nathan was very familiar with those.

A large object stood on a platform in the center of the room covered by a tan tarp. Brad smiled at Nathan and climbed the ladder next to the scaffolding that fit around the project like a cage. He carefully picked up the bottom of the covering and carried it with him on his ascent. At the top, arms out to his sides, he flung the drape off of his creation letting part of the material rest on the metal housing.

Before them stood a muscular, life-sized American Indian brave. One foot was propped up on a rock. The moccasin-clad foot on the ground was balancing on the ball and toes. The left arm was bent at the waist and the right arm was extended to the sky, fist open.

"I want to put a spear in his right hand, so I've left the palm open," Brad said simply.

Nathan walked around the sculpture, head and eyes focused upward. "Why did you decide on him as your subject?"

"Well, I love the West. And the many tribes have called the West home for centuries. I've always been interested in their culture. They have such strength. I wanted to show his strength and courage. And I wanted to strive to make him as lifelike as possible."

Again, Nathan's mouth hung open in admiration. In the moment he forgot where he was, why he was there, the only reality being the figure that stood before him. So real, yet it was of clay. Nathan could only stand in silence. He finally managed to say, "This is incredible. How did you get the folds in his loincloth? And the six-pack abs? He almost looks alive."

"Well, now that's the whole idea, isn't it? I mean unless an artist is going for abstract. For some of us we want our subjects to look real. Did you ever hear what Michelangelo said about his marble sculptures?"

"Yeah. He felt that the figure was fully formed inside the stone, and he was just chipping the rock away to set the image free."

Brad smiled. "Exactly. Fully formed. We want them to look real."

"I don't know that I could ever do this. Make the stone, or bronze, look like material draping over his body."

"'Course you could, Nate. It's called learning. There's a lot of research that goes into a piece before I even get my hands on the clay. I go to the library or online, look in books for inspiration, for topics, subjects. I calculate measurements. Then, it's trial and error. You get someone to teach you. And then you practice. You might throw a lot away. You might get angry and break stuff. But one day it all comes together. And then..." he said looking up at the Indian brave and holding his hands open and out to his sides, "and then, you have something like this. It's an amazing feeling. Accomplishment. Poetry. Art. Then you're done, and you go on to the next project."

"I don't know." Nathan shook his head.

Brad climbed down to the floor and came over to Nathan, placing his hand on the young man's shoulder.

"And in case you missed the part about learning and teaching, here I am. Willing to teach."

"Why are you doing this for me?"

"I see the passion burning in your eyes. Follow your art, Son. But, there's just one catch," Brad said, again with one of his frequent smiles.

"I can pay for lessons. That's no problem. I'd want to pay you for teaching me."

Brad was quiet for a few seconds. "Now, Son, don't insult me. This is the older generation passing down what I know to the younger generation. In fact, I'm also teaching Tad so you are welcome to join us. But if you want to talk about money, I will. And it's not you paying me. It would be the school paying you."

Nathan was totally confused. "What do you mean?"

"I've been teaching classes at the community college. All kinds of art. I put on demonstrations, but I'm wanting to slow down. I'm seventy-five, you know, and I could use an apprentice."

Nathan was speechless. The turmoil in his mind running over and over was how would he explain this to his father. There would be consequences, no doubt about it.

"You might've noticed my Tilly. She had a stroke a couple of years ago and also might have the onset of Alzheimer's. Sometimes she forgets things like our son Ryan being gone. Luckily, she still knows me and Tad and our other kids. I want to be here more for her in our later years. This will get you off your ranch for a while and get you involved with our local art community. Then when you have free time, come here and work with me and Tad."

Nathan never had his mouth open so much in one day without any words coming out.

"I also work with a gallery in Santa Fe. It would help me to have someone who can be my liaison. Haul pieces for showings, stuff like that. It's getting where I can't leave Tilly by herself. If she can travel, we usually spend the summers there. You could use the guest room, be our house-sitter when we're not in town."

Just then Tad entered the barn. "I heard my name, Grandpa. What's going on?"

Again, Brad's smile lit up the room. "I was telling Nathan about my college class and also about him working with us here, like you and I discussed. You're busy with high school." Brad turned to Nathan. "He's our youngest grandkid and a senior this year. I'm thankful for the opportunity to teach the next generation. What do you think? And you're okay with Nathan hanging out here. Am I right, Tad?"

"Right as rain, Grandpa. We can all learn from each other. Can we start now?"

They all laughed. Nathan had to admit the young boy's enthusiasm was contagious.

Brad grabbed Tad around the shoulders almost in a wrestling move. "How'd I get so lucky to have a grandson like you, Mr. Theodore?"

Tad grinned and hugged his grandpa. "Must be your right living. God is rewarding you."

"I didn't always live so right, Tad. You know the old stories."

Nathan was still a bit in shock and finally found his tongue. "I can't thank you enough, Brad. Are you sure about all of this?"

"Of course." Grabbing Tad again, he said, "We're sure. Aren't we, Tad? You'll always be my blood relative apprentice. Nathan can assist me at the college. Then when you're ready, you can apprentice there."

"Sure, Grandpa. One hundred percent sure." And with that, Tad shook Nathan's hand.

"There's lots of opportunity for both of you here, if you want to learn," Travers said. "Assist at the college or I can introduce you to the art scene in Santa Fe."

Suddenly in the doorway, Carli appeared. "Wow!" She looked up at the towering Indian brave. "That's amazing! Did you make this, Brad?"

Nathan grabbed her hand. "He did. It's an incredible piece of work."

"And one day Nathan will be doing work like this." Brad placed a hand on Nathan's "good" shoulder and they both smiled a smile of camaraderie and gratefulness.

Nathan saw Carli's questioning look. "I'll explain it all to you on the ride home."

Chapter Twenty-Seven

Carli followed Nathan to the truck. He opened the passenger side and said, "Get in." As she walked up beside him, he suddenly lifted her off her feet and swung her around. He bobbled a little as he wasn't in the best form. She grabbed hold of his arms to steady herself and in stilted, out of breath speech, said, "Nate! Put me down. Be careful. You'll hurt your shoulder. Where's your sling?"

Thankful they had parked out of sight of the Travers' front windows Carli was embarrassed by Nathan's sudden display of affection.

"I'm going to study under Brad and learn everything I can. This is huge, Carli!" His smile was as big as a Cheshire cat, in a good way.

He set her down on solid ground but wasn't done yet. Grabbing her around the waist, he bent his head and planted a firm kiss on her mouth. Holding it there for a few seconds, his lips were warm and searching. His eyes closed but hers were wide open in shock.

"Nate! Slow down. I need to catch my breath."

She pushed against his chest.

They had kissed before. Maybe once. Or twice. She couldn't remember. It wasn't that memorable. No sparks whatsoever. This one was different though. For him. She could tell he was serious.

"Carli, I'm so glad you're here! This is about my art. Things are finally starting to happen. And I want you to be a part of it."

She pushed against his chest until he released her and she took a step back. Her forehead wrinkled and her face scrunched into an incredulous expression.

"Nate, I'm truly happy for you. I really am, but this is something you have to do. It doesn't involve me."

He held her door as she climbed in.

"What about me being the designated driver?" He didn't answer, just walked around to the driver's side.

She glanced through the back window at him and could tell she had knocked some of the wind out of his sails. Was he worried about their relationship, or was the pain on his face due to the shoulder injury?

Driving down the road, at first, they were both quiet, consumed by their own thoughts. Occasionally, Carli stole glimpses of him. Things were moving way too fast for her. Had he lost his mind? The last thing she wanted to do was to lead him on and make him think she wanted more. She didn't. She didn't know what she wanted. She'd been avoiding this discussion, but maybe it was time to tell him how she felt.

"Nate, look..."

But then he jumped in, both of them starting at the same time, their words jumbling.

"Carli, I've been thinking..."

"Nate, I've got to tell you..."

"Let me go first. Please."

She took a deep breath, stared out the window, then back at him. "All right. You first."

"Look, I'm sorry. The kiss, I mean. I'm just pumped about Travers and my art. It's something I've thought about, dreamt about, my whole life. It's who I am. And I'm glad you were here."

He stared at the blacktop ahead. "Carli, looking at this road makes me think of my life's path. I've got to follow it. It's my dream and I can't keep it bottled up inside any longer. And then there's you." He muttered, his head straight, his eyes never wavering from the road ahead.

Her stomach flipped over a bit and she didn't want him to continue. But she knew he would. He had to. The time spent with Brad Travers had given him courage in some way. Carli froze, her breath stuck in her throat and it was everything she could muster not to stop him from talking. She didn't need anything else to complicate her life. Why couldn't their friendship stay the way it was?

"I've liked you since the first time I saw you walking into my parents' home at the barbeque for my sister. You were the prettiest girl in the room. I remember everything about that day, Carli. You came with Lank, but he was off with an old girlfriend. He left you by yourself. And you were new in town, didn't know anyone. So, I stood beside you, at the request of my mother I admit, but then we talked and laughed. I drove you home when

Lank acted like a jerk. I'm the steady one, Carli. I'll always be there for you."

He pulled the truck to the side of the road and turned the ignition off.

Looking into her eyes, he said, "I know I can find the courage to pursue my artwork with you by my side."

Carli closed her eyes. This handsome, kind Texas cowboy might be the answer to her dreams, but the break-up and betrayal from her past in Georgia was still too fresh on her heart. She didn't know what she wanted.

"Nate. You're my best friend in Texas. Anywhere actually. There's no one back in Georgia. I care about you. And treasure our friendship. I'm so excited for your passion of art, but this—'us'—is moving too fast for me. You should follow your dream. Wherever it leads, with or without me."

She placed her hand on his forearm and he turned his head to look at her. "I really admire you, ya know. You've got some gumption to move halfway across the country and start a new life. I can see us together, Carli. You don't have to be alone anymore."

"What are you trying to say, Nate?"

"I think I'm falling in love with you." He looked longingly into her eyes.

No words formed in Carli's mouth. She honestly did not know how she felt, other than this was a great friendship, with total trust like with no one else before. Is that love? Is that enough to commit a lifetime to one person? She thought she knew. Back in Georgia love had been true and wonderful, she had thought, but then the betrayal almost did her in.

He remained quiet when she didn't reply, then started the truck and pulled back on to the main road.

Lord, help me. Show me what's right. Help me to make the right decisions. And not to hurt anyone. Carli had learned a lot about faith over the past several months from Lola and Buck. It was time she tried to live it more in her life. Sometimes you can't do everything on your own. As much as she wanted to be in control. But sometimes that control got her into trouble. She needed to release the reins. Trust God to help her.

Arriving at the Wild Cow, Carli knew she didn't want to let Nathan leave after he had just poured out his heart and soul, and she basically rejected him. So, before she got out of the truck and let him drive away, she said, "Please come in for a minute, Nate. I'll make us some tea or coffee. I want to talk a little more."

"I'll come in for just a few minutes. Then I've got to get home. I'm sure my father has a list of work lined up since I've been gone most of the day."

As they walked to Carli's front door, Lank approached fast like he was marching on a mission.

"Where the heck have you two been?" His voice curt, his angry eyes focused on Carli.

"What's the matter with you?" She spun around to face him and could see he was upset, but what business was it of his where they had gone today?

"Well, your horse is going stir crazy. Before you know it, he'll start cribbing on the fence. You just up and leave all your responsibilities."

Yep. He was mad. Hopping mad. Carli wondered if there was more to it. But before she could find out, Nathan stepped between her and Lank.

"You don't talk to Carli like that." Nathan's tone was low and deep. "She's your boss and she had plans today. With me."

Based on the fury that clouded Lank's face, that just added fuel to the fire.

"Look, man. This is none of your business. It's between me and her." Lank's eyes darkened as he thrust a finger out and poked Nathan's chest. "Why don't you climb back in your truck and get out of here?"

"I'm making it my business. That's no way to talk to a lady." His voice rose as his hands tightened into fists about to explode.

Lank inched even closer.

"This is between Carli and me."

Carli had never seen Lank so angry before. And Nathan was bowed up like some cave man protecting his woman. She was stunned transfixed on the strange scene in front of her as it played out.

Then Lank shoved on Nathan's chest. It was enough to detonate Nathan's timebomb.

The two men scuffled, Lank swinging first and then Nathan returning the jab. Lank responded with a gut punch, and Nathan lunged until they both hit the ground. Lank tore at Nathan's shirt in a fury and Nathan pummeled Lank's face.

A few expletives were mumbled, and then Nathan grunted.

Carli saw the pain that flashed across his face and yelled. "His shoulder! Lank, stop it! Both of you! You're acting like idiots."

Lank hopped to his feet, his eyes never leaving Nathan's face.

Nathan had trouble getting up, but Carli lent him a hand under his elbow.

The two men stood, covered in dirt, and wiped at their bloody mouths.

"Are you all right, Nate?" Carli asked as she tried to touch his arm, but he pulled away.

"If you're okay, I'll be going now." And he turned and headed for his truck.

"Nate, wait." Carli didn't know why she said that, but it seemed like they had more to talk about. Or maybe it was her guilt?

"Thanks for going with me today. I'll call you later."

Lank dusted his jeans off and picked up his hat. "Couldn't take it, I guess."

She was fuming, walking towards Lank, and put her finger in his face. "You! What in the world is wrong with you?"

Lank's attitude was simmering down somewhat like a chastised kid. "Well, he butted his nose in. If he hadn't gotten in the middle of us like that."

Carli wondered if there was more meaning behind his last statement but decided to ignore it.

"I will not tolerate any fighting on my ranch, Lank Torres. In fact, I've a good mind to fire you!"

Again, Lank's temper flared evidenced by the rage that filled his eyes. "Well, if that's what you want to do, boss lady, go ahead. Do it! I don't need you and I don't need this job. In fact, I'll make it easy for you. I quit!"

Carli watched Lank's back until he disappeared through a gate at the corral. Overcome with emotion, she sank into one of the rocking chairs on her front porch. What a day. No matter. Buck would hire Lank back again before supper, and he'd be around tomorrow to do something again to make her angry. She noticed a pattern beginning to emerge.

Time stood still as she watched the light slowly fading from the sky. It was a beautiful spring evening, but her heart was too troubled to really notice. She pulled her jacket closer around her and listened to the soft nickers of the horses. She recognized Beau's right away. She thought about going inside to make a cup of hot tea, but before she left her rocker, Lank's pickup truck came roaring by. The passenger seat and the second seat inside the cab were piled high with stuff. She couldn't tell what. In the bed of the truck, she could see a roping dummy and several saddles. Her shoulders slumped. Of all the stupid, arrogant cowboys in the world she had to employ this one. The idea was to leave all her troubles behind in Georgia. Would her life ever get easier?

Chapter Twenty-Eight

A week had gone by since the fight between Lank and Nathan. Carli hadn't spoken to either one of them, and she still felt numb and lost. All she knew how to do to give herself a reason for waking up each morning and getting dressed was to submerge herself in the work of the ranch and her genealogy research. The heck with men. There was no winning or reasoning. They were always trouble.

She leaned back in her chair and propped both feet on one corner of her desk. Now she felt suddenly alone again. Nathan was a good friend to hang out with, and Lank was always around. Alone, except for Buck and Lola. They were the one constant in her life. And, of course, God. She was trying once again to learn to trust Him, but it was hard sometimes. Why did it seem like a daily challenge? She had always been a worrier and second-guessed herself, doubting her decisions. It's what she was best at.

Nathan had given her space over the past week, but, hopefully, not for good. He had some tough decisions to make about his own life. Fueled by the inspiration he felt after leaving Brad Travers' studio, now was the time to tell his parents. If he didn't do it, Carli realized he never would. He'd spend the rest of his life doing the job he was born to and would hate every minute. It made her sad to think his talent would go unnoticed. She missed his daily phone calls.

And Lank? She had no idea where he was.

Her heart hurt. Was everything falling apart? Had all her decisions been the wrong ones? Would she end up losing her grandparents' ranch and everything they had built? A cloud of doom somehow slipped over her world.

The desk in the back den of her grandparents' house was covered with papers. With a heavy sigh she swung her legs to the floor. Leaning on her elbow, her head propped up by her other hand, she scrutinized invoice after invoice while her mind still thought of Nathan and Lank. She wasn't making much headway with the bills.

A knock sounded, and Lola walked in. Carli couldn't help being a little short. "The prices from Farmer's Supply Store keep going up! Why is that? And when did we buy a new pressure washer? And corral gates? I'm going to have to talk to Buck about this. We're not even halfway through the year. I never realized how much it costs to run a ranch."

"Yes, and we only have one payday. In late fall when we ship, that's when we make our money. I know you have a lot going on right now, Carli, and I've been praying for you. What's really the matter? The ranch business never seemed to bother you this much before."

"What do you mean, Lola? Look at all these bills! Of course, it's the ranch."

Lola took a couple steps towards Carli, placing a hand on her shoulder. "I know it's a big responsibility, and I would have never passed along the bill paying to you if I'd known how upsetting it would be. But it'll work out. It always does. It's the nature of the ranching business. We have good years and bad."

Carli ran her fingers through her hair and shuffled some of the papers. "Well, this must be turning out to be one of the worst years on the books."

"Is something else bothering you? Do you think maybe you're upset about Lank and Nathan? Lank told Buck what happened."

"I don't really want to talk about them. They both acted like idiots and left, hardly even looked back. It's really for the best."

"Carli, life is complicated. Humans are complicated. We get our feelings hurt. We have tempers. And jealousy. Did you ever think Lank might be jealous of Nathan and that's what caused the fight?" Lola eased into the leather chair.

Frowning, then smirking, Carli spun her chair around to look at Lola. "Lank's a hothead! Only thinks of himself. Besides, he quit. I'll just hire someone else. Must be easy to find ranch hands around here."

"Not one with the kind of loyalty Lank has for the Wild Cow. Buck told him to take a few days and cool off. He'll be back. We really need him. Calves are dropping. It's a busy time."

"Loyalty? He quit! And he says things on purpose just to get a rise out of me."

"You've got to learn about men's pride. God de-signed them that way. To be strong, fighters even, to guard and protect their families. In this case, he was defending what he thought was his—you. I wonder if he sees Nathan as a threat."

Carli swallowed the lump in her throat. Lola was digging way too deep, and her personal questions made Carli uncomfortable. So, what if Nathan had said he was falling in love with her? What did that have to do with the employees on her ranch? There was so much she hadn't told Lola. So much she wasn't sure she could.

"When you fired Lank, he had to stand up for himself so he turned it around and said he would quit instead. That was pride, a way to save face, to be a man. Sure, sometimes stubborn pride gets in the way and I'm sure God would want them to be humbler at times. But all in all, just remember, God designed men and women differently. We might not understand them, and they might not under-stand us, but God did figure out that at times we can come together and really complement each other and make up one another's 'better half' as they say."

Hmph! Sounds good on paper. But real life is way different.

Carli rolled her eyes and pushed around the stack of invoices.

"Looks like you don't believe me. Just trust me when I say, men do not talk about their feelings. You have to be direct and ask, otherwise you'll nev-er know what's going on with them. You can patch this up."

"But where does that leave women? Are we supposed to let men be the fighters and we cook the dinner and clean the house and forgive everything? These men are being jerks. Why do I have to be a perfect angel and they don't?"

Lola laughed. "None of us are perfect angels. Or any kind of angels, period. We're flawed human beings who make mistakes every day. God just wants us to realize we were designed differently and to accept those differences and try to help the other person be the best they can be. Is that so difficult to comprehend?"

"I don't know what to do or say to either of them at this point." She shook her head. Carli was having a hard time understanding anything in her life now. It all seemed to be turning upside down.

"Sometimes it's not always about you, Carli. People are dealing with things we can't even imagine. I have every confidence you'll sort this out. Oh, and the reason I came over is to make sure you're riding with us to church on Sunday."

"Yes, thanks. I'll see you guys then."

Her cellphone's ringtone sounded with a horse's whinny. Juvenile? Maybe, but it made her smile every time she heard it.

"Hello?"

"Carli?" Lexi's mother's voice sounded a little shaky and upset.

"Emily, is everything okay? What's going on?"

"It's Lexi. We had a huge fight. She didn't want to help me with chores. And I said something about her torn jeans and the losers she's been hanging around with. I told her no chores, then no party and no leaving this house. She ran out. I wondered if she might be heading your way. I'm not sure. Just wanted to give you a heads up."

"I'm glad you called. But ranch headquarters is a good thirty miles from Dixon. How would she get here?"

"Hitchhike maybe? I'm not sure. Or ride with one of her friends?"

"We'll keep an eye out for her, Emily. Don't worry. And if she does show up, I'll give you a call, okay?"

"Thanks, Carli. She really looks up to you."

Carli ended the call and looked at Lola. "Remember Lexi, the girl who came to ride? She's missing. Her mother thinks she might head this way."

"I'll put Buck on alert," Lola said.

Carli imagined all the possible places Lexi might go, but she wasn't that familiar with the area yet and didn't know much about teenage hangouts. Lexi's mother must have noticed how much the girl loved horses to think she might show up at the Wild Cow. Carli took a deep breath and went hunting for her boots. Might as well join the search party. With everything else on her mind, how much more trouble could a teenage girl be?

Chapter Twenty-Nine

Instead of remaining in her house worrying about where Lexi might be, Carli decided to go for a ride. It would keep her busy and she could watch for Lexi too. She thought about the phone call from Lexi's mother; their conversation ran over and over in her mind. She couldn't think of any reason why a teenaged girl would run away to the Wild Cow Ranch, but maybe Emily knew her daughter better than Carli did. She saddled Beau and led him through the corral gate.

As Beau trotted a good stretch away from the ranch's entrance, Carli thought of how mixed-up things had gotten lately—Nathan and Lank's fight, then their sudden exit from her life. Were they afraid to come around? She could make no sense of what was going on in their minds. She missed Nathan, as a friend and confidant. And now she'd been dragged into the middle of Lexi and her family. Who knew what kind of drama was going on in her young life? But Carli wanted to help. Maybe she could prevent more heartache for Lexi, or just lend a compassionate ear, one that could relate to her struggles without judgment.

Up ahead a plume of road dust drifted skyward, evidence of a vehicle coming her way. And it was moving fast. She slowed Beau to a walk, urged him out of the road and across the bar ditch, gently pulling to steady his reins. "It's okay, Beau. Easy, fella."

As it approached, she saw it was older model bright blue Camaro. It slid to a stop, gravel and dust rolling out from behind the vehicle. Beau took a few antsy steps at the rumbling muffler, but Carli kept him calm. The passenger window was open, and Lexi leaned her arm out.

"Hey, Carli."

"Lexi? Your mom's looking for you. What are you doing here?"

Lexi rolled her black-lined eyes and rested her chin on her arm. "Thought I'd come and brush a horse." She pointed her thumb to the driver. "I want to show him where I come for riding lessons."

"Who's your friend?" Carli asked as she bent down to see a spiky-haired young man.

"This is Raven."

"Hello, Raven. Now that's an unusual name."

The young guy didn't really look at her but instead grunted a low sound.

"It's his battle tag. He's a gamer," said Lexi.

Carli looked into Lexi's eyes. "You are welcome here anytime, but you need to call your mother first and tell her where you are. Drive slow on this road and don't scare Beau. I don't want him to spook and dump me."

"Sure, Carli. We'll see you at headquarters."

Raven lurched the car a little and it kicked up

some road pebbles, which caused Beau to jump.

"I said slow!" Carli yelled after them. As they drove away, she could hear Raven laughing and saying something that sounded like, "Oops, my bad."

Carli watched them drive on ahead and kept Beau walking slow and steady until the car had a head start. She didn't want to get anywhere near that bucket of bolts or the juvenile delinquent driver. After a few minutes she nudged Beau into a safe trot.

Shaking her head, Carli wondered what the appeal was for some girls, and women, to go for the "bad boy". Was she going for the bad boy with Lank? And was he really that "bad"? She mulled it over—Lank was a hard worker. Definitely loyal to the Wild Cow, following Buck's and her orders to the letter, grateful and kind to Lola and others. He was close to his sister, and his mom too, who had recently passed away. He nearly gave up his life to fight the barn fire and was heartbroken to lose his horse Blackie. He had searched for Carli and didn't give up until he found her lost in the snowstorm where she could have died.

In fact, Carli couldn't think of any "bad" thing he'd ever done, except he made her act like a stark raving lunatic. Maybe it was just his smart-alecky jokes at times or the way he bucked her authority. Or maybe it was that she wanted to be in control of everything. He did know more about cattle and ranching than she did, and she really hated to have to fire him again. That was getting to be so annoying. Could she ever have an equal, more easygoing relationship with Lank and why did she spend so much time thinking about him? She pushed that irritatingly handsome face out of her mind.

Right now, she had to deal with the two teenagers who stood next to her barn. She hoped she could be a proper role model for Lexi and, if need be, chase Raven off her property if he displayed any troublemaking behavior.

She dismounted near Raven's car and held Beau's reins. Lexi wore her usual black ensemble, but this time her hair was neon pink, and she wore thigh high boots with a short skirt. She had added new piercings at the top of one ear and one side of her nose.

"So, what's going on with you, Lexi? Have you called your mother, yet?"

With eyes rolling upward, Lexi sighed. "She's driving me crazy. Won't let me do anything. Always wants me doing chores."

"Yeah, a real drag," Raven grunted as he flicked a cigarette butt on the ground. Carli glared at him, so he stomped on the butt three times, then ran his fingers through straight, long black hair. Black nail polish and silver rings on every finger and all black clothing to match, with a chain hanging down one side of his pants. Jet black hair hung below his shoulders, and the top stood straight up in spikes. He had the most unusual green eyes that were lined with black smudges and dark gray eyeshadow on the lids. Carli was surprised to see intelligence in those eyes when he raised his head to meet her gaze, but nothing friendly was there. He winked.

Carli eyed Raven warily and looked at Lexi. "Are you here to see Sally?"

Lexi nodded her head, a very slim spark of interest showing in her eyes.

"Get a lead rope then." Carli spun on her heels and walked into the next pen where Sally slurped water from the trough. The morning sun cast light into the water making the goldfish glint bright orange and gold. They did a good job eating the algae and kept the tank clean.

Lexi appeared at her side, rope in hand, and gently draped it over Sally's neck. Carli couldn't help but notice the shy grin on her face. Yeah, horses will do that to you.

Lexi led Sally over to the saddle house, tied her to a rail, and disappeared inside.

Raven watched, leaning against the fence. He pulled another cigarette from his pants pocket and stuck it in his mouth.

"Sorry. No smoking around the horses," Carli said to Raven. "We battled one barn fire, and that's one too many." As Lexi walked closer to Sally with a brush in hand, Carli stood in front of both of them, hands on hips, and then directed her comment to Lexi. "I'm calling your mother if you're not."

This time it was Raven doing the eye rolling. He looked at Lexi. "What a crock. I didn't drive you all the way out here to watch you brush some stupid animal. You said we were gonna race some horses."

"Don't even think about lighting that cigarette." Carli's eyes narrowed.

He held the cigarette in his fingers and got menacingly close to Carli. "Look, lady, no one tells me what to do and I don't need your b.s. rules."

"Raven, I think you need to get off my ranch." Carli didn't back down and didn't let any fear show in her eyes. She stared directly at the kid. She needed to get Lexi away from him. Then she turned and kindly said, "How about you, Lexi? Do you want to stay and brush Sally? I could drive you home."

Raven gritted his teeth. "If you don't come with me now, you can forget about Friday night."

Lexi looked from one to the other, then settled on Carli. Quietly she said, "Could I stay?"

Carli thought she might have heard Raven grumble the b-word but she couldn't be sure.

"Of course. I'll call your mother right now." Carli punched in the number before Lexi changed her mind. She told Emily about her daughter and ended the call.

In a flash, Raven was in his loud muffler Camaro and blasting down the gravel road, kicking up a cloud of dust bigger than the one he had arrived in. Hip hop music thumping from his car stereo. Carli let out the breath she didn't realize she was holding. Inside, a shiver of panic ran through her. That could have turned out worse, but he was gone now.

Carli could visibly see the tension leave Lexi's body as she focused on the horse. She put her hand on the girl's shoulder. "I'm glad you stayed. You're always welcome here."

Sally turned her head to watch the young girl, nudging Lexi's shoulder with her nose.

"Why are you hanging out with him? Do you like him?"

Lexi shrugged her shoulders. "He's okay."

"Maybe he's the easiest way to irritate your mother."

Another shrug of the shoulders. Silence.

"You are so lucky, Lexi. I didn't have a mother who cared about where I was. Your mother bugs you because she loves you." Carli couldn't tell if her words meant anything or not. Talking to a rebellious teenager was like talking to a fence post, actually a fence post was much easier. She was heartened that Lexi had showed up out of the blue to spend time with the horses. That was a good sign. Maybe she could win the girl's trust after all.

Suddenly they heard more gravel crunching on the driveway. "Hope he's not coming back," Carli mumbled as she turned to see who it was.

But it wasn't the goth kid returning for his little girlfriend.

Feeling relief and irritation all at the same time, Carli whispered to no one in particular, "Lank."

Okay, Lord, just help me be nice.

Chapter Thirty

Carli stood like a statue. Arms folded across her chest, she watched Lank park his pickup, get out, and amble towards her. She wasn't sure she could do this. Still angry at him, she couldn't help but notice the dark stubble that shaded his jaw. Darn it. Why did he look so good to her? Sheepish look in his eyes, no smile. Her stomach fluttered.

Buck had returned to the corral and offered to assist Lexi on brushing Sally, the bay horse she was bonding with lately. Carli turned her full attention to her ex-ranch hand. She walked closer and met him at the corral gate.

"What're you doing here, Lank? Did you forget something?"

He was slow to start and fiddled with his hat turning it round and round.

"Carli." Those blue-gray eyes looked up at her while his head tilted downwards. "I kinda lost my temper."

That might count as an apology. Carli may have lost hers too, but she wasn't going to admit it.

Losing her cool around this irritating cowboy was something she seemed to be doing a lot of lately.

Lank waited a minute for her to respond. She didn't so he kept talking. "If I said I'd like to come back, will you have me?"

Have him? Truthfully, she wanted him to stay. She didn't want to fight anymore. But how would this work? How could they ensure it wouldn't happen again?

"We'll have to talk, Lank. I mean really communicate. Honesty, no games, no temper, no teasing. Can you do that?"

"Naw. I don't want to do that. On the drive over here, I was thinking about asking you to hire me back. That's what I had planned, but I've since changed my mind."

"You have?" Carli felt her stomach fall to her knees. She looked at the ground so he couldn't see the disappointment in her eyes. Lank leaving for good? She'd really done it this time.

"I got an offer from a buddy in New Mexico. Think I'll take the job."

"You will?"

"Yeah, it's obvious you don't want me around. I just cause you a lot of trouble and I don't understand why. I think it's best for me to leave."

He stepped closer and brushed a lock of hair from her cheek. She swallowed the lump in her throat. His burning eyes bore a hole right into her soul.

"New Mexico?" was all she could manage to murmur.

"I'll miss you," he muttered back, and then he broke into a wide grin. "Not really! Buck called me last night. You're still my boss and I'm still the thorn in your behind." He laughed. A deep throaty, belly laugh.

She felt irritation from his mocking tone, but then she saw the humor in those eyes, and she couldn't help but feel relieved. "Is this your idea of better communication? Lank Torres, you're an idiot." She slapped his shoulder.

"What are you kids laughing about?" asked Buck as he joined them.

"I told her you hired me back for the second time." Lank raised his eyebrows and displayed that stupid smirk of his.

"Oh, right." Buck turned a sheepish grin to Carli. "Sorry, Little Jean. I know you fired him again, but we really need him around here. He knows this ranch like the back of his hand. I should have checked with you first, and I'm sorry."

Carli looked from one to the other. They both apologized. That's two apologies in one day from two Texas cowboys. She was on a roll. "You're both idiots." She couldn't be mad, not with the look Lank was giving her now. They all laughed.

"What's on the agenda today, boss?" Lank looked at Buck. Then he quickly swung his face around to Carli. "I mean, boss?" His head swiveled from one to the other and back again.

"Are we going for a ride today, Carli?" Lexi nudged her horse over to where the rest of them stood.

"Yes, ma'am. Let me get saddled up." Carli hurried to the saddle house.

When Carli was ready, she jogged Beau next to Lexi's horse and together they edged out of headquarters, taking a path through the horse pasture towards the creek. Leading the way Carli said, "I want to stay close to the road. I can't take a long ride today, Lexi, but at least we can enjoy the time we have. And the weather's so nice. Not much wind."

"Yeah."

"I think Sally likes you. She goes really smooth for you."

The girl smiled just a little and patted the horse.

"Lexi, what do you know about the guy that drove you out here? Have you known him very long?"

"Not too long."

"Does he go to your school?"

Lexi hesitated, then said, "Not anymore."

"What does that mean?"

"He's not in school anymore. He works on cars."

"How old is he? Did he graduate?"

"Seventeen. He had one more year to go but had to drop out to get a job."

"Does he live at home?"

"Not anymore. His dad gave him some trouble."

"Where does he live?"

"With some other guys."

"Your mom loves you, Lexi. And I worry about you too. That's why it seems we might ask a lot of questions. It's not to pry into your business, it's because we care. People in the world can be mean and are not what they seem to be at times."

The girl remained silent as she steered Sally down a cow trail into the dry creek bed. They were walking the horses now. It made it easier to talk.

"Have you thought about what you want to do after high school?"

More silence, but finally, she said, "Maybe work with horses? I love animals."

Carli smiled at her. "Sounds great. You'd be good at it. Maybe I could give you a job here. We've got lots of animals."

"Really? What kind of job?"

Carli was encouraged that Lexi showed a spark of interest.

"Well, I'm not sure yet. I'd have to talk with Buck. Maybe brushing the horses. Maybe giving them a bath. Or feeding. There's always work to do around a ranch. How about helping me with the riding school if and when I ever get more students?"

"That'd be great. Thanks."

"I told your mom I'd drive you home later. But I've got to say, that wasn't right for you to run off and not tell her where you were going. Sorry if you think I'm butting my nose in your business. She's your mom and she deserves some respect. I know you want your freedom. I remember what it was like. But she only wants the best for you."

With her head hanging down, Lexi said, "I know. But she doesn't let me have any fun."

"You are so lucky to have a mom who cares about you. You'll understand that one day. You can learn a lot from others around you or you can close your ears and make your own mistakes."

"What do you mean?"

Carli led the way as they crossed a flat stretch of grass to just off the side of the road. Where they stopped under a couple of trees afforded a bit of shade, the only oasis for miles around. They didn't dismount, just got comfy in their saddles. Carli hated to lecture the young girl because she felt like they were building trust. She didn't want to run her off before they could even become friends.

"The best example I could give you, Lexi...or maybe she's the worst example...is my birth mother. As a young girl she liked having a good time, hanging out with kids some people might call 'wild'. She started rebelling against her parents, lying, staying out overnight, all kinds of things. Eventually, it caught up with her."

Lexi stared at Carli. "Like the Prodigal Son story?"

"Yes, you might say that. The only thing is my mother didn't have a happy ending. All that partying and rebellious behavior led to her getting pregnant, with me. She ran away to California and...I'm sorry to say she got addicted to drugs and died. I was raised by foster parents since I was a baby. My mother's bad choices not only ruined her life but also made my life challenging. It's taken all these years to come to terms with her abandonment of me. I've only been able to do it with God's help."

Lexi looked very sad. All she could say was, "Wow. But what does that have to do with me?"

"We all have choices, Lexi. Respect others, or not. Curse, do drugs, steal, or not. Have unmarried sex, or not. If we make bad choices, they could lead to bad consequences. Like my mother. The choices you make can affect others who care about you. Choosing the right friends is half the battle."

Lexi stared at her. "You mean Raven, don't you?"

"I don't want to judge him. I thought he was disrespectful, reckless even, like the cigarettes. Is he a true friend?"

Lexi remained quiet, thoughtful.

"Why don't we head back now? We need to brush the horses off, feed them dinner soon, and I need to drive you home before it gets too late. Okay?"

"Sure."

"And, Lexi," Carli looked over to the girl, "I'm sorry if I sounded preachy. I'm not your mom. I just care about you and want to help."

As they walked the horses back to headquarters, their quiet camaraderie was abruptly jarred by the sound of a vehicle motor and it was approaching fast. Carli looked back and saw a cloud of dust.

"Hey, Lexi! I came to give you a ride home!" shouted a kid from the rolled down window.

It was Raven and he wasn't alone. Another young guy was in the passenger seat. His arm was hanging out his window and he appeared to be holding a beer can.

"Slow down!" Carli yelled to them.

Raven's face took on an angry mask at the command.

He yanked the steering wheel, and the sports car left the road and began circling the horses.

"Easy, Beau." She steadied the reins without pulling on them. If she stayed quiet, he would, she told herself.

"Lexi, just sit back. Sally's pretty calm."

"You boys have had your fun. Now please, leave my ranch." Carli said it in a deep, commanding voice not letting the fear show in her face.

"We ain't no 'boys', lady!"

Raven continued to drive recklessly. He pulled the steering wheel and shot off into the grass, making "donuts", leaving the pasture torn up behind him.

As they came around for another pass near the horses, the passenger boy yelled, "Yeehaw!" and threw something at Sally's rear. That was too much for her and she gave a couple small bucks.

"Hold on, Lexi. Sit back and try to gently pull her head up and to the side."

"Yeehaw! Ride 'em cowgirl!" the boys continued their taunts as Raven revved his motor.

Before Carli could do anything to gain control of the situation, Sally turned her head towards the barn and headed that way in a brisk jog, then lope. Luckily, Lexi held on.

And, Beau, who had become laid back during his stay at the Wild Cow after seeing cattle and coyotes, couldn't stand it anymore—the boys' wild antics, and then Sally's bee-line home—so he headed that way as well. Carli thought about disciplining him and making him stand still, but she figured she may as well get going after Lexi and Sally to help if need be. But she wouldn't let Beau run full out, uncontrollably, just an easy lope and she spoke reassuring words to him the whole time.

They hit headquarters at a fast clip, and she reined Beau to a stop. Lank held Sally's reins, and Lexi stood beside the horse, pale with tear marks streaking her face.

Buck met Carli at the corral. "What's going on here?"

Carli answered before even dismounting from Beau. "You need to run off a couple of kids for me. I've asked them to get off my ranch. We could have been hurt. Lexi, are you okay? They threw a beer can at Sally's butt! And they tore up the grass with that old sportscar."

Lexi said quietly, "I'm okay now, Carli."

"You held on and you're a good rider. That could have been a bad situation. Now let's take care of the horses and get ready to take you home."

Carli was more than a little relieved to turn over the situation to the men, but there was so much more she wanted to tell Lexi. She hated to keep hammering on the girl, but good grief. They could have been seriously injured. All she wanted to do was provide a place for kids like Lexi to come and ride. A safe place. No drama. Maybe this was another sign from God. Maybe she just didn't have what it took to deal with teenagers.

Lank and Buck hopped in a truck and drove off. Carli could see Raven's car as it turned into headquarters. It stopped as Buck pulled his pickup truck alongside. She would have given anything to be a fly on the wall to hear that conversation.

Carli and Lexi brushed and fed the horses and started to head to Carli's truck to drive Lexi home when they heard a whimper, or something.

"What was that?" Carli turned around sharply, frowning at the strange sound.

They both tiptoed towards an empty stall. Peering over the top they discovered a bundle of black and white fur, whole body wiggling, and smiling canine face.

"A puppy? What're you doing in here?"

"Awww, she's so cute," Lexi cooed. "Can I go in and pet her?"

"Well, I'm not sure who she belongs to, but I guess you can."

"I wonder what her name is." Lexi blossomed with puppy love.

"L.J." In walked Lank. "Lily Jane. I got me a dog."

Lexi's arms were full of puppy, gyrating and licking her entire face.

"Looks like she's trying hard to make sure she can stay." Carli couldn't help but smile.

"I'll help take care of her," Lexi offered a plea, full of excitement.

"Just might be one of your first jobs on the ranch, but you'll have to ask Lank first."

She studied Lank as he watched his puppy, fatherly pride beaming on his face. Carli was never allowed pets growing up, and after she moved out on her own, they just seemed like so much of a handful and extra time she didn't have. Buck had told her that Lola was highly allergic, which is why they didn't have a ranch dog. With everything else going on, Carli added high-maintenance teenagers and now Lank had a puppy. She shrugged. Oh well, the more, the merrier.

Chapter Thirty-One

It had only been a short month, but Carli poured most of her efforts into figuring out all what was needed to run an equine program for at-risk children. The weeks rolled by since that disaster on the first Saturday in April. Now it was the first Saturday again, and she was expecting a few new kids this time based on inquiries to the public page. Luckily, she found more horses for the students. Older, calm demeanor. She was anxious for the kids to meet them.

The riding school preparation was in addition to learning about running the Wild Cow Ranch, and also doing some heritage searches for her birth father before closing her eyes at bedtime. Everything was zapping her strength, mentally and physically, but she also felt invigorated and enthused. She wanted to do all of it and felt driven towards her goals. Maybe, just maybe, she had figured out God's plan for her life. But then hanging over her head was Nathan's profession of love, and the argument between him and Lank. She still couldn't figure that one out, even though she replayed the incident over and over in her mind.

For the equine program, she contacted the group in Oklahoma that had a similar one established for many years with lots of children participating. She also spoke to a woman with the Department of Family Services to get an idea about the kinds of kids she'd be dealing with, if her program ever grew. During the telephone conversation, Carli couldn't believe her ears. How could parents hurt their children like that? Rage and enormous sadness welled up inside of her. This program might be harder than she thought. Could she handle it? That old self-doubt always reared its ugly head, but she had to learn to trust in her faith and push onward.

As Carli walked towards the corral to get ready for the kids, her stomach did a somersault of dread at seeing the sheriff's cruiser parked in front of the Wild Cow Ranch cookhouse. What now? But the idyllic scene of Buck, Lola, Lank, and the sheriff all laughing and playing stick tug-o-war with the new puppy immediately dispelled any worries.

"What are y'all doing? Besides roughhousing with—er..."

"L.J.," Lank offered. "Lily Jane."

"Right, L.J. Hello, Sheriff." Carli extended her hand.

Sheriff Anderson stood and dusted off his khaki uniform. "I'm here about those kids who were acting up the other day on the ranch. Buck called and told me about it."

L.J. wiggled over to Carli and commenced to biting and tugging on the bottoms of her jeans. She tried to pull her leg away, then looked to Lank and just said, "Lank, your dog?"

"Oh, sure, I'll put her in one of the stalls."

"Thanks." She surveyed the tiny bite marks and a new rip in the bottom of her pants. Great.

Lank left but Buck and Lola stayed with Carli and the sheriff.

"I found out more about that kid," the sheriff started. "We know who Raven is. Real name is John Andrew Gibbons. Dropped out of school. Been in juvie trouble before. Rough home life. Dad's not a good role model. Not sure who his passenger was but we can make an educated guess."

"I don't want to get them in real trouble, Sheriff. Can you maybe put a scare into them, and make sure they don't come back here? I'm also hoping to convince Lexi to stay away from them." What Carli said was true. She didn't want the boy to end up back in juvenile jail again, but he needed to understand he couldn't drive around terrorizing people. And Lexi was way too young for him.

"Young people have minds of their own," the sheriff said. "As much as their parents might warn against their choice of friends, sometimes they end up doing just the opposite."

"That's for sure." Carli thought of her own mother.

"But, Carli, there's something else you should know. Raven was picked up a few months back for possession of methamphetamine. Because he's underage he was let off with community service and drug counseling, but it's on his juvenile record. When he turns eighteen, all bets are off. If he's still messing with that stuff by then, he could go to jail for quite some time."

"Oh, no," Lola said quietly.

Carli shook her head back and forth and pressed her lips together. "I had a bad feeling about that guy. I sure don't want Lexi getting mixed up in his lifestyle."

"I'll go find him and his buddy and try to put the fear of God into them about trespassing on the Wild Cow." Sheriff Anderson tipped his hat to Carli and Lola before climbing back into his cruiser.

"Good luck with that," Buck said. They all waved as the sheriff drove away.

In the barn Carli watched Lank cradling L.J. in his arms like a baby. A big baby, not a tiny puppy, which looked to be a couple of months old. He was nuzzling her and whispering. Her heart did a flip flop. The more she resisted him, the stronger the pull.

"So, what's the story with that bundle of fur, Lank?"

With a handsome smile he glanced at her and then explained. "Sis found her on the side of the road along with a couple of siblings. No momma around. The pups are about eight weeks or more. A vet checked 'em out, but my sister can't have any pets at her apartment. My nephews were devastated. Her friends took the other two, but she said this one looked perfect for me, on the condition my nephews can visit her any time."

"Boy, are you a sucker. Your nephews get a dog but you get to feed and train it." Lank looked at her in surprise, as if the idea had never crossed his mind. Carli laughed at the expression on his face. "She is a friendly little thing."

"We'll make her into a ranch dog. She's a Border Collie, or at least that's what she looks like. They're really good at herding cows and earning their keep. And I heard you say something to Lexi about helping out with L.J. That's a great idea."

At that the dog scrambled out of his arms and full body wiggled towards Carli.

"And maybe you can help, too?" There was his mischievous smirk she found so hard to resist.

The dog was on the attack again with Carli's jean cuffs. "Hey, you little rascal! Quit it. You're gonna tear a hole in my pants."

Scrambling to keep her footing, Carli gave up, landed on her bottom, and wrestled with the pup who still had some razor-sharp puppy teeth. She held its kicking paws in a vice grip. "I'm not gonna let you go, you wild thing!"

Suddenly the black and white dog looked up into Carli's eyes and relaxed its squirming as though it liked being held by her. Then slowly licked her chin.

"Oh, boy," Lank said, "you might be done for. I think L.J. is claiming you as her owner."

"What? No. I've never had a dog before. Wouldn't know what to do with one."

"Well, you feed her, pet her, throw the ball or stick if that's what she wants, pay her vet bills, and let her protect and love you. And you love her back."

Carli gazed into his gray-blue eyes and almost swooned but shook that silly feeling from her mind as best she could.

"I thought she was your dog, Lank. You're not trying to pawn off your responsibilities on me, are you?"

"No, of course not. I'll help. And Lexi will help. How 'bout we see how it plays out? See who L.J. chooses as her human?"

The dog roused out of its temporary rest in Carli's arms and started roughhousing again, so much so that Carli fell flat on her back with the dog jumping on her stomach and chest and licking her face again.

"Quit, quit, you little rascal! Lank, don't just stand there laughing. Help get your dog off!"

"Now don't tell me you can't handle a little bitty puppy dog like L.J." The beginnings of a smile tipped the corners of his mouth as he tried to grab the dog off Carli. He kneeled on the ground next to her.

She kicked at him gently with her boot. "Stop laughing! You're just egging her on."

But she couldn't help smiling and soon they both were laughing as the dog went from one to the other.

"C'mon, help me up. We've both got work to do."

"Since you mentioned work, I guess that means I still have my job." Again, that charming smile.

He reached out to help her up and yanked a little too strenuously so that she ended up with her palms against his chest. He held her arms to steady her footing. They both stayed in the embrace for a couple of extra seconds until Carli pushed back. He resisted for a minute. There was a boldness in his stare, and she felt an overwhelming urge to lay her head on his shoulder, but, of course, didn't.

"Ahem, excuse me, you two. Carli, I think some of your kids are arriving," Buck said.

She felt her face grow warm at the sight of Buck standing there awkwardly looking at the ground.

Then she gave Lank an angry scowl and pushed away.

Lank released her and took a step back, but she didn't miss the humor in his eyes. "You want to take your dog with you?"

That smart-aleck smirk on his face she had seen more than a few times still irritated her.

"No. She is not my dog."

Lank's deep belly laugh followed her as she walked towards the cookhouse to greet her riding school students.

Chapter Thirty-Two

Lola rested an elbow on the corral fence and nodded her head when Carli walked her way. "Are you ready for this?" she asked.

"After that last Saturday I'm not sure if this is what we should be doing. But it can't go any worse, right?" Carli shrugged and leaned up against the fence next to her.

Lola laughed. "You never know."

"I wonder if Bianca will be allowed to come back. Her mother wasn't too happy that we had a Bible study." Carli felt bad about offending someone, but she couldn't change the past. "Maybe I should call Bianca's mother and explain."

"All we can do is plant the seeds, but then it's between that person and God. It's in His hands now and we can certainly pray that Bianca is allowed to come back. Do you want to have a Bible study during your riding school?" Lola asked.

Carli nodded her head.

"Then, that's what we'll do." Lola patted her arm.

Carli wished she had Lola's confidence and sense of self.

Buck joined Carli and Lola as they watched a boy, about thirteen-years-old, step out of a van. Carli thought he looked like a feral animal, eyes darting side to side, head down, mouth clenched tight, but his eyes perked up when he saw the horses.

Another car pulled to a stop and Carli watched a little girl, with a wild, headful of fuzzy curls, hop out.

Carli walked closer. "Hi, my name's Carli. Who are you?"

"I'm Shauna," was the quiet reply. "I'm eight. Can we ride the horses now?" Excitement practically rushed out of every pore. She couldn't stand still or stop the wide smile that covered her face.

"Hang on there, young lady. We'll get to that soon enough." Buck laughed at the overeager girl.

Carli turned to the boy. "You must be Jared." She smiled at his mother.

Within a few more minutes Lexi was dropped off by her mother. While Lola and Buck kept the kids occupied, Carli introduced herself to the mothers and answered their questions. With all the paperwork in order, she turned to greet the second class of LoveJoy Riding School students. She brushed clammy palms on her jeans and took in a deep breath. After giving riding lessons for almost a decade in Georgia, she couldn't figure out why this new venture had her nerves on edge.

Nathan pulled up in his truck, got out, and walked towards Buck and Lola. Carli hid her surprise, turning her focus to the kids. She hadn't talked to Nathan since he and Lank had swung at each other like two hot-headed clowns.

Everyone gathered in a semicircle as Carli gave her introductory speech.

"Hello and welcome to LoveJoy Riding School and the Wild Cow Ranch. We're so glad to have you here today. We'll learn about horses and I think you'll all have a good time. I'm Carli. This is Mr. Buck, Mrs. Lola, and Mr. Nathan. They are all here to help us. We just have a few rules. No yelling, especially around the horses. Keep your voices soft and low. Horses can sense your fear. No hurting the horses or each other."

"What about keep your hands to yourself?" Shauna interjected.

"Yes, for sure. Definitely. Is that one of the rules from your school?"

The little girl nodded her head.

"Thank you for reminding us, Shauna. Would you like to be the first to meet our horse friend? I can show you how to pet him."

The little girl hesitated but stepped up. "What do I do? Will he bite me?"

"You just reminded me of two more safety rules. Don't hold your fingers out to a horse like this. He might think they're something to eat. In the future, when we feed carrots or apples, we'll hold our hands flat like this. And don't stand behind a horse. It could spook him. We don't want you to get kicked. Watch your feet so you don't get stepped on."

The girl said, "Sounds dangerous. He'll hurt me."

"You just need to know about safety. These are big animals. Some of them weigh a thousand pounds. So, we have to be careful. But mostly, they're gentle and sweet. Here, take your hand and hold it under his nose. Let him smell you first. Then you can pet his shoulder. Like this. See, he's soft."

"Ooh, that tickles. His nose wiggled."

"He likes you," Carli told her. She turned to Lexi. "I could really use your assistance today. We've got some new kids and it's their first time here. I need someone your age to help me."

Lexi still scowled and mumbled to herself, but she peered at Carli rather than looking away.

"What do I have to do?"

"You can stand next to me. You're closer to their age. They might trust you more. Little by little, we'll all learn about horses."

"I know what you're doing, by the way. Making me think I'm gonna help you, but really you want to play shrink on me. Trying to be my friend but you just want to warn me about Raven. You're just like my mother."

Carli walked closer to the girl and dropped her voice to a low murmur. "You're a smart girl, Lexi. But I'm no counselor and I'm not your mother. I haven't figured out my own life yet. I'm glad you like horses and I'm glad you came back. I think you'll enjoy your time here and I really hope we can be friends. As far as Raven goes, he's not welcome on my ranch."

After a big sigh, the girl let out, "Sure, I'll help."

Carli watched the busyness as everyone pitched in, adults and kids alike. A common interest brought together by the horses who clearly enjoyed the attention. She noticed the smiles on every face. The moments of laughter, and the looks of concentration as they focused on their tasks. Lexi and Lola worked to show Jared and Shauna how to brush their horses, and Nathan ran in between, helping find saddles to fit each kid and getting tack for everyone. Buck leaned against the fence, watching. Her heart lightened as she felt more determined than ever to make this riding school work. Deep down, she knew it was the right path for her.

Carli approached Nathan with a wide smile. She decided to keep the conversation neutral. "Nate, thanks for helping today. I saw how good you were with that little girl."

"Shauna? That girl's a pistol. Funny, too. She kind of took over, was showing me what to do. Although I don't think she's been around horses much. I like her. I'm glad to be of some help."

"I'm surprised to see you here today. You haven't answered my texts." Carli leaned her back to the fence next to Nathan.

He looked straight ahead and didn't turn to acknowledge her. "The last time I was here, as I recall, I professed my love and you called me an idiot. Thought I'd give you some space."

"Yeah, well…" Carli stammered. "Don't take it personal. I called both of you idiots."

"You got that right about one of us being a bigger idiot than the other."

"Honestly, I'm still confused over the whole situation. I'm not sure why you two got so angry at each other."

Nathan laughed. "It's not the first time Lank and I had words that turned into fists. We all grew up together, his sister and my siblings. We have a history, but I apologize for getting you involved and for my behavior."

"I accept your apology. As far as the rest, I am flattered that you expressed your… uhmmm, interest. You are a great friend, but I don't know what I want right now. Everything is moving too fast."

"It's all right. You don't have to decide anything. Yet. But that doesn't mean I'm not gonna try to convince you otherwise." He pushed off the pipe rail and walked away to help the young boy Jared with his saddle.

The morning passed in a blur. Carli didn't take the kids on a trail ride because of the two youngest but instead kept them close in the corral working on going and stopping. From the looks on their faces, the kids had a blast. And Lexi even seemed to be enjoying herself.

After horses and tack were put away, Carli stood with the new boy Jared as they waited for someone to pick him up.

"Your mom must be running late."

"She's not my real mom." He answered with a deep frown. "She's my foster mom."

Carli hesitated. She didn't want to pry but was curious about this quiet young man.

"Did you have fun today?"

"I guess," was his short reply.

"I'm glad." She had the same problem reading him as the other kids. They didn't show much excitement or joy about being at the ranch, other than the light in their eyes when they worked with the horses. She did see that, but still questioned her efforts. Was she making a difference in their lives? Could she make a difference?

He suddenly turned his face to her and smiled a snaggle-toothed smile. "My dad knocked my teeth out."

Carli's heart dropped to her knees and she was stunned into silence. She didn't know what to say, or how to respond. Before she could think of anything, a car topped the hill and drove into ranch headquarters. A mix of emotions and thoughts were rambling through her brain.

Before Jared reached the car, he stopped and turned to Carli. "Can I come back here?"

With relief and tears burning the backs of her eyes, she smiled at him. "Of course, you can. You're welcome here anytime, Jared." The little boy wrapped his arms around Carli's waist. He squeezed her tight. She felt as though she might burst out crying before he let go of her. Through misty eyes she waved and watched them drive away.

Lola and Buck came out of saddle house with Nathan.

"Thanks for your help this morning," Carli glanced at her ranch foreman, but Buck suddenly stopped, his face turning a shade of ashen gray. Lola didn't notice. She kept walking.

"Buck!" Carli ran towards him. "Buck, are you okay?"

Nathan caught the ranch foreman just before he hit the ground.

Chapter Thirty-Three

Lola spun around in the corral at the Wild Cow Ranch and dropped to her knees next to her husband. "Buck. Tell me what hurts." She gently patted his cheeks, but he didn't open his eyes. "Thanks for catching him, Nathan."

"I'll bring my truck around. Let's get him to the hospital." Nathan ran to the fence and flung himself over it in one fluid motion, not taking the time to unlatch the gate.

"What's going on? Is he okay?" Carli grabbed hold of Lola's arm who was cradling Buck around his shoulders.

Lola's eyes were glassy from unshed tears, but she was also in "take charge" mode.

"I dun want no hors-pi-tal." Buck's eyes fluttered open for a minute as he leaned on Lola.

Lola held her husband. "You just hush, old man. We're taking you to the ER. No argument."

"Carli's eyes glistened, her heart raced, and her hands trembled. This place couldn't run without Buck. And she couldn't lose him.

About that time Lank ambled out of the saddle house, but then broke into a run dropping to his knees next to Buck. "What happened?"

"Here's Nathan with his truck now. We've got to get Buck to town. Can you follow us, Lank? Carli, you can ride with us." Then looking from Lank back to Carli, Lola asked, "Would that be okay?"

Both of them simultaneously nodded. "Sure. Sure."

With Nathan on one side and Lank on the other, they gently eased Buck to his feet. He got a little agitated and fought them, trying to regain his balance. "I can walk on my own." But then doubled over in pain. "I'm fine. Y'all don't need to fuss over me."

"Yeah, you look real fine." Lola shot her husband an angry glance. "Put him in the pickup, boys."

They half-carried Buck to Nathan's vehicle, loaded him in the front seat, and Carli and Lola piled in the back. "My purse!" Lola hollered.

"I can bring whatever you need to the hospital later. Let's just get Buck to town." Lank shut her door and nodded to Nathan who peeled out before Carli's door was even shut. She leaned towards the middle using the momentum of her body to swing the door closed, thankful she didn't end up in a heap on the gravel. She leaned up to look at Buck. His face was gray, his eyes closed, but he didn't seem to be in too much pain.

On the drive, Lola didn't cry but stared off into the distance through the window. "I don't know what I'd do if I lost Buck. He's my life, my world, my best friend. Please, God, please heal him and keep him safe."

"Yes, we'll pray, Lola." Carli grabbed her hand and they locked fingers.

"We've got to think positive, have faith." Nathan maneuvered through an intersection with horn honking and turned onto the blacktop towards town.

Carli tried to hold her emotions in check. She couldn't lose Buck. Eyes closed she mustered the strongest internal prayer she could. He was the only real father figure in her life.

Growing up with the Fitzgeralds hadn't been that bad. As a toddler, it was comforting for Carli to be tucked in at night and cared for by them. She couldn't remember, and didn't really know, her birth mother who had given her up.

Looking back on her childhood, Carli was very grateful to the Fitzgeralds who started her on horse riding lessons when she was around five years old, before first grade started. They recognized her passion and encouraged her.

Carli remembered one childhood friend in particular, a red-haired girl named Patty. Carli noticed the little girl had a mommy and daddy who brought her for riding lessons. Little Patty wore shiny new riding boots, skinny pants, and an oversized black velvet helmet. Carli came to the barn in faded blue jeans and sneakers, until she earned enough allowance to buy her first pair of real cowboy boots. But she had fallen in love with horses then, it didn't matter what she was wearing.

Carli remembered that Patty's parents always stayed for the entire lesson, cheering. On the other hand, the Fitzgeralds made a habit of dropping

Carli off at the barn, said they had errands to do, or a doctor's appointment to attend. After all, they were older than most of the parents around. Again, Carli told herself she didn't care. At least she got to learn as much as she could about horses. And her four-legged friends always returned her love, no questions asked, or judgments made.

When the lesson ended and Patty's parents took her home, oftentimes the Fitzgeralds were late to pick Carli up. She'd sit on a hay bale and dream about her life. Maybe one day she'd have a horse of her own. Maybe her real mommy and daddy would come back for her and cheer her on in a riding competition. She leaned back on the hay and looked up at the white clouds, thinking of so many things. Sometimes her riding teacher noticed the foster parents were late again, so she'd ask Carli to help with some chores—rolling the cloth bandages used on horses' legs or folding the white English saddle pads and stacking them neatly.

Eventually, one or both of the Fitzgeralds would pull up to collect her and take her home. Most days they didn't offer any explanation for being late. Or if they did, it might be something like, "The doctor kept us waiting forever." Carli never put up a fuss, just figured that's the way it was, and actually, she found being with the horses and around the barn to be the most fun of her young life. She later realized it was this experience and knowledge that had given her the confidence to begin giving riding lessons in Georgia and open her own business.

As the years ticked by, Carli progressed in her riding ability and became active in horse showing. The Fitzgeralds couldn't afford to send her to every show so when Carli was a teen, she took on part-time jobs around the barn and then at a feed store so she could earn money to pay for her own show expenses.

Anyone would say she had a good life, a good upbringing, even special perks like riding and showing horses. What child wouldn't love that? And Carli was grateful to the Fitzgeralds. She told herself, and them, how thankful she was, time and time again. But even though her homelife offered security, the result was that Carli had taken care of herself for as long as she could remember.

It seemed there was always one piece of herself missing. She knew that, now more than ever before, as she looked at Buck slumped in the front seat of Nathan's truck. His previous gray pallor had changed to red-faced and he was sweating profusely, his speech somewhat mixed up as he kept trying to tell them no "hors-pital".

She never experienced a heartfelt connection with the Fitzgeralds like she had with Lola and Buck. She missed having a father who cared for her deeply, loved her unconditionally. Right now, Buck was the closest thing to a real father for her. And it would devastate her if anything ever happened to him.

Someone had thought to call ahead, probably Lank, because when they pulled up to the hospital a team was waiting on them with a wheelchair. With looks of concern on their faces, several of the nurses called Lola by name and asked Buck where he hurt. Everything happened in a blur after that, as Buck was whisked inside and the rest of them collapsed into well-worn, straight-back waiting room chairs. Within minutes, Lank joined them.

Nathan found the vending machines and brought everyone a hot cup of coffee. Carli couldn't help but grimace at the bitter taste, and then hoped Nathan hadn't seen the look on her face. They sat in silence, each lost in their own thoughts, Lola occasionally wiping tears from her face.

Lola suddenly stood. "Prayer circle, now." Without a word they grouped around Lola and joined hands. She looked at Lank and nodded.

Lank prayed.

Carli's eyes blurred and she couldn't quote a word he said, but when they all ended with "Amen," she thought it was the most beautiful prayer she'd ever heard, and her heart was comforted. She stared at the ranch hand. That cowboy was certainly full of surprises.

Nathan's phone buzzed and he answered. "At the hospital with Buck. Yep. I understand." His face turned dark red and Carli could see a jaw muscle flex as he gritted his teeth. "My dad. He needs my help. I hate to leave y'all, but I've got to go." He turned to Carli. "Call me later and let me know how he is."

"Sure." She gave him a small smile.

"Thanks, Nathan. I really appreciate all you did today." Lola stood and gave him a hug.

"See ya, man." Lank nodded.

Carli watched their exchange with interest. Apparently, all the fist punching had been resolved, whatever that had been. She should just forget it. No matter how much time she spent going over that situation in her mind, she'd probably never understand it. Men.

The antiseptic smell of the hospital was soon replaced with the pleasant aroma of buttered popcorn as a volunteer emerged from an office to operate the machine. Carli studied the lobby. They had driven to the next larger town over from Dixon as it was a little closer than the trauma center in Amarillo. Lola explained they could stabilize him here and take him on to the bigger facility if necessary. She, Carli, and Lank were the only ones in the lobby at this time of the afternoon on a Saturday. A few people walked through turning towards the hallway with patient rooms. Carli lost track of the time, and the doctor finally came out to speak with Lola. She stared into his tired face, grabbed onto Carli's hand, and squeezed.

"Mrs. Wallace, your husband is going to be fine."

Carli felt as though the entire building swayed in a collective exhale, a giant breath it had been holding.

"We think it was a case of angina where blood flow and oxygen are restricted to the heart, maybe a panic attack thrown in. Those can both be very debilitating and feel like a heart attack. Maybe a little acid reflux, which is intense heartburn. The good news is it wasn't a stroke or heart attack."

"Oh, my, thank you, Doctor. Thank God. When can I see him?"

"He's resting now, and the nurse is changing his IV fluids. In a few minutes, I think. I might keep him overnight for observation and run some more tests in the morning. I'm a little concerned about his elevated blood pressure. Acid reflux can make you feel like you're having a heart attack. We'll need to talk about his diet."

After the physician walked away, Carli quietly asked, "Acid reflux? What did he eat?"

"Well, you know, Buck likes his hot stuff. I made tamales like I normally do, but he adds jalapenos and hot chilis, and who knows what all when my back is turned. And he loves salt and onions. If he has acid reflux, coffee can be bothersome; it's acidic. He may have to make some huge changes."

"Wow, what's left?" Lank chimed in. "I doubt Buck is gonna start eating salads. And a panic attack? He is the calmest, most laid-back man I know."

"Well, he may just have to make a few changes!" Lola was stern. "I won't have him scaring me like this. Or taking risks with his health. I want him around for years to come. Wait till he gets home. I'm gonna be watching him like a hawk. And you know what, Carli? One day soon it might be time to talk about Buck taking on fewer physical duties around the ranch. It may be Lank's turn to step up to the plate. Think about it. Buck and I are not getting any younger."

Carli had never seen Lola like this—wound up and marching forward on a campaign for good health, all fueled by intense love for her husband.

"I want to stay here with Buck overnight. When they move him to a room, I could nap in a chair. You two go on back to the ranch."

"You sure you want to do that, Lola? You don't have anything with you—toothbrush, PJs," Carli pointed out.

"We can come right back with anything you need," Lank offered.

Lola nodded. "I'll be fine. The nurses can probably find me a toothbrush. You go on home. I'm not leaving him."

"I'll bring my truck around." Lank hugged Lola and left through the sliding glass doors.

"Someone can come pick us both up tomorrow as soon as they release him to go home. And, Carli, thanks for staying with me. You mean the world to us, me and Buck. You're like the daughter we never had."

The two women hugged and then Carli headed outside to the parking lot, her eyes glistening as she thought of Buck and Lola and how much they meant to her.

Lank parked under the portico, and Carli climbed in.

"I'm worried about Buck and Lola. And you," he muttered.

Things were crashing in on her—all her fears about losing Buck, and everything that had been on her mind about the ranch. She felt herself almost collapsing.

Leaning on Lank, he put his arm around her and held her close. Her face buried into his shoulder, tears dampened his shirt.

"Oh, Lank, I was so afraid we might lose him."

He stroked her hair and held her head to his chest. "It's okay now, Carli. I've got you. Don't worry. He'll be fine."

"Thank you, Lank, for coming." She looked up into his smoky-blue eyes that were filled with compassion.

Draping her arms around his neck, she didn't want to let go. They sat there for several moments while she regained control of herself. She was always the tough one. No emotion. No girly tears. But this had shaken her to the core. She was learning more and more every day about what it meant to be part of a family.

Chapter Thirty-Four

The pillow was soft, squishy, and cool. Carli buried her face under the covers. Just one more minute. But a crick in her shoulder made it impossible to fall back asleep. Stretching her neck, she reached to flip her long hair around from under her. She savored the big mattress glad she had added a four-inch pillow top cushion to it when she had first set up the room.

Was that whining? Scratching at the side of the bed. Oh geez, the dog. What dog?

Rolling over to the side of the bed to peek through one eye, full on licking to her face commenced.

"What are you doing here? S'pose you have to go out now, huh? Can't you let me sleep, dog? Please."

The black and white furball wiggled from tail to nose tip, with a smile Carli couldn't ignore.

"I guess my nap is over. All right, all right. Let's go, just for a minute."

Carli flung her legs to the floor and stepped into fuzzy pink Ugg slippers. Earlier she had gotten comfy in her favorite green flowery/froggy PJ bottoms, a reminder of her Georgia days, on sale at Belk Department store. An extra-large, extra-long, gray sweatshirt served as a robe over her tank top. What an outfit. She didn't care and didn't think she'd run into anyone. Lola and Buck were still at the hospital and Lank was probably out doing chores.

"Make it quick," Carli instructed as the wiggly ball of fur hopped and spun in front of the door. For the life of her, she couldn't remember its name. R.J.? L.J.? Lank had called her something else besides the initials. Lily! That was it.

"C'mon, Lily. Let's go out. Now don't run off. Just pee pee and right back in. Okay?"

The dog was so excited—jumping, whirling, wagging, panting, smiling.

Carli couldn't help but smile also. This pup was super cute. How could anyone witnessing this explosion of life not smile? As a kid she had asked for a dog but the Fitzgeralds always said no. "They make such a mess," her foster mom had said. "Dog hair everywhere. Usually not even housebroken. Who's going to take care of a dog? Surely not me."

Just about every child she knew—in school, at church, at the horse barn, everyone—had a dog, cat, gerbil, goldfish, some kind of animal. Not her. As much as she begged, Carli never won the debate. So, she stopped asking. Stopped hoping for a dog, instead focused on her horseback riding and dreamt of the day she could afford a horse of her own.

She followed the bouncing fur ball out into a bright, late afternoon. If it hadn't been for the worry about Buck in the back of her mind, she would've lingered on the porch for a while. As she admired the white clouds drifting across the bright blue Texas sky, the jingle of spurs approaching jolted her attention. She turned around as the dog scampered towards Lank. Oh, geez! Carli clutched her sweat-shirt closer across her chest and hustled to gather up the frisky pup. "Why is your dog in my house?"

Lank scooped L.J. up into his arms. "She ran off. I found her on your front porch, but she kept begging to go in, so I let her."

"You opened my house and let your dog in? Into my house? What is wrong with you?" Forgetting about modesty as she only focused on picking up the dog, she stomped closer, which left her sweat-shirt to its own devices, flying open.

Lank's eyes surveyed her cuteness. "You never lock your door. Nice outfit, cowgirl. Frogs? And could you find a pinker pair of slippers?"

"The pinker the better is my motto." She had really come to dislike that silly, smart aleck grin. So why did it make her heart flutter? She bent down to grab hold of the rambunctious animal that was all wiggles, tongue, and sharky teeth. Lily spun around and around between them, nipping at the toes of Carli's house shoes.

"Owww!" The pup nipped right through the slipper into Carli's toe. "I'm just trying to get my dog. I don't have enough hands!"

"Your dog? Is that what you just said, Ms. Jameson?" Now he chuckled.

"Uh, huh. I don't know. I guess she's your dog." Shaking her head, Carli punched his arm and turned towards her house. "Take your dog, Lank. I've got to get dressed and find out if Lola needs anything. Can you manage without Buck for a few days? Or however long the doc says. When Lola calls, I'll go pick them up."

"Aye, aye, captain," he saluted with a grin, wiggly pup in his arms.

Inside she poured a mug of coffee, started to check her iPad for emails, when she noticed her cellphone buzzing. The hospital, and she had missed it. Darn. She tried the main number and asked for Buck's room, but no one answered.

Out of her stretchy frog pants, teeth brushed, dab of lip gloss, hair drawn up into a ponytail, she threw on jeans, Tee-shirt, and boots—and flew out the door.

As she walked to her vehicle, she looked across the compound and first saw his strong back stretching a white Tee-shirt to its limits, his long denim-clad legs kneeling, torso bent at the waist as he maneuvered a tool on the tractor. His voice reached her ears in the calm air. Was he praying? Talking to the tractor? She heard a one-sided conversation.

"Now, lady, don't you worry. You're very important to me. I'd do anything for you. You know that don't you?"

Heat rose in Carli's chest, up through her neck, eyes squinting. What did he say? He'd do anything for her? She was about to turn and leave when he noticed her standing there.

Grease-covered hands, he crooked a shoulder to cradle a cellphone to his ear. "Okay, Lola, I'll tell her. She's right here. You guys take it easy and we'll see tomorrow."

Lola? She tried to hide any surprise or awkwardness so he wouldn't see it plastered all over her face. Was it jealousy? Wonder if it had been a girl? What about earlier this afternoon and how she felt in the safety of his arms at the hospital when she nearly collapsed and lost it right there in the parking lot?

He looked at her, and they stood in an awkward moment of silence. An idea made his face light up and he walked closer. "Are you jealous, Ms. Jameson? You thought I was talking to another girl?"

"No. Why would you say that? It doesn't surprise me you talk to our equipment, though." She giggled. "I missed Lola's call. What time should I leave to pick them up?"

"You don't have to go now, Carli." He stood and faced her. "She has everything she needs, and Buck is demanding to go home, so he's much better. That's why Lola called. Some members from their church wanted to help so they've got a ride home in the morning."

Carli wanted to outline exercises for the riding school students. That hug from Jared had motivated her. But then she looked at Lank and thought of how he had held her so tight, so comforting in the hospital parking lot and let her cry. She needed to say something to him about that.

Lank knelt down again next to the tractor and got back to his ratchet and grease.

"I guess I was really freaked out with all the excitement. I was afraid we might lose Buck. He's been such an important person in my life ever since I first came to Texas. He's always there for me. Almost like a father. And I was so sad for Lola, to think what it would be like for her to lose him. It was all so scary."

He still didn't say anything but turned slightly to look at her.

When she saw his blue-gray eyes, she went on. "Thank you for being there for me, Lank."

Quietly he said, "Always," then went back to his work.

Her heart filled, but her mind was conflicted. Stay or go?

"I'll see you later. I've got work to do."

She thought she heard him murmur, "Mm-hmm."

What she hadn't told Lank was that she never let people inside her life or heart as much as she had with Lola and Buck. She always guarded herself before. No friends, no complications. But now, her barriers were coming down. The Wild Cow Ranch family had grabbed her and they weren't letting go.

Chapter Thirty-Five

For the thousandth time, Carli looked at the old phone book with the address and listing for what she thought was her birth father's family home. She hadn't the nerve to drive by it in Dixon yet. But she would. It had to be them. She forced herself to return the book to its place in the cabinet, an effort to get her mind off the possibility of ever meeting her birth father. Like somehow a dark space could erase it from her mind. She turned on her computer. While she waited for Buck and Lola to return home from the hospital, she needed to work on riding school business.

Carli loved lists, so she made one for the equine school. Reading about therapeutic riding, maybe she could use some of the ideas. She'd get a few of those colorful, foam cylinders—swimming "noodles" that people held onto in the water. Attach them to a tree, five or six across, and horse and rider could walk through them like a beaded curtain entryway. It was a great way to desensitize horse and rider, teach patience and calm.

She typed on her iPad:

• Hula hoops for horses to step through on the ground.
• Pieces of plywood to use as a bridge for horses to walk over.
• Mailboxes to open and close.
• A corn toss-like game using Beany Babies.
• Balls to catch.
• Big exercise balls for horses to walk around.

What else did they need? Some websites showed kids and horses dressed in costumes for holidays, Halloween especially. That would be fun. She'd seen photos of horses covered with sheets, holes cut out for eyes and ears. Hopefully, the trailing sheet wouldn't spook anyone. Carli chuckled at her unintended pun.

The older girls crossed her mind. Where would Lexi and Bianca go for this kind of fun? Did Dixon have a teenager hangout? When she was young, she was always at the horse barn, but the other kids in her school went to dances, bowling alleys, and movies. None of those activities had held any appeal for her. No one ever invited her anyway and it was all in the past now.

Maybe the teens would just need mentoring time—cleaning tack, cleaning the barn, cleaning the horses, riding, hanging out. And hopefully, talking about whatever was bugging them at home.

Carli's cellphone buzzed. She saw the name and said to herself, "What now?" Then she hit the speaker button. "Hello, Sheriff. How are you?"

"Carli Jameson." Sheriff Anderson was all business and usually skipped the niceties. "I've got a girl named Lexi in custody, says she's one of your riding students. She's asking for you instead of her mother."

"I'm on my way."

Carli clicked off the computer and located her purse and keys, turmoil in her mind about the riding school. Trouble with a student made her doubt everything again. If she hadn't invited the girl to the Wild Cow, then she wouldn't be involved in whatever was troubling this young lady. Lexi had a mother after all, and Carli felt that getting involved in their family issues might complicate things and make the situation worse. How could this ever end well?

Every time she felt on track something derailed her spirit and sent her off course. Is this really something God wanted her to do, or was she trying to bring a part of her old life from Georgia to Texas? And through the riding school she now added the complication of Lexi. Whatever it was, she needed to decide and either commit to these kids or drop the whole thing. She didn't know which.

Barely noticing the colors of the setting sun, she sailed through the little town of Dixon and parked her truck near the small Sheriff's Office. It would be dark soon and with the absence of light the evening would get cooler. She forgot to grab a jacket. Then she remembered to pray a quick plea that Lexi was all right. She'd been learning that with intentional practice, praying was becoming somewhat of a habit.

"Lord, please help Lexi and please help me to say the right things to steer her out of trouble and onto the right path. Lead her in the right direction. Thank you."

She yanked on the heavy door and walked into a beige world that smelled of fruity disinfectant trying to mask an old musty building.

Inside, Sheriff Anderson shook her hand and offered her a seat.

"We've been following that kid, John Gibbons—'Raven'—and came across him and Lexi walking in town, looked like they were headed to a bar. Lexi's underage, you know. When we searched him, we found pot and meth. She was clean. Technically, she wasn't arrested but I brought her in to give her a scare."

"Is that legal, Sheriff?"

"In a small town like Dixon, I'm the law. I didn't lie to her. Said I wanted to bring her to the station for questioning. She voluntarily agreed."

"What's gonna happen to Raven?"

"He's got priors. But he's not eighteen yet. He'll probably go back to juvie for a while, but his big brother sprung him already."

"Can I see her?"

"She's only fifteen. I'm obligated to contact her mother, but in order to calm her down I promised we'd call you first."

"Thanks, Sheriff. We will call her mother. Let me speak with Lexi for a few minutes first."

Carli walked through the door a deputy held open into a small, secure room where Lexi sat hunched over a table, her head resting on her arms. The room was cold, bare, and beige. It was everything she could do to not burst into tears when she saw the young girl sitting there all alone.

"Lexi?"

Tousled hair, red marks on her face from leaning on her arms, and teary eyes, Lexi straightened in the chair but didn't say a word. A flash of relief showed on her face, and then as if embarrassed, her eyes went downcast.

"Are you okay?" Carli walked closer.

"Yes."

"I'm so glad you're all right." Carli dropped into the chair across the table. "We have to call your mother and let her know you're okay. She must be worried. How long have you been gone?"

"I texted her yesterday, said I'd be spending the night at a girlfriend's."

"Lexi, remember the talk we had about life decisions?"

"Yes."

"Where do you think you'll end up after all the lies and hanging out with a guy who does drugs and gets arrested?"

"I dunno."

"Here, Lexi." Carli raised her hands to point to the whole room. "This is where you'll end up. In jail! Raven's gone. Somebody paid his bail and you're still sitting in jail. He left you here alone." The situation made Carli furious, but then guilt washed over her as she saw a tear run down the girl's cheek. She hated to nag someone when they were at their lowest, but reality is the pits and Lexi needed some real-world lessons. "I thought you liked horses and my ranch."

"I do."

"Well, you can't do the things you love if you're messing up like this. Your mother will never trust you if you keep lying."

Lexi avoided Carli's stare at first, looking all around—down at her hands, watching some speck on the wall. What in the world was going on in the girl's mind, Carli had not a clue. And then Lexi gazed into Carli's eyes. Silence hung in the room like an awkward shroud, but Carli was not going to give her any sympathy. She just hoped and prayed Raven hadn't turned her into an addict yet, if she was doing drugs with him.

Finally, Lexi whispered, "Okay."

"Follow your heart and don't let others lead you into something you don't want to do. The right path is not the easy one. I need a promise from you, Lexi."

"What?"

"No more Raven."

Again, the girl's eyes darted in all directions, thinking it over, what it meant. But then, in an almost inaudible sound, she said, "Okay." That was good enough for Carli.

"Good decision. Welcome to the rest of your life."

Chapter Thirty-Six

Easing out of the parking lot Carli hated to leave Lexi sitting by herself in that cold and bleak room at the jailhouse. But she wasn't the girl's legal guardian. Lexi finally agreed she should call her mother to come get her, and Carli offered to wait but Lexi said no. She'd face her mom, which was surprisingly the most adult thing she'd done since Carli had known her. Still, Lexi's wide, sad eyes haunted Carli and she thought about going back inside.

Without consciously thinking about it, Carli automatically pulled her pickup truck into a space in front of the B & R Beanery. At this late hour, she was surprised to see the lights on. She could really use a friend's shoulder right now and hoped Belinda was working and not Christy, that annoying girl who apparently had a sharp memory when it concerned anything relating to Nathan's past. With mind and heart weary, Carli hopped out of her vehicle and walked into the smells of roasting coffee beans plus a faint touch of cinnamon. The aroma always brought a smile to her face. Belinda appeared from the back and greeted her with a look of surprise and returned the smile.

"Carli! I'm so glad to see you. We haven't visited in weeks and weeks. Sit right here." She motioned towards a back table where papers and unopened envelopes surrounded a calculator and small lap-top computer.

"I know." Carli laughed. "I've missed you too. You're here late."

"Working on the books and roasting some beans, plus it's Saturday night. This is my life. What can I get you?"

"Give me whatever amazing new concoction you're working on with a double shot of espresso. It's been quite the day."

"Oh, goody. Stories to tell." Belinda bustled around behind the counter as Carli plopped onto a barstool at a high-top table.

"You have no idea." Carli hung her purse on the back of the chair and scooted up closer to the table. She stretched out her legs on the stool next to her, crossing her feet at the ankles.

Within minutes Belinda set a Texas flag mug down, complete with lid and straw. "This is nice." Carli should have said hot coffee, but a frappe might be good too. She leaned over and placed her lips on the straw, taking in a big draw.

"Mugs are new. That one's on the house."

Carli sat bolt upright, her cheeks puffed out from the icy cold drink that assaulted her mouth. She swallowed. "That's not coffee!"

"No, ma'am. That's a smoothie. Yogurt, berries, vanilla, and coconut milk. You really shouldn't be drinking a lot of caffeine right now. And by the way, how is Buck?"

Carli made a face but took another drink. She was parched. "I hear Buck is doing really well. Comes home tomorrow. Lola's making some lifestyle changes for him. That should be fun, watching those two work out his diet."

"And the riding school?"

Carli let out a heavy sigh. "It's growing, more slowly than I'd like. There is this one girl. I just came from Sheriff Anderson's office."

"Hang on, I need a drink for this one." Belinda disappeared behind the front counter and hurried back, holding a giant mug and settling onto the stool across from Carli. "Okay, continue."

Carli told Belinda about Lexi, and the troubles she'd had with Raven. She talked about the other students who had shown up and about the future of the riding school. She had so many doubts about the entire venture, yet she felt strongly she should keep at it.

"Be patient." Belinda sipped and swallowed. "Word will get around."

"I'm still making inquiries about horses that might be good for the kids to learn on. Checking with horse rescues and several owners of sale barns have their eyes on the lookout for me. If you hear of any, let me know." Carli talked about the problems the project brought and her doubts about making a difference in the kids' lives. It felt good to clear her head and talk to a friend. Belinda was a good listener. Carli slurped the last of her smoothie. It was a relief to have shared so much. Her troubles seemed a little less daunting after she talked about them. Always a big worrier, she sometimes made problems bigger in her mind than they really were. She told Belinda about the opening of her riding school and Belinda responded in the same way Lola had. "Teenagers."

Carli asked, "Can I have coffee this time around? A double shot."

"Do you think it's wise?"

"What do you mean?"

"With your condition and all." Belinda held up a finger as she stood to flip a switch on the chrome contraption that took up one corner of the room. She opened a lid, turned some dials, and seemingly satisfied with the results, sat back down.

The front door chime tinkled, and a young couple walked up to the counter. Belinda hopped off her stool. "Be right back."

Carli had no idea what she meant by condition. She hadn't had a horse wreck of any kind. Hadn't been sick. She just wanted a good jolt of B & R Beanery coffee and then she would be on her way.

"What are you talking about?"

"You know." Belinda pointed at her tummy. "The baby."

"You're pregnant! Congratulations, but why can't I have caffeine?"

"No silly, not my baby. Yours and Nathan's," she said with a sheepish grin.

"What are you talking about? Nathan and I are just friends."

"I love you Carli, but don't lie to me," Belinda said in a very annoyed tone. "You have to face reality. You need to plan a wedding and you're going to be a mommy soon. The time flies by faster than you can ever imagine, and before you know it, you'll be holding that sweet baby in your arms."

Carli took a breath. Belinda's words sounded familiar. Hadn't Carli just told a young lady sitting in jail about the real world and the consequences of one's decisions?

"Listen to me. Nathan and I are not having a baby," she finally said. "We're friends. Well, he wants to be more, but I can't decide. Where did you hear this?"

"Christy told me."

"Christy? That blonde girl who filled in for you one day when Nathan and I came in? She knows him from high school. Why would she think I'm pregnant?"

"She heard you and Nathan talking about a birth certificate, said y'all were making plans for the future."

"No! She's wrong." Carli's hands came down on the tabletop with a forceful slap making Belinda jump. "It's not true. I found a birth certificate at my grandparents' house and it's mine. I was telling Nathan about it." Shock registered in Carli's brain. "You didn't tell anyone else, did you?"

"I may have mentioned it to Lola," Belinda said with a sniff.

"Lola knows? And she didn't say anything to me? Well, if it's just the two of you, that's not too bad." Carli exhaled and leaned back in her chair. Maybe she was overreacting.

Belinda lifted her mug and took a long sip, putting it back on the table. "Crazy Vera told me she heard it at Jack's Grocery, and she's really good friends with Nathan's mom. But maybe she didn't say anything."

"Wait. Doesn't Christy work at the Chamber of Commerce office? Wonder how many people she comes in contact with in any given week."

"Nothing much goes on there. This is Dixon after all." Belinda took another sip and then snapped two fingers. She looked up. "Oh, I just remembered. They did have their chamber banquet last week."

"What does that mean? How many people think I'm pregnant with Nathan's baby?" Carli watched her friend gaze out the front window of the coffee shop. "Belinda?"

"The annual banquet is just a little dinner for all of the businesses in the county. Christy worked the registration that night. This is just my guess, but I'd say the whole town and most of the county knows by now you're pregnant with Nathan Olsen's baby."

"Oh, no!" Carli buried her face in her hands. "I really need caffeine now, and I'm not paying for it."

"Right away. Double shot, I know." Belinda slid off the stool and hurried behind the front counter. She didn't try to hide the silly grin that spread across her face. Carli glared at her and suddenly her chest tightened, and she couldn't breathe. She was choking. She leaned over and put her head between her legs as she gulped for air.

"Calm down. You're having a panic attack," said Belinda with a hint of amusement in her voice.

"What am I gonna do?" Carli stood and paced around the table. "I can't deal with this right now. Nathan is already bugging me, says he's falling in love, which is ridiculous. And Lank is acting weird, plus trying to trick me into bonding with his dog. My ranch foreman's health is bad. And I have the riding school. If this gets out, parents won't let their kids come to the Wild Cow for lessons. LoveJoy is done before it even gets going. This is horrible!" She sat on the stool and leaned back to stare at the ceiling.

"Stop talking for a minute. Take a breath, Carli." Belinda walked up beside her and placed a mug on the table before placing a hand on her shoulder. "The universe is not ganging up on you. I promise. In nine months, they'll know the truth."

"Nine months!" With trembling hands, Carli wrapped both around the hot mug and took a long sip. The aroma was enough to calm her nerves, but then another shot of panic seared through her mind. "Tomorrow is lunch at the Olsen's and Nathan invited me. I hope he doesn't hear this from his mother before I can talk to him! What'll I do?"

Carli dropped her face to the table and covered her head with her arms.

"You may think it's so, but this is not the end of the world." Belinda stood and walked around the table. "Listen to me. Welcome to life in a small town. You're not the only one having troubles, and the problem is we know everything about everyone's troubles around here. Or at least we think we know it all. You're not the only one who is misunderstood. We're all slammed with illness and tragedy, facing life as it comes."

"But this is so bad." She'd tell Nathan and they'd have a good laugh, but deep down he wasn't Carli's main worry. The only face she saw in her mind was Lank's. Chances are he'd already heard the rumor and chances were even greater he'd never speak to her again. Ever.

"Sometimes life can be overwhelming, but it's all

in how you face it." Belinda placed an arm around Carli's shoulder.

"I can't handle this. It's just too much. I have a lot going on right now."

"Carli. Look at me."

Carli lifted her chin and looked into Belinda's face.

"Take a breath. Give your worries to God. Clear your mind. Now, what is the first thing you need to do?"

Carli breathed in, exhaled, lifted her mug, took a few more sips to fortify her strength, and set it back on the table with a deliberate gesture as she thought.

"I need to warn Nathan his mother may think she's going to be a grandma. And I probably need to talk to Lola and Buck," she finally said, her voice soft.

"That's my girl. This will all work out. Choose joy. Let God handle the rest. It works every time."

With a newfound spurt of energy and purpose, Carli slid out of the chair, grabbed her purse, and turned towards the door. She could fix this. She would fix it. Suddenly spinning on her heels, she turned to Belinda and gave her a hug. "What a day."

"Love you, my friend." Belinda didn't stifle the giggle that escaped from her lips as Carli swung open the door and hurried to her pickup truck.

Chapter Thirty-Seven

Carli drove through the one traffic light at the corner of Main Street and Main Avenue in the little town of Dixon thinking hard about her friend's advice. Push the worries away. Let God carry them. He's strong enough to handle whatever's bothering you. It wasn't until after she had gone through the intersection that she wondered if the light was red or green. No matter now. There was something she had to do.

One of the things she excelled at was worrying. And if there wasn't anything to worry over, she could probably invent something. Owning a stable and riding business in Georgia had certainly provided her with a lot of stress—how to pay the bills, how to make a profit, how to juggle the equine business and horse showing with her job at the realtor's office. And she fretted over her students too—not only about their performances but also what kind of people they were growing up to be. But Belinda was right, as she thought about her life. Everything usually worked out, no matter how many sleepless nights she spent or how much effort she put into trying to manipulate a situation. It was never as bad as she imagined in her mind. And all that lost sleep! Trusting in her faith was a new concept for Carli, but one she was determined to work at and learn more about.

The address came to mind as she pulled into a parking lot, so she punched it into the map app on her phone. An address that had been burning in her brain for some time, ever since she'd found the stack of old phone books in her grandparents' cabinet—606 Maple Street in Dixon.

She followed the GPS instructions and pulled up in front of a low-roofed house. Numbers on a rusty, crooked mailbox confirmed she was at the right place. A dead tree stood sentry in the front yard, weeds made up the lawn, and even grew in the cracks of the driveway. At the end of the drive towards the back of the lot, a long-neglected garage door hung crooked. The once white clapboard was now partially chipped away and glowed a dull gray in the evening twilight. She was surprised at the unkempt, ramshackle condition. The lot was a good size with ample room on either side of the house, and from what she could tell, a spacious backyard. There didn't seem to be any activity on the quiet street.

Carli sat in her vehicle for a moment, staring at the house, and glancing in the rearview mirror at the neighborhood behind her. There were no cars driving past, or anyone about. She slowly stepped out and walked up the broken cement drive. Lawn furniture and a wooden table with peeling paint stood on the front porch, seemingly undisturbed.

For how many years?

She dared to step on the boarded steps and walk across the front porch, pausing to glance through the picture window. She used her phone to shine a light inside. Good gosh! It was as though time had stood still. The room was tastefully furnished, two overstuffed easy chairs, and a burgundy sofa appointed with knitted white doilies on its arms. A marble-topped table held a Tiffany glass lamp, and the fireplace mantel was covered with knickknacks and framed photos. Carli squinted but couldn't make out the faces. Was her father in a photo with other family members? Ancestors she never knew existed? She moved to the next window, and the next and the next, covering her mouth in surprise at what she saw through the dirt-caked glass.

She wanted to see more and thought about going inside. It certainly appeared like the house had been abandoned. At the back door she wiggled the doorknob. It didn't budge. Was it locked or stuck?

A gravelly voice behind her made her jump. "You don't look like a burglar. What're ya doin' anyway, nosin' all over?"

Carli whipped around and cast the beam of light at an old man. He was big, with big glasses, a big stomach, and only a few sprigs of white hair on his shiny, bald head. The flabby midsection looked as though it was about to burst open his stretched, plaid shirt.

Her heart still hadn't slowed down. "I'm, uh, uh, I'm not a burglar, sir. I was looking for the people who lived here. The Miller family. Do you know them?"

"No one's lived here in at least ten years. All dead."

Carli almost felt tears forming. She clenched her teeth, but managed to ask, "Do you live around here?"

"'Cross the street. Who ya lookin' for?"

Carli didn't know if this man was friend or foe. In fact, his size frightened her not to mention they were standing in almost pitch dark. She kept an eye on where her escape route might be if she needed one.

"Have you lived there a long time?"

"Prob'ly forty years, if not more. I've seen a lot around here in my time."

Carli's mind reeled. She wanted to ask him so many questions. But she was afraid. Part of her wanted to run and hightail it out of here. Then again, she knew she should seize this opportunity. *Please, God, give me some courage right about now.*

"Uh, did you ever know a man by the name of Taylor Miller?"

The man's eyes squinted. He was quiet for a bit, sizing her up. Carli almost felt she could see the wheels in his head turning, thinking things over.

"You mean J.T.?"

"Yes, yes, J.T. Do you know him?" Carli was about to jump out of her skin. She imagined Taylor Miller might appear behind her at any minute.

"Yeah, I knew him. Everyone knew J.T."

Carli felt like this guy was either stringing her along or maybe it was just difficult to extract information from him. Like pulling a long rope. Where was the end of it?

"Do you know where he lives now?" There, she said it. Now she had to prepare herself for the answer.

"He moved away. That's all I know."

Carli turned before he could see the tears in her eyes. "Thank you for your time," she said over her shoulder as she hurried to her truck and sped home.

During the drive back to Wild Cow Ranch headquarters, Carli thought about what the old man had said about the Millers. She ran their short conversation over and over in her mind. "They're all dead," he said, and yes, he knew J.T. Knew. Did that mean her birth father was dead too? But the man had mentioned that J.T. had moved, so did that mean he was alive and well? Carli wished that she had taken the time to calm down and ask him more questions. But he was so creepy, and the empty house was creepy. Her first instinct was to get away as soon as possible. Maybe the trail to meet her birth father had already grown cold, but she had to hold on to that slim chance of hope.

Weary in spirit, Carli parked under the carport at her grandparents' house and climbed out. She needed to talk to Buck and Lola first. Small town life was good in so many ways. She still couldn't believe all of the neighbors that had showed up to help search for her in the snowstorm, but then there was the crazy rumor mill. Didn't people have more important things to do? What a mess! A simple conversation in the local coffee shop with a friend had mushroomed into a flippin' scandalous tale. The thought made her cheeks burn. The rocking chair on her front porch held promise of a silent refuge while she sorted out this mess and formulated a plan.

Instead of sitting still, she wandered inside and, in the darkness, gathered up the trash. After carrying it out, she decided to clean the house from top to bottom. That would keep her busy until Lola and Buck got back home tomorrow. She would talk to them first thing in the morning. She ran the conversation over and over in her mind. There wasn't any easy way to say it, other than to say this was a horrible rumor and not true. And so unfair to Nathan and his family. He must be furious at her.

Nervous energy took over. She made herself a quick sandwich and sat down at the computer to check riding school inquiries and dig into more of her birth father's genealogy. After seeing his childhood home, she was more than ever determined to find him. Time flew by, and she yawned and looked at the clock. It was well past midnight.

Before turning off her computer for the night, she decided to research horse shelters. She had an idea she might be able to locate Itchy, Lexi's horse they'd given up, but she didn't have her hopes high. Still, he might be a great addition to the remuda for the riding school and a nice surprise for Lexi.

As late as it was, a hot shower sounded good and an hour later she was warm and snuggled under the covers. The worry of the ridiculous pregnancy rumor was still on her mind, but with a heavy sigh she resigned herself to the fact that she'd face it tomorrow, with God's help.

Chapter Thirty-Eight

The light streaming in through the slits of the blinds made Carli blink. She stretched and yawned. For a second she thought about what to wear to the Olsen's. Maybe she should find something dressier than jeans and chided herself for not asking Nathan. But maybe he wouldn't know the dress code. Guys usually said, "Wear whatever you want. It'll be fine."

She went to the kitchen to make a cup of coffee, found her slippers, and wandered to the front porch rocker. Closing her eyes, she pushed anxiety from her mind and enjoyed the morning. The birds were usually at their noisiest first thing but were strangely quiet now. She wondered what time everyone would be leaving for the Olsen's. Maybe she could hitch a ride with Buck and Lola. The drive would be the perfect opportunity to clear up the baby rumor and thinking about it made her frown.

Draining the last drop from her mug first, she then ambled back inside to get dressed. She took her time, trying on several outfits and decided on dress slacks with a bright purple western shirt and concho belt. Grabbing her purse, she strolled towards the cookhouse and was surprised to find Lola's SUV gone. It was then she thought about looking at the time on her phone. It was late afternoon! How had she slept so long? The stress of the last few days must've caught up with her body.

Carli never wore a watch and the alarm clocks left behind by her grandparents were so ancient, she never made the effort to reset them. Time didn't seem to be an issue here on the ranch. She woke when the sun came up, went to bed when she got tired. And the days soon passed into weeks. She really needed to get a modern, workable alarm clock. And even more strange, why hadn't Nathan called?

She jogged back across the compound towards her pickup truck, purse bumping against her side, hopped in, and hurried to the Olsen's ranch. She could drive faster but it would take longer if she went the roundabout way by pavement. Instead opting for the dirt road, she'd have to stop and unlock a wire gate. Passing through Crazy Vera's place whom she shared a fence line with and then the next ranch over was the Rafter O pasture, land that had been in the Olsen family for at least five generations.

Lots of cars and trucks were parked in unorderly fashion surrounding the sprawling ranch house. Apparently, this was more than a family lunch. Not only was it his mother's birthday, it was also Mother's Day weekend, another excuse for Nathan's mom to entertain. She loved cooking and feeding a big crowd. They found more reasons to celebrate than any other family Carli had ever known. It suddenly dawned on her, was this to be a brunch or a dinner? So much had happened over the last few days, she couldn't remember. Either she had missed it or she was right on time.

Busting through the door, all heads turned when she entered the abruptly silent room. It was obvious that conversation had just stopped. A crowd was quietly milling around the family room. Nathan had an arm resting on the fireplace mantel. He smiled and walked her way. She heard Lola's laughter from the kitchen. Buck turned and looked at her, a strange expression of sympathy on his face. Nathan's sister Angie nodded, but didn't leave the tall, dark-headed man she was standing with.

It was at that time Nathan's mother emerged from the dining room. "Carli. Honey. Come sit down. Can I get you a glass of iced tea? A pillow for your back?" She gripped Carli's arm and led her over to an easy chair where she gave her a little nudge. Were those tears in her eyes?

Carli sank back into the soft, leather chair. "Sorry I'm late."

"We're putting it on the table just now. Your timing is perfect, but you can rest for a few minutes if you need to."

Nathan stood by her side, strangely silent. After several more moments, Mrs. Olsen announced, "Come on everybody. Let's eat."

She stood, Nathan grabbed Carli's hand and led her to the far end of the long dining table, set of course to perfection. Smells of yeast rolls drifted from the kitchen. Deer antlers surrounded mason jars filled with sunflowers and extended down the middle. Blue Willow china, an abundance of silver-ware at each place setting as well as a bread plate, dessert plate, and water and tea glasses. A wagon wheel chandelier shed bright light over the entire scene. Nathan pulled out a cowhide-covered chair for Carli at his right and he took a seat next to the end, where his dad sat. Buck and Lola, the Olsen family, and a few couples Carli had seen around town but wasn't sure of their names, were all in attendance. About eighteen people gathered round.

"Let us bless the food," said Skip Olsen, Nathan's dad. Just before he began, the front door banged shut, spurs jangled in the entry hall, and Lank appeared from around the corner. He took a seat at the far end, opposite Nathan and Carli. The blessing was brief but moving.

"Lunch is served." Lola balanced two casserole dishes followed by Nathan's mom who carried a huge pot of beans. They arranged more dishes and food on the sideboard, and then Mrs. Olsen nodded to Nathan. "Let's start at this end."

Nathan allowed Carli to go first, and she grate-fully filled her plate with tender brisket, coleslaw, pinto beans, along with a few other sides she didn't recognize but looked too delicious not to try. Lola came up behind her and gave her a squeeze. "Glad you're here. Everything's going to be all right."

Carli glanced at her for a moment, wondering what she meant but dismissed it after she sat down and started eating. The dishes and fancy setting seemed out of place for barbeque brisket, but Nathan's mother loved pulling out all the stops and making everyone feel like kings and queens.

The air seemed thick with tension and the room

quiet, as silverware clinked against china. Maybe everyone was just hungry. Carli pushed the concern from her mind.

"There's pecan pie and blackberry cobbler," announced Mrs. Olsen as she cleared a spot on the sideboard for the desserts.

"Which would you like?" asked Nathan.

"Pie please, and thanks." Carli smiled.

He returned with pie for her and a bowl of cobbler for himself. He grinned when she eyed his bowl. "You can have a taste if you'd like."

She giggled. "Great." She dipped her spoon into his bowl and brought it to her lips. As she did, she glanced up to see Lank watching her from the far end of the table. His face was red as anger glinted in his eyes, but then he changed to a look of utter sadness as he watched her. She'd ask him if everything was all right after the meal.

"Can I have your attention everyone?" Nathan stood and gently tapped his spoon against his tea glass. There really wasn't much talking, again strangely quiet, but Carli looked up at him. "Mom. We are all here today to celebrate you, and, as usual, instead of relaxing you've outdone yourself. The meal was delicious. Thank you."

Claps and agreements followed.

"You're sweet, but I had some good help. Thanks to Lola for assisting in the kitchen."

Mrs. Olsen put an arm around Lola who said, "Anytime, but it was mostly all you."

"I want to give you something I made. Happy Birthday and Happy Mother's Day." He handed her a bright pink bag. She genuinely seemed surprised, and pulled out an intricate, delicate, copper-colored, long-stemmed rose made from metal. She beamed with pride. "It's beautiful. You made this, Son?" The look of surprise shone across her face.

"Which brings me to the next thing I want to say." Nathan cleared his throat. "I have an announcement to make."

The faces around the table were frozen in place, no one uttered a word. Nathan leaned on the table as if to find courage, and then he glanced at Carli and winked. She smiled back but had no idea what he was about to say.

"We know already," said his mother with great exuberance and a wide smile on her face. "The best present you could ever give me. I'm going to be a grandma!"

Carli choked on a bite of pie, coughed and sputtered, and then covered her embarrassment with her napkin. The town rumor was running amok.

"What?" Total shock appeared on Nathan's face as he looked at Carli. She couldn't stop herself from glancing at Lank. He smirked and then shot Carli a look of anger, disappointment, almost hatred. He didn't seem surprised which meant he had heard the rumor too.

"When's the wedding, big brother?" asked Travis.

"No, wait." Nathan held up his hands. "There's no wedding."

"You sorry loser." Angie jumped up from her chair so fast it turned over backwards hitting the tile floor with a thwack. "I should smash your face in."

Voices started all at once with some congratulations in between Angie's griping at her brother. Lola's voice rose from the den. "You can get married at the Wild Cow!"

"I'm trying to tell you, I've made a decision about my future. I'm leaving town." Nathan's voice was drowned out by the chattering around him.

"What's this nonsense? Of course, you're marrying Carli. You're not going anywhere," Skip Olsen said firmly and then turned his attention back to his bowl of cobbler.

Carli watched the chaos for a minute and then climbed up on top of her chair. She stood and placed two fingers between her lips, giving a shrill, piercing whistle that stopped the chatter instantly.

"I am not pregnant!" she shouted. And then glanced down the long table to see that Lank's chair was empty. Her heart sank. She got off the chair and turned to Nathan. "You are a dear friend, but I'm not going to Santa Fe with you. That is what you've decided, isn't it?" She moved closer to Nathan and took his hands. "You're going to pursue your art, aren't you? I wish you all the best, but I've got to go now and take care of something. Before it's too late."

She rushed to Buck's side. "Where did Lank go? I have to talk to him. Right away."

"He left early to ride in a rodeo. Stay on highway 287 and it's three towns over."

"Go get him, Carli," whispered Lola.

She nodded. "That's what I intend to do. Say a prayer for us."

"Always." Lola smiled.

"Name of the town is Happy," Buck called after her.

Chapter Thirty-Nine

"Carli. Wait." Nathan's voice followed her to the entry hall of the Olsen's ranch house, just before she placed a hand on the front doorknob.

Carli turned to face him. "Nate. I'm sorry."

"I went over and over what I wanted to say to my parents, and that's not anything like I had imagined the conversation would go."

"What a mess this is. I feel bad. I ruined your announcement."

"Back there I said there was no wedding, but I didn't mean it. I'll help you raise this child."

For a moment Carli was shocked. So, it seemed, Nathan believed the rumor too. "You think it's true? You think I'd do that? I thought you knew me better."

"It is a shock, but we will get through this." He stepped closer and wrapped his arms around her.

She pushed him away, almost feeling betrayed. "Listen. It's not true. It was a horrible rumor started by that waitress at the coffee shop. Remember when I showed you my birth certificate? She only heard part of our conversation and repeated it to Belinda and then to the entire town, apparently."

"There's no one else? I hoped we would eventually find our way, but I didn't want to rush you."

"There's no one. At least not at this moment." That last part escaped from her lips before she could stop. An awkward silence followed as he met her eyes. "There's no us either, Nate. I think you should pursue the passion you have for your art wherever that might lead."

"You're right. I had already decided that before you blurted it out."

"I'm sorry."

"It's okay. Now I'm forced to talk to my father about it. But Carli, we can make this work. Come with me to Santa Fe. When we move back our children can run the Rafter O and the Wild Cow."

"If you're not happy on the back of a horse, then this life will never be satisfying for you, Nate. Why be miserable every day because that's what your father wants? Don't let your talent go to waste. You can't be everything to everybody. Make a decision. Your art or the ranch."

"You're right, Carli. You of all people should know what it's like to leave everything you've ever known and follow a dream."

"I've got to go." She turned and opened the door.

"Wait. Tell me the truth."

"The truth is there's no baby on the way."

"That's not what I'm talking about. Say his name and then admit it to yourself."

Carli's heart thudded in her chest and her mouth turned too dry to speak. She glanced down at the tiled floor to avoid Nathan's eyes.

"You knew?"

"I had a suspicion because I knew it wasn't me, and I could see the looks you gave him. I just didn't want to admit it to myself. It would make my life so much simpler if we could make this work."

"I know. You are kind and funny, a great horseman, good looking."

"Go on," he said with a laugh.

"You're perfect, Nate, but you're not in love with me. Be honest with yourself. I will always treasure your friendship." With that she rose to her tip toes and gave him a kiss on the cheek. He squeezed her tight and reached around her to open the door wider.

"You're right, Carli. Friends it is. Follow your wild heart, Carli. Grab your future and never let go."

Tears stung the backs of her eyes, but she turned and jogged to her pickup truck without a wave or a glance back. The directions Buck had given her raced inside her mind, "Stay on highway 287. Three towns over."

She roared out of ranch headquarters and forced herself to keep her speed reasonable on the caliche-topped dirt road until she reached the blacktop. And then she pushed it wide open. "Can I pray for no Highway Patrol, Lord? It would be much appreciated."

***

Nathan stood on the front porch for a moment with mixed emotions as he watched Carli driving away. Part longing, part relief. With a newfound purpose clear in his mind, he turned to head back inside. It was time for him to find his future too.

Now or never. He had to face his father.

As he emerged from around the corner, the guests were eating pie and drinking coffee but all heads around the dining table snapped in his direction. The room erupted.

"Are y'all engaged?"

"Where did Carli go?" his sister Angie asked.

"When are you moving to New Mexico?"

His father's booming voice rose above the others. "You are not leaving this ranch, Nathan."

The room silenced.

Skip Olsen stood at one end of the dining room table and Nathan walked closer to him. "Dad. Hear me out first."

"What are you thinking?" His father rarely showed a temper. In fact, he was the most even-keeled man Nathan knew whenever a crisis arose, but the hard glint in his father's eyes proved that this was not one of his calmer moments. Skip Olsen was furious with his firstborn.

"Let's hear him out," Buck's calm, commanding voice interrupted the strained silence.

Nathan paused to stare at his father. He knew what had been tossing his insides into such a jumble lately. Carli had made him see that life offered all kinds of possibilities, and now he was torn. He knew his dad wanted him to do the ranch business, take it over, be the head of the family when his parents were gone, like his father had done, and his grandfather before him. But Nathan wanted to pursue his own dreams. The desire to be something different burned in his gut. He knew that he would be a success. Become an artist like Brad Travers.

His dad's dream was the ranch. Nathan's dream was to follow his art.

But how could he make his father understand?

"Hon, I think we should hear what he has to say." His mother stood at Nathan's side and put her hand on his arm. "Go ahead, Nathan. Tell us what you have to say."

"Mom. Dad."

Silence. The room grew unbelievably hot, the guests remained motionless, as if with bated breath. Some felt awkward listening to the family business. But many of the friends were like family and had known Nathan since he was a baby. No one even blinked. Nathan pulled his chin up, stood a little straighter, and took a deep breath. "I'm moving to Santa Fe."

"Is Carli going with you? Is that the best place to raise a child?" This coming from Travis. Leave it to his little brother to make the situation worse.

Temper flared inside Nathan. "There is no baby. Carli and I are friends." His voice boomed louder than he had meant, so he took a calming breath. "I know it sounds crazy, but I have an opportunity in Santa Fe that I can't turn down. I'll be able to work and learn from some of the best artists in the Southwest."

"That's the stupidest thing I've ever heard," his father said. "We've got branding soon. Long days in the saddle and flanking calves will get you to come to your senses. I don't know what's going on with you, Son, but you'll get through this. We'll get through it together."

"My mind is made up. I'm giving you my notice, Dad. I'm not working at the Rafter O any longer."

"This ranch doesn't run on its own. You are lucky to have the kind of life this place provides for you, and now you're throwing it all away." Skip Olsen met his son's stare eye to eye, his face red. "Generations before you, hardworking people, gave their sweat and tears to make the Olsen ranch a reality. You're stomping on all of their memories, on our legacy."

"Over and over and over, I've heard you say that a million times. I'm not stomping on anything. I'm well aware of how this ranch operates. I know how lucky I've been to grow up here." Nathan didn't want to hurt his family but he felt a strength inside him building.

"I said no." Skip's voice came out hard, low and mean. His word was final at the Olsen house.

"Dad. I'll help you." Angie stepped in between them, laying a hand on her father's arm. "I'm here. And Travis is here. We're not going anywhere."

"She's more of a cow man than I'll ever be," Nathan said. "Angie never misses a count. She can tell you where each one of those bulls came from and what year they were purchased. Travis is the best roper and flanker in the county. He's always been better than me. You have a good crew here, Dad."

"Listen to the children, Hon."

"You don't need me." Nathan put an arm around his mother as she wiped a tear from her face. "Mom, Dad, you always taught us that God gives us the desires of our heart. I believe this is what's happening for me. You had my life planned out to run this ranch, even before I was born. But I can't do it. God gave me this dream and ability. It's the one thing that makes me happy."

Skip Olsen looked at his firstborn son, nodded his head. And quietly said, "I'll consider it, Nathan."

Stubborn to the very end, his father, but at least he gave an inch although he'd be the last to admit it. Nathan knew he had won. Maybe not the war, but perhaps this battle.

"Thanks, Sis." Nathan gave Angie a big hug. "Finish your desserts everyone. And you're all invited to my first gallery showing in Santa Fe one day."

Applause erupted from the guests.

"I call dibs on Nathan's horse and saddle." Travis sat down and shoveled an oversized bite of cobbler into his mouth, chewed, and then looked up. "Mom, can I move into his room?"

Without saying a word Nathan turned and grabbed Travis into a headlock, dragging him out of his chair.

"Don't wrestle in this dining room, boys," Mrs. Olsen said. They all laughed.

Nathan knew he would miss these moments more than anything in the world, but the world was waiting for him and he was ready to get started.

Chapter Forty

Thanks to the friendly convenience store attendant a couple miles back, Carli finally saw the rodeo arena up ahead. But before she could get through the gate to parking, the sounds of a siren interrupted her thoughts as an ambulance blared behind her. She had to pull to one side and let them pass.

At the entrance she ignored the greeting of the gatekeeper, instead dug in the bottom of her purse for money to cover the parking fee and shoved it into his hand.

Finally, she parked her truck in a grassy lot, hopped out, and weaved her way through the cars, trucks, and livestock trailers. She had to find Lank and set things right with him. The notion that he thought badly of her caused her stomach to twist in knots. He had to know the truth.

Wandering through the dust and noise that rose above the crowd, she took a moment to peek at the arena. Team roping was underway, so she turned and searched the sea of cowboy hats for Lank's face. Up in the stands, more cowboy hats on guys and girls, smiling faces but no one familiar. Wandering past the concession stands, she made her way towards the holding pens. Taking note of every face shaded by a hat, bodies perched on railings. She walked through the middle of several clumps of cowboys. Some tipped their hat to her, some casting friendly, interested smiles her way, but she didn't pause long enough to engage in conversation. With a disappointed sigh she turned and walked back the way she had come.

"Vera!" Finally, a familiar face. Carli saw her neighbor Crazy Vera standing at the concession stand. She towered over everyone around her, most especially from the tall hat and feather. The older woman turned at the sound of her name.

"Carli, girl. Want something to drink?"

"No, thanks. Have you seen Lank?"

Vera handed over her money before answering. "You just missed his ride."

Carli followed her towards the stands. Vera stopped and turned to her, a frown on her face. "It didn't end well."

"I need to talk to him."

"He's gone by now. The ambulance left about ten minutes ago."

"Ambulance? I pulled over to let it pass."

"That's the one and Lank was in it."

"What? Was he hurt bad? Where'd they take him? Do you know?" Fear crept over her causing her throat to close. She felt dizzy.

"So many questions. Easy, girl. You're as pale as a ghost. You don't need any stress in your condition. He'll be okay, but I can't believe he tossed aside his promise to his momma and climbed back on a dang bucking horse. His poor momma must be rolling over in her grave, God rest her soul."

"Vera! Are they taking him to the hospital in this town?" Carli walked closer and grabbed her neighbor by both shoulders. Her first instinct was to shake the living daylights out of the woman until she could find out what she wanted to know. But Vera had her on size and weight. It would have been like trying to budge a Sequoia.

"Maybe your blood sugar is too low? I'll buy you a snack. You need to keep up your strength. You're eating for two, ya know."

"There is no baby. Nathan is moving to Santa Fe. The rumor about us started at the coffee shop based on parts of an overheard conversation and then the Dixon town gossip train ran full speed and out of control. Dependable form of news, but not always accurate. Listen to me! I have to talk to Lank."

"How does Lank play into this? What has you so upset?"

"I think I love him." Carli let out a breath. There. She'd blurted it out without even thinking. What a disaster this was going to be, no matter how things might work out. Vera's eyes widened and then a slow grin covered her face.

"Come with me." Crazy Vera grabbed her by the scruff of her shirt and half ran, half dragged her towards the parking lot. As they approached Vera's truck, Snot the bloodhound raised a droopy-eyed face up from the back and wagged his tail at Carli. Vera opened the back of the truck bed and Snot jumped out and walked around to the passenger door.

"Get in. You'll have to ride in the middle because

Snot always sits by the window." Vera shouted as if Carli wasn't just on the other side of the truck. "And hold my drink."

Carli held Vera's soda and with her other hand pushed the dog away to avoid a slobbery tongue on her cheek. They roared out of the parking lot, turning into a residential area, Vera weaving right and then left. "I'm taking a shortcut. Now they may have just taken him to the local hospital, but if they took him on to a larger medical center we'll find out."

What would she say to Lank when she saw him? Admitting your undying love to an employee is hardly appropriate, and what if he didn't feel the same? They couldn't ever work together once those three words escaped her lips. It would be torture seeing him and knowing he didn't love her back. What a mess. She'd have to fire him. Again.

The notion that he might be seriously injured slammed into her brain and caused tears to bubble up in her eyes. Houses and yards and traffic passed by blurry in her vision. She absentmindedly laid an arm across the bloodhound in the seat next to her, pulling him closer. The thought of sobbing into his neck crossed her mind but she concentrated on breathing in and out to get a check on her emotions.

Vera practically jumped out of the truck before it stopped rolling under the portico, and Carli followed still holding Vera's drink from the rodeo concession. "Emergency" blinked bright red next to the sliding glass doors.

"Was that cowboy brought here?" Vera asked, her voice booming in the sterile, orderly space. A nurse looked up from behind the counter. "Yes. Room 35, but are you family?"

"You're dang right we are!" The nurse raised curious eyebrows but didn't argue. Vera turned to Carli. "Go get your cowboy."

"You bet I will." She passed the drink to the big woman with frustration, not knowing why she was still carrying it around, and looked at the nurse who pointed a finger towards the hall behind her.

Walk, don't run, she reminded herself, but she couldn't stay calm. She busted around the corner, swerving to miss an orderly who pushed an empty wheelchair, and barreled through the door without even knocking.

Lank appeared to be asleep, but breathing, his chest rising and falling as the air made a wheezing noise. One arm was in a sling and one eye was swollen shut. His cheek and forehead marked with deep purple bruising. Peaceful. He looked so serene and Carli was filled with joy, giddy and sharp, at the sight of his face. She froze and stared, memorizing every line weathered by the outdoors. A black curl covered one side of his forehead and dark stubble shaded his handsome face. She stepped closer and couldn't help but reach out and caress his jaw. She let her hand trail down his good arm and then clasped his hand in hers.

After a moment he slowly opened one eye, saw her face, and lifted his good eyebrow. She smiled at him.

"I need to tell you something, Lank Torres," she murmured.

He turned his face into the pillow. "Go away." He jerked his hand back.

Carli drew in a deep breath. This wasn't going to be easy. He was so ornery he'd make it difficult. But she had to tell him how she felt, even if they could never be a couple. Even if he hated her.

"You just listen. I'll talk." She leaned over him so in case he did open that one good eye again, she'd be in his line of vision. "You left the Olsen's before you heard my news." She poked him on the shoulder. "There is no baby."

He kept his eye shut. "So? What has this got to do with me?" he mumbled.

"I wanted you to know." She eased onto the bed next to him.

"I'm sure you and Nathan will have many long years together. Don't send me an invite to the wedding."

"That would be an interesting marriage since he's moving to Santa Fe and I'm staying here. There's no wedding. There's no baby. Can you drop the arrogant attitude for once and just listen?"

Lank turned his head and finally opened his good eye. She met his gaze, couldn't think of what she needed to say so she leaned in to plant a gentle kiss on his lips. For once this smart-mouthed cowboy was speechless. She giggled.

"I know I said we needed to keep it professional, employer and employee and all that, but I've changed my mind. When I moved to Texas, I wasn't looking for a new relationship. I just wanted to learn about cattle ranching and find out about a family I never knew. I didn't expect to find love. But here you are. Whether you feel the same or not, I think we should be honest with each other." A tear slid down her cheek. She'd laid bare her heart and soul. They were in his hands now.

His hand gently caressed the side of her face and his thumb wiped the tear away. "I'm just the ranch hand. A dirty, rotten, tough cowboy is what my momma always said. I don't have ambition to be anything else. But if I'm being honest, I have loved you from the first moment you climbed out of that truck with the Georgia license plates and started ordering me around."

"You seemed furious with me that day. I had no idea you were interested. And then today, I saw the anger and hurt on your face when you looked at me. Why did you come to the Olsen's today?"

"No matter how much I hated the thought of you and Nathan building a life together, there's no way I'd miss a meal at the Olsen's," he said with a sheepish smile and shrugged.

Carli laughed. "Promise me one thing."

"Anything," he said as he reached for her hand.

"We have to communicate. No more conflict between us. But I might have to dock your pay for this latest stunt. Why would you climb on the back of a bronc again and risk life and limb?"

"It seemed no one cared if I lived or died. You and Nathan were starting a life together. When I'm on the back of a bronc I can forget. I only have to focus on that moment. It's the rush."

"Like I said, I might have to dock your pay for being so stupid."

"Will there be a bonus since I'm dating the boss?"

"A bonus? What kind of bonus?"

Lank sat up in his hospital bed, a muscled arm pulled her closer. "This." His lips covered hers, firm and demanding, and she was helpless to control the flutter in her heart and that tingle that spread through her like a heat wave reaching all the way to her toes.

When she finally came up for air, she mumbled, "I love you, Lank Torres."

"I know you do, boss lady."

Acknowledgements

Thanks to the cowboys and cowgirls, ranchers, farmers, and countless busy, hardworking folks who have crossed my path, both past and present, and who continue to inspire me. Their stories of joy, heartache, and unwavering faith prove that the human spirit undeniably endures.

Thanks to Lauren Bridges and the CKN Christian Publishing team for the opportunity. Your efforts are greatly appreciated.

To my co-author Denise. There is no doubt in my mind that God sometimes steers us in new directions and places certain people in our path. Thanks for your creative spirit, dedication, and willingness to travel along this challenging and rewarding journey. Here's to the work and words behind us and hoping there are many more to come.

– Natalie Bright

Acknowledgements

For the most part, writing is a solitary endeavor. But there are still many who contribute to the production of turning ideas into words, into stories, into books. Heartfelt thanks to: A holy and loving God for creating each of us with unique talents and for staying by our side; my wonderful co-author Natalie Bright for her expertise and treasured friendship; many friends connected with the Western Writers of America; Wolfpack Publishing and CKN Christian Publishing; and so many others.

Award-winning bronze sculptor Chris Navarro was the inspiration for characters in this book, Follow a Wild Heart, who are driven to follow their passion of creating art. At a young age, Navarro was eager to learn about sculpting, much like our character Nathan Olsen and his mentor. Please visit Navarro's website: https://www.chrisnavarro.com.

Another bronze sculptor, Deborah Copenhaver Fellows, was the inspiration in our first book in the Wild Cow Ranch series, Maverick Heart. The sculpture of the cowgirl that our character Carli Jameson loves so much is actually in the Booth Western Art Museum in Cartersville, Georgia. Please see Deborah's website: https://www.fellowsstudios.com/deborah-fellows.html.

Amy Wilmoth Watts is another artist who follows her passion. In addition to her paintings appearing in a Santa Fe, New Mexico gallery, and the Booth Western Art Museum, she is a for-real cowgirl, a cattle rancher with her husband James in Statham, Georgia, and dog, cat, and horse mom. Amy has a heart as big as the planet for people and animals, and I am thankful to count her as my friend. See her art at: https://www.instagram.com/amy.watts.art/.

And be sure to visit the Booth Western Art Museum in Cartersville, Georgia, when you get the chance. https://boothmuseum.org.

Thank you, Dear Reader, for spending time with us on the Wild Cow Ranch.

– Denise F. McAllister

Take a look at A Place Called Destiny by Emma Easter

Twenty-five-year-old Rachel, nearing the end of her pregnancy, makes an urgent dash to flee her polygamist husband Mike Caldwell and his embittered first spouse Olivia. Pregnant with her first child, a product of her troubled forced spiritual union with Mike, Rachel knows if she doesn't escape her unholy relationship both her and her child will never be free.

She has been unable to accept this way of life and feels it is not right for her to act as a barrier to Mike and Olivia and the sanctity of their marriage. Her escape plan fails, due to Fallow Creek, the polygamy commune she lives in, employing a security detail of young men who guard against escape.

With help from the unmarried pastor Keith Thorn, of nearby town Destiny, they are reminded that with faith, love and trust in God's plan they can achieve anything.

AVAILABLE ON AMAZON

About Natalie Bright

With roots firmly planted in the Texas Panhandle, Natalie Bright grew up obsessed with the Wild West and making up stories. The small farming community where she lived gave her a belief in hard-working, genuine people and a firm foundation of faith. She is the author of books for kids and adults, as well as numerous articles.

This author and blogger writes about small town heroes with complicated pasts and can-do attitudes, who navigate life's crazy misfortunes with humor and happy endings. A passionate supporter of history and libraries, Natalie loves exploring museums and collecting old books. Her ranch photography is featured in a chuck wagon cookbook. She lives on a dirt road with her husband, where they raise black and red Angus cattle and where the endless Texas sky continues to be her inspiration.

About Denise F. McAllister

Lovers of the West can be born in the most unlikely of places. For Denise F. McAllister, her start was in Miami, Florida, surrounded by beaches and the Everglades.

After being in the working world for some years, Denise F. McAllister decided to apply her life experience and study for her B.A. in communications and M.A. in professional writing. She loved going back to college "later in life" and hardly ever skipped a class as in her younger years. Growing up in the suburbs of Miami, Denise credits her love of horseback riding and showing in Atlanta, Georgia (15 years) for her heartfelt connection to all things Western.

Denise's faith is important to her and she loves to write about characters' journeys as they navigate real-world challenges. She prays that readers will enjoy her books, but most importantly experience a blessed connection with their Creator and Heavenly Father.